BAY OF DEVILS

By Grahame Shannon

Print Edition:
ISBN: 978-0-9958685-3-3

FOREWORD

Everything in this book is true, except for the parts I made up.

In 2008 my wife and I took our sailboat on a trip to Alaska. According to her, it wasn't a vacation. It was an expedition. We visited all the places described, including Thomas Bay.

I did live in Vancouver's West End in 1968, so the landscape is as my memory recalls. It's a city where buildings are torn down and replaced at a fearsome pace, so many of the places described have been re-developed at least twice since then.

Some of the characters are based on real people, but anything they say or do is fictionalized. If you knew me in that era, you might be in here, but no promises!

I have taken some liberties with the timing of events in Vancouver and the geography of Southeast Alaska. Many people have helped me with the technical and navigational details, so naturally, any errors are theirs.

I have attempted to write in the style of the times, so please note that gender roles and some behaviors portrayed do not represent my current attitude.

I want to thank my editor, Marial Shea, for her excellent and good-humored assistance. Thanks also to my beta readers, who gave gentle suggestions and criticism of the first draft.

PROLOGUE

SS Princess Sophia
Cabin 17
October 25, 1918

If found, please deliver to
Miss Elizabeth Hadley
1618 Barclay St. Vancouver, BC

My Dearest Elizabeth,

It greatly distresses me that this may be the last communication you will ever receive from me. I am grateful for the affection and respect you have bestowed upon me, despite the difference in our ages.

On the afternoon of October 23rd, I embarked on the voyage from Skagway back to Vancouver, hoping to see you again, but that evening the ship hit a rocky reef at full speed. We are grounded hard on the rocks of the Vanderbilt Reef in rough seas, fog, and rain. I am writing this in my cabin, but we have been advised to remain in the public areas in case of a rescue. The electric lights are still on, but it is thought the generator may soon be submerged, and all power will be lost.

Several ships have come by, and rescue attempts have proved useless due to high winds and seas. I fear the ship will soon founder, and due to the angle we are lying at, the lifeboats cannot be launched. Chances of survival are, in my opinion, dismal, although, as is my nature, I remain hopeful.

I plan to put this letter in a metal flask I have and throw it into the sea. Chances of it being found seem greater than if it goes to the bottom with the ship. The flask is sturdy and watertight, so it should survive, although I most likely will not.

Lizzie, I have left my will, properly inscribed, with my solicitor, Jan van Holgren, at his office in Howe Street. I have left the bulk of my modest estate to you, with a few dollars to each of my surviving relatives. I hope this will be of some small comfort to you.

I have something else I must tell you. I spent the greater part of the summer prospecting for gold in the area in and around Thomas Bay, Alaska. The gold rush is long over, and to my knowledge at the time, no significant quantity of gold was ever found there. Nevertheless, as a geologist, my examination of the rocky terrain in the area led me to believe it was a likely spot to find veins of gold.

I used a rented gas boat called Scurry, with a small engine, a sleeping cabin, and a coal stove for heat and cooking. Behind it, I towed a canoe for shore excursions.

In any case, I found no gold but did find a curious cave high up along the eastern side of a long narrow lake. The cave entrance was hidden by brush, and I discovered it only by accident when an animal of some sort ran out as I approached. I pushed aside the undergrowth and saw the entrance, just big enough for a stooped man to enter, perhaps four feet high and three wide.

Inside it was pitch dark except for a bit of diffused daylight right at the entrance. Fortunately, I had a US Army electric torch, which I obtained from an outfitter in Skagway. Although not extremely bright, it threw a decent beam. Once inside, the cave opened out into an area perhaps ten feet wide and as much as thirty feet deep. At the far end, it tapered down. There were some signs of human habitation. I could see a blackened area surrounded by stones where there must have been a fire. There was one charred and battered saucepan, half-buried by the fire, which, while old, was clearly of modern manufacture. I pulled it out of the dirt and examined the bottom. There was a faintly stamped maker's imprint, square, and filled with Chinese characters. Underneath were the letters BCCHK 1896. I assume BCCHK means British Crown Colony Hong Kong.

I searched the cavern for further artifacts and found only a few bones, whether human I could not determine. Suddenly a low moan arose from deep inside, like a large animal in great pain. A cold sweat of fear came over me, and my heart raced. I felt an urgent need to get out. As I scrabbled for the entrance, I tripped on something partly buried in the gravelly dirt of the floor. My foot was caught on a small protrusion of what appeared to be leather, cracked, and worn with age. Instinctively I pulled at it with my right hand, and it came loose from the dirt. It was a pigskin bag, closed with a knotted thong. It was heavy and made a muffled rattle when shaken. I took it with me as I hastened away from that fearsome place.

Once outside in the sunshine, I ran for a few hundred yards until I was at the edge of the lake. I sat on a rock to recover. The fear gradually subsided, and my heart returned to normal. After a few minutes, I started to open the leather bag. The knot was tight, but I managed to loosen it and extract the contents.

Inside was a carved sandalwood box a bit larger than a cigar box. It had tarnished brass hinges, and a brass hasp held closed with a matchstick. It was intricately carved with ornate patterns, seeming to represent flowers and leaves. There was a single carved Chinese character inscribed in a circle. I had seen a similar box once in Batavia but did not ask its origin.

I started to open the box with care, as it seemed fragile, and I didn't want to destroy it. As I did so, an overwhelming feeling of trepidation and terror came over me, and I closed the box. After a few minutes, I tried again and caught a glimpse of something shiny inside. But the feeling of terror was even stronger, and I closed the lid. This time I put the box back in the bag and tied it with the thong. I wanted to return it to the cave, but fear prevented me.

Although I have been in combat during the Boer war, even wounded, I never felt the sort of terror that this place and that box occasioned. I espied a boulder with a flat top, which overhung in such a way as to form a deep recess, sheltered from the rain. I placed the bag under the rock and made a pile of stones to hide it from view. I planned to return another time, armed, and with at least one other person, and open it then. I marked the location by lining up three large rocks about a yard apart in a line pointing at the site, and about five yards away. They also point the way to the cave beyond.

I ran the considerable distance back to the beach, jumped in the canoe, and paddled back to where Scurry was anchored across the bay. I got underway and headed for Petersburg. The next day I recounted the story, without mention of the box, to a fellow in the hotel bar. He told me that Thomas Bay was known as the "Bay of Death." It was considered by the locals to be haunted, and few would venture there. The place was the scene of a massive landslide that wiped out a large Indian village in 1750. He also told me of crazed prospectors coming out of the area in terror, after being chased by hairy creatures with long claws. He called it "the Devil's Bay" and vowed he would never go there.

I decided to abandon the box, and my gold prospecting, to come home to you. Because of bad weather, it took me several weeks to get to Skagway to return Scurry. Princess Sophia was due to leave the same day, and I just managed to book a ticket. At the time, that seemed lucky, but now I know it was not.

Lizzie, I can't tell you how important you are in my affections, and how it sorrows me that I will never see you again.

I'm praying that you will get this letter, which I will now throw overboard. The lights are flickering, and the groaning of the ship's plates as they grind on the rocks below is getting more strident. I must get up on deck.

With all my love,

Jakob B. Holcomb

Princess Sophia was lost with all hands on that day, at 5:50 PM, confirmed by stopped watches found on some of the bodies. More than 350 passengers and crew perished. The only survivor was a small dog, believed to belong to a wealthy couple aboard, that was able to swim to a nearby island and found a few days later. It remains the most severe maritime disaster on the BC and Alaska coast.

CHAPTER 1 – SEAN, MAY 1968

It was warm and cozy in my bunk. I rolled over and reached out to put my arm around Suzy. My head thumped on the bulkhead, and I woke up groggily—no Suzy. My fuzzy brain shook itself like a wet dog, and reality returned. Suzy was in Toronto. Our romance was over.

I should never have asked her to marry me. When I said the words, her eyes had shown love, pity, and fear. Not all at once, but one at a time, in that order. The dazzling woman who could climb a mast in a gale and swim a mile was afraid of me! Or at least afraid of committing to me.

I unfolded myself out of the vee-berth and stumbled to the chart table to check the time on the ship's clock. The hands pointed to 2:17, but it was daylight outside. I forgot to wind it. Again.

I found the key and wound the clock. Then I looked around for some clean clothes. There was a choice of long or short khaki pants and long or short-sleeved blue cotton shirts. Looking through a port showed nothing but grey, so I chose long in both categories. After slipping into my topsiders, I pulled on a light windbreaker. Climbing the steep companionway ladder, I remembered to duck and avoided a collision with the stainless tubing supporting the dodger. I clambered out of the cockpit and vaulted over the lifelines on to the dock. It wasn't as graceful as it sounds. My shoe caught on the top line, and I narrowly avoided a faceplant. The shoe came off and landed in the sea. I fished it out, shook it, and put it back on. It squished a bit as I walked.

I turned back to admire my boat. *Tangled Moon* was a beauty: a 41-foot Olin Stephens sloop built by Nevins in '38, with no expense spared. The decks were laid teak almost an inch thick. The long trunk cabin was painted white with a varnished mahogany eyebrow. An inlaid gold leaf cove stripe and broader white boot stripe accented the double-planked navy-blue hull. All the deck hardware was bronze, which would look splendid when polished—if that ever happened.

I found the old yacht chained and padlocked to the dock at Clay's Wharf, having been seized by the sheriff. I inquired at the office and found out it had belonged to a well-known stock promoter who had recently disappeared without a trace, taking a lot of investors' money with him. The boat was for sale, and I negotiated a price I could manage, about half as much as a small house in the suburbs. The bank loan had payments of two hundred and ten dollars a month. I found moorage in Coal Harbour and moved aboard. That was in 1967.

Walking up the slope from the marina toward Denman Street, I took a shortcut through the remains of the old Georgia Auditorium. Only the concrete walls and floor remained, and inside was a jumble of temporary sheds and various boats under construction or repair. I passed Wright Mariner, a local marine store, a place I often hung out. Laurie Wright always had the coffee ready. But the shop was closed, as it wasn't yet nine.

I crossed Georgia and continued up Denman to the Shipmate Café. It was the kind of place you could charitably call a "greasy spoon," located on the ground floor of a boxy brick commercial building. Locals called it the "Shitbait". The hinges squealed as I pushed the door inward.

"Sean Gray! I haven't seen you in ages, maybe as much as twelve hours. Are you still an asshole?"

Coffee was twenty-five cents, but Brenda's abuse was free. I had no snappy comeback. I needed a shot of caffeine first.

Brenda brought me a thick mug of black stuff that resembled used motor oil but did smell a bit like coffee. With a liberal dose of cream, it could be consumed. She looked quite attractive in her waitress uniform; a sort of sailor suit with a short skirt. Her blonde hair was tied back in a bun. She was just a little too curvy to be fashionable—more 1958 than 1968.

I was nursing my coffee and eating a slice of buttered toast when the café door opened again. The place was quiet early in the morning, so I noticed who came in. This woman was tall, black (a rare sight in Vancouver) and slim, with a long neck and fine features. I couldn't guess her age, but since she was wearing a very well-tailored business suit and expensive-looking shoes, I assumed she was a professional of some sort. In the moment before she spoke to Brenda, I made up a history. She was a career diplomat from Ethiopia, posted to Vancouver, and exploring the neighborhoods to decide where to live.

The moment she ordered, I knew I was wrong. Her accent was pure Bajan, with an overtone of British education. She ordered an Earl Grey and a muffin and said something to Brenda, which I didn't quite catch, but I thought I heard my name. Brenda jerked a thumb in my direction and said, "Talk to that clod."

It wasn't every day a beautiful stranger walked up to me with a smile on her face. The last time, it was a bill collector, which was what I expected when she reached into her purse. I had a momentary flash of imagination in which she was pulling a gun on me.

Instead, she looked directly into my eyes and pulled out a card. Her eyes were a surprising bright blue. I wiped my face with a paper napkin and stood up.

"Sean Gray, at your service," I said. Probably should have bowed or something, but I didn't.

"Darya Hubert." She handed me the card and sat down at my table.

The card said:

Darya Hubert, BA, LL.D
Attorney-at-Law

At the bottom was a phone number, nothing else. I stared at it for a moment.

"A lawyer? What can I do to help you?"

She looked down at the table, as though composing her thoughts. When she looked up, she spoke softly. "I heard about what you did for Mrs. Haskell."

"I found her missing cat, that's all. No big deal."

Darya smiled, revealing straight white teeth with a slight gap in the front, and her eyes glistened with amusement. "I heard the cat was solid gold with ruby eyes."

"That's the rumor."

Mrs. Haskell had me sign an agreement not to reveal that the cat was only gold plated, and the rubies were glass.

"I also heard that you have a boat. I need your help."

I stood up. "We'd better continue the discussion upstairs in my office."

I raised my eyebrows in the direction of Brenda, who was leaning on the counter, paying close attention.

Brenda turned around and started polishing the coffee urn, something never seen before. Darya followed me out of the shop and up the narrow stairs to my office. The old-fashioned oak door had a frosted glass panel with "Anson Investigators" engraved in the glass. It was there when I rented the office, and it was too expensive to change. The rest of the office was also pretty much as I found it.

Darya looked around the room. I had a large oak desk behind which was my wooden swivel chair. Beside the desk were a big old steel filing cabinet and three wooden guest chairs. On the side of the room opposite the entry were two unmarked oak doors. One concealed a toilet and sink, and the other a private back room where I kept boat stuff. The floor was well worn Douglas fir planking.

Darya walked over to the tall bookshelf, which occupied a space between the two doors. She perused the titles on the shelf at her eye level.

"Nietzsche, *Freddy the Pig*, Proust, *Hardy Boys*, Agatha Christie, Conan Doyle... you have eclectic taste in literature."

I said, "Don't forget the *RCA Vacuum Tube Manual*. That's my favorite."

I sat at my desk and waved her to a chair. I thought I better clear up the false impression made by the sign on the door.

"I'm not a licensed investigator. Technically, I'm an archaeologist." I pointed to the wall behind me where three diplomas were displayed, all from ICS.

Darya said, "None of those is for Archaeology. I see Electronics, Diesel Mechanics, and Watch Repair." She had sharp eyes. Most people couldn't read them from over there.

"As I said, I'm *a technical* archeologist. I dig up old technology and fix it."

I pointed to the typewriter on the side extension of my desk. "That is the only IBM Selectric in the world with a teak case. The original broke when it was thrown from a second-story window. It missed me. Anyway, to the point; how do you think I can help you?"

"A client of mine just received a letter that was sent to her almost fifty years ago."

"The Post Office can be slow. I can't be expected to do anything about that."

She ignored me, and reaching into her purse, took out a Xerox copy of a hand-written letter. The writing was old fashioned but legible. I took the hint and read it. Several words, which seemed to be the names of people and places, were blacked out.

The contents excited my interest, but I played it cool. I asked if her client had the means to pay for my time, and she asked my rate.

I usually charged eight bucks an hour for repair work, but this was likely to be a long job, so I decided a daily rate would be more appropriate. The figure of sixty dollars entered my head, but I said, "One hundred a day plus expenses."

"Agreed. My client will be pleased."

I should have asked for two hundred.

With that out of the way, we went back down to the café and sat with some more coffee

I asked Darya, "Do I detect a Bajan accent?"

"Yes, I'm surprised you recognized it. Most people think I'm Jamaican. I came to Canada from Barbados when I was seventeen. I won a scholarship to McGill."

I said, "I was born in Grenada, and I can usually recognize a West Indian accent. My Dad could tell what part of an island you were from. The family moved to Canada when I was a child."

"I don't meet many West Indians here. With your sandy hair and light eyes, I took you for a white guy. What did your father do in Grenada?"

I laughed, "I'm as white as they come in Grenada. My Dad was a planter. His family was there for a couple of hundred years."

She looked serious for a moment. I imagined she thought that I was a descendant of slaveholders. I suppose that was true, though nobody in the family ever mentioned it.

I said, "You have blue eyes."

She nodded. "Yes, almost everyone in my mother's family has them. It's rare, but not extremely so."

I changed the topic and asked her about law school. She was a fairly recent graduate. Still, she had to be a few years older than me. I surmised that race might have something to do with why she ran a one-person firm.

We parted on friendly terms, and I looked forward to seeing her again.

CHAPTER 2 – ELIZABETH'S LETTER

Elizabeth Hadley
1618 Barclay St.
Vancouver, BC

October 12, 1918

Dear Jakob,

I am mailing this letter care of General Delivery, Petersburg, Alaska, in hopes that it may reach you there, but I know there is a chance you will not receive it.

It appears the end of the war is in sight. The Americans have made a big difference. After the battles at Amiens and Cambrai, allied victory seems certain. What peace will bring, I cannot say.

Jakob, your affectionate letters have disturbed me. It appears that you have attributed to us a relationship that is far more serious than I had supposed. You have even hinted at betrothal.

Mother feels you are anything but a fitting suitor. Despite your valiant service in the Army, especially at Vimy, your wounds, and your medals, she is not impressed with your prospects.

As you know, we operate a boarding house out of necessity. Since the death of my father, Colonel Hadley, our income has been insufficient to maintain this house without taking in boarders.

I am sure it did not escape your notice that all our boarders are young women of pleasing appearance. This is not accidental. Mother chooses them with great care. All of them have admirers who contribute financially to their upkeep, and the rent is a proportion of their income.

Since prohibition came into effect last year, there is great demand for drink. One of the regular visitors is Captain van Zant of the steamer Den Hoorn. He can provide a reliable supply of Batavia Arrack, a type of rum, at a reasonable price. Because of this, we have begun serving the men drinks in the salon, where Mother has had a mahogany bar built, and business is thriving.

The Mayor and the Chief of Police are occasional visitors, and as a result, there are no legal issues,

Captain van Zant has taken a great interest in me, and I must admit that I find him a congenial character. He calls on me whenever he is in town, and we sometimes take a turn through Stanley Park in a carriage. Occasionally he rents a motorboat and treats Mother and me to an evening at the Wigwam Inn. We have also been to the cinema together. He has many amusing stories of adventures in sailing ships before he switched to steam.

I have reason to believe that Captain van Zant may propose to me soon, and I'm confident that Mother will accept him. I thought it would be prudent to let you know this, so there are no unpleasant surprises upon your return.

Yours in friendship,

Elizabeth

CHAPTER 3 – LOOKING BACK

After Darya left, I went back to the marina and got my car from the parking lot—a blue '65 Mustang convertible. I had just bought it up on the Kingsway for under a thousand dollars. Never buy a convertible on a sunny day! I missed the leaks in the top, and the rust already starting around the wheel wells. Duct tape patched the leaks, and I ignored the rust. It did run well.

On my way down Georgia Street, I made a mental list of what was known about the case. *A doomed geologist found a box and reburied it, somewhere in Alaska.* Princess Sophia *sank. The contents of the box were unknown.* It wasn't much, but I hoped I might find more at the library.

In those days, I used the Vancouver Public Library a lot. In fact, I met Suzy there in the "Boating" section, where we both reached for Eric Hiscock's *Cruising Under Sail* at the same time. We ended up sharing the book…

There was a vacant parking meter on Burrard. The meters were new and demanded an outrageous amount for an hour. I found a quarter and paid up. Inside, I breezed by the front desk and went straight to the newspaper archives. Because I knew the date, it didn't take me long to find the story of *SS Princess Sophia*. The headline on the Alaska Daily Empire read: "PRINCESS SOPHIA SINKS AND 350 SOULS PROBABLY PERISH."

Alaska State Library, Photo Collection

THE ALASKA DAILY EMPIRE

"ALL THE NEWS ALL THE TIME"

| VOL. XII. NO. 1350. | JUNEAU, ALASKA, SATURDAY, OCTOBER 26, 1918. | MEMBER OF ASSOCIATED PRESS | PRICE TEN CENTS |

PRINCESS SOPHIA SINKS AND 350 SOULS PROBABLY PERISH

There were articles galore in many newspapers, but nothing about Jakob Holcomb. Bodies washed up on beaches for weeks afterward, and some names were given in the paper, but no Holcomb. I learned that it was still considered BC's greatest maritime disaster, although it happened in Alaska. It wasn't well known because it occurred in wartime when thousands were dying in Europe. The flu pandemic and the end of the war made more headlines at the time. I made photocopies of many of the articles, at a nickel a page. Expenses were accumulating, although I didn't officially have the job.

Then I tried to find information about the "Bay of Death", but I didn't have any luck without a geographical location. I gave up and went around the corner to the Devonshire Hotel for some lunch. When I saw the prices on the menu, I left and went back to the car. Then I drove over to Kitsilano, where parking was free and found a phone box. I called my friend Brice Pickett. Brice had an amazing memory and read a lot of books about boats and maritime history. I called him at the ship's chandler, where he worked. He had heard of the *Princess Sophia* disaster but had nothing to add to what I found at the library.

"What about the 'Bay of Death?' Or the 'Devil's Bay?' It's in Southeast Alaska, but I don't know where exactly."

"That sounds like something I should know about, but it doesn't ring a bell. I'll ask around and call you tonight. I have to get back to work."

In his daily work, Brice encountered captains and crew from all sorts of vessels, including towboats and fishing boats that plied the coastal waters up to Alaska. Somebody would know.

I went up to Broadway and had lunch at the Aristocratic. It was a proper diner where burgers and sandwiches were served by friendly uniformed waitresses. I had a grilled cheese on sourdough. The coffee was better than Brenda's. Of course, pretty much any coffee was better than Brenda's.

After lunch, I called Darya's law office. To my surprise, a recorded voice answered—the latest technology. There was no point in leaving a message because she couldn't call me back. Just as I was hanging up, she came on the line.

"Hello? This is Darya Hubert."

"Darya, this is Sean Gray. Have you spoken to your client about me?"

"Yes. She'd like to meet you. Would tomorrow morning at your office work?"

"Sure. Is 9 AM alright?"

"See you there."

I drove back home and parked the car at the marina lot. Down at the boat, I gave the bilge pump a few strokes, but no water came out. Then I went below and lay on the settee for a minute to collect my thoughts. I must have dozed off. The phone woke me up. It was a regular home phone, which plugged into a socket on the dock. I answered groggily.

"This is Sean."

"It's Brice. Eva asked me to invite you over for dinner. I have something for you. You can come over anytime now."

"Okay. That sounds great! I'll be over in ten."

Brice's wife, Eva, was a petite blonde with a dazzling smile and a killer body. All that, and a great cook too. They lived on the next dock on an Alden designed, Lunenberg built sloop called *Mersey*. We often sailed in company.

Looking at my watch, I saw it was after six. I washed up and put on a clean shirt before heading over. I took a bottle of Mateus out of the bilge. It was drizzling, but the sky was still light. I had to pick my way along the dock carefully. Some of the planks were rotten. Power was provided by a series of extension cords running to shore. The management had promised new docks and wiring some time back, but I wasn't holding my breath.

The *Mersey* was a lovely sight. Her beautiful lines were marred only by several bags of sails, a crab trap, and a chimney on the cabin top. Living aboard a small boat forces some compromises. Not all the boats were as tidy as Pickett's. Several were ferro-cement hulks in various stages of construction or decomposition. Some newer fiberglass boats like Cals and Ericsons were interspersed with old Chris-Craft and lesser-known makes made of wood. Most were in poor repair. The nice ones were across the harbor in the Royal Vancouver and Burrard Yacht Clubs.

I knocked on the deck, then climbed aboard. Brice slid the companionway back and removed the drop-boards so that I could descend the steep ladder. As I did so, I handed him the wine. Eva had to move aside since the galley was right at the companionway. She greeted me with a hug and a peck on the cheek.

Moving forward, I let out a small cry as my forehead made sharp contact with a deck beam. Eva and Brice didn't react. They were used to it. The *Mersey* had exactly six feet of headroom under the beams. Both Brice and I were taller than that, but he never seemed to bump his head. Rubbing my forehead, I sat down at the saloon table while Brice poured the wine.

The boat was warm and cozy inside. Eva had made curtains for the ports, and the formerly dark wood interior had been painted in a cream color, leaving the mahogany finish on the trim and drawer fronts.

Eva was taking a tuna casserole out of the oven of a new Dickinson diesel stove, which provided heat as well as cooking capability. Through the winter, it was always on, but at that time of year, they would light it only in the evenings.

After we were seated at the table, I told them about Darya and the letter. They listened attentively. Eva asked a question.

"Did you see the flask the letter was in?"

"No. The letter I saw was a copy with some words blacked out. That includes the location."

Brice said, "I think I can clear that up for you."

He brought out a small book, more of a booklet, really.

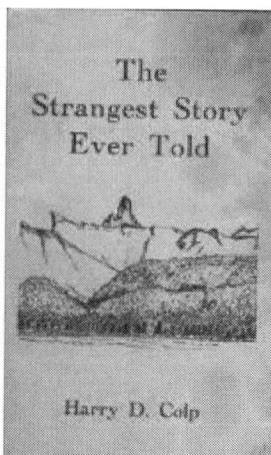

The story inside was only a few pages long, so I read it on the spot. It took place in 1900. It tells the tale of a prospector named Charlie who found quartz, hinting at a large gold deposit near a crescent-shaped lake. This is a partial quote:

Charlie gave his fellow prospectors the story on his finding the quartz and then said, "I thought I would climb the ridge directly over the ledge and get my landmarks. Right there, fellows, I got the scare of my life. I hope to God I never see or go through the likes of it again.

"Swarming up the ridge toward me from the lake were the most hideous creatures. I couldn't call them anything but devils, as they were neither men nor monkeys—yet looked like both. They were entirely sexless, their bodies covered with long coarse hair, except where the scabs and running sores had replaced it. Each one seemed to be reaching out for me and striving to be the first to get me. The air was full of their cries and the stench from their sores and bodies made me faint.

"I forgot my broken gun and tried to use it on the first ones, then I threw it at them and turned and ran. God, how I did run! I could feel their hot breath on my back. Their long claw-like fingers scraped my back. The smell from their steaming, stinking bodies was making me sick, while the noises they made, yelling, screaming, and breathing drove me mad. Reason left me. How I reached the canoe...is a mystery to me.

"When I came to, it was night, and I was lying in the bottom of my canoe, drifting between Thomas Bay and Sukoi Island, cold, hungry, and crazy for a drink of water. You no doubt think I am crazy or lying. Never let me hear the name Thomas Bay again, and for God's sake, help me get away tomorrow on that boat!"[1]

The book mentioned in the introduction that the area was known as the "Bay of Death" after a massive landslide in 1750 wiped out a native village, killing over 500 people.

I said, "That certainly sounds like the place. Thanks for that."

Brice refilled our glasses. "There's more. The old guy who gave me this book said there are two schools of thought on the story. Apparently, it's still a common topic for debate in Alaska. One group believes Charlie made it up to discourage other prospectors and steal the gold from his partners. Another group believes he stumbled on survivors of a sunken ship carrying Chinese laborers to the canneries. If they were marooned there for a long time, they might have been in a bad way. Mountain goats are common there, and they could have been wearing untanned goatskins. That would account for the stench. Add to that untrimmed hair and nails, and shouting in an unknown language, and you can see how a fellow could think

---

[1] Colp, Harry D. (1900) *The Strangest Story Ever Told*

they were devils. They probably thought he would rescue them."

I was speechless for a moment while I digested this. There were other possible explanations. Chinese laborers were certainly imported to the area to work in the many salmon canneries. And the pot Jakob found supported that theory. A trip to the Maritime Museum was in order.

We finished the evening with a game of cards. Then I went home to my empty bunk.

CHAPTER 4 – POLAROID

In the morning, I awoke early. I could hear the clang of halyards on aluminum masts, indicating a brisk wind. The sun was streaming in the port above my bunk and warming my cheek. I peeked out and saw a bright blue sky with a few fluffy clouds scudding along—another glorious day in paradise. I rolled out of the vee-berth. On my bare feet, the cold teak floor reminded me that it wasn't quite summer, so I dressed quickly, put on a jacket, and went up the dock. I continued up Denman to Davie Street. My buddy Sid Engelmann lived in a recently erected high-rise.

Sid was a school friend from Edmonton and a collector of old things. He had cameras dating back to the last century, wind-up phonographs, and odd musical instruments. For example, he had an electric zither, and a two-string Oriental violin called an "erhu." That wasn't why I went to visit him. His apartment had a shower with plenty of hot water.

He wasn't a morning person, so I never called him before ten. He had given me a key, so I could slip in quietly and use the shower, which I did. I had to move some negatives hanging from the curtain rod to dry. The bathroom had no window, so he used it as a photographic darkroom.

As I dried off in the living room after my shower, the bedroom door creaked open. Sid was a big guy, as tall as me but a few pounds heavier, wearing striped flannel pajamas and fuzzy slippers with bunny ears. He covered his eyes and moaned, "For God's sake, put on some clothes!"

I didn't answer, and he continued past me to the tiny kitchen, where crashes and curse words accompanied the sound of the news on his transistor radio—the usual stuff. Riots in Paris, student protests against the Vietnam war, a big plane crash, missing hikers on Mount Seymour, and the Montreal Canadiens won the Stanley Cup.

By the time I had dressed, Sid had produced two steaming cups of coffee. He handed me one, and we sat down on the couch. Then he started his morning rant.

"You can't get a decent cup of coffee and a bagel in this town. The clubs only have rock or folk music. What about Jazz and Bluegrass?"

"Bluegrass? Seriously? This isn't Kentucky. And the cave has Jazz sometimes. I saw Mitzi Gaynor there." I wasn't a serious music fan.

When he finished, I told him about the letter and what I knew about *Princess Sophia* and Thomas Bay. I promised to show him the book later, as it was still on the boat.

"That sounds like you'll be taking off on one of your crazy adventures. Don't try to include me. I swore off death for Lent."

"You aren't Catholic," I said over my shoulder as the door closed behind me. Then I went back and knocked on the door.

"Now what?"

"I forgot that I need to borrow a camera."

I just had time to go back to the boat, hang my towel to dry and grab *The Strangest Story Ever Told*, and head up to the office. As I passed through the Shipmate, I called out to Brenda, who was reading a copy of the *National Enquirer* with the headline "Sasquatch to run for Congress."

"Brenda, could you please bring up a pot of coffee and three cups to my office? I have company arriving soon."

She snorted, "Sure thing, right after I finish the paper. Maybe by tomorrow."

It was worth a try. Maybe I should have left a tip the last time.

Ten minutes later, Darya came up the stairs. The door was ajar, so she came straight in.

With her was an older lady dressed in a tailored suit of black and white houndstooth fabric. I later found out it was by Chanel. She wore white gloves and white high-heel shoes. Her hair was blonde and waved like Lauren Bacall's. I figured she must be in her seventies, but she was still a beauty. She stood not much over five feet tall, even with the heels. Trim of line, she moved with a youthful flair.

"This is Elizabeth Hadley," Darya said. Miss Hadley slipped off her right glove and held her hand out to me. I wondered if I was supposed to bow and kiss it but settled for a light shake.

"Charmed." She sounded as if she meant it. Her accent had a slight British inflection.

"So glad to meet you," I said. Just then, Brenda appeared at the door with a carved wooden tray on which were a silver coffee pot, cream jug, and sugar bowl, along with three delicate cups and saucers. I tried not to look surprised. She put it down on my desk and handed us each a cup. I swear she even curtseyed before taking her leave.

"Thank you, Brenda," I called out to the empty doorway.

"Very elegant," said Miss Hadley. I was so stunned it was left to Darya to pour the coffee, which she did with great poise. When they were both seated, I told them what I had found in my research and showed them the book.

Darya said, "I'm impressed that you figured out it was Thomas Bay and found those stories about the place." She shuddered visibly and shook her head. "Very scary."

"Miss Hadley, do you have the original letter with you?"

"Call me Lizzie. Yes, I have it here." She reached into her purse and removed an unmarked envelope. The edges of the letter were curled as if it had been rolled up. It read as expected, with Thomas Bay and Petersburg in places blacked out on my copy.

I looked it over carefully for any other clues, but found nothing, "Lizzie, why are we here? What do you want to accomplish? These events took place fifty years ago."

Lizzie leaned forward with passion in her green eyes. "I want to mount an expedition to Thomas Bay and find that box and its contents."

"But why? Chances of finding the box are slim, and the contents are likely of little value. Probably some Chinese trinkets if the story about cannery laborers is true."

Lizzie responded, "Call it closure. I want to get some idea of what poor Jakob experienced that frightened him so. He was a brave man, in robust physical condition, yet something there terrified him. I want to know what it was."

"So, this is a quest for understanding? No other agenda?"

"None.'

"And you want me to lead the expedition?"

"Yes. I'll finance it, and you can take any other people you need."

"It's over a thousand miles from here. Are you proposing that we go by boat? It would take several weeks to get there in my sailboat. It's too dangerous to travel at night, so eighty miles a day would be the best we could expect."

"No. You will take my boat, *Lady L.*"

"That boat belongs to you?" I was shocked. The *Lady L* was an old classic motor yacht, moored directly across from my boat at the Royal Vancouver Yacht Club, next to the Boeing family's *Taconite*, which was about 120 feet long. *Lady L* was perhaps a bit shorter but not much, and similar in style, with an upright stem and fantail stern.

"Yes. It was built in 1928, originally called the *Malachite*, and belonged to a mining promoter. He went broke in the crash of twenty-nine, and my husband bought it cheap in 1932. Come to my house tomorrow, and I will tell you more about the history. We can also discuss financial arrangements."

Lizzie was a much wealthier person than I had expected. There was a chance the expedition would be a lot of fun, even if unsuccessful. And it would help me pay my bills.

"Alright, but before you go, something is bothering me. I want to see the flask the letter was in and determine why it was suddenly delivered after fifty years. Did you see the person who delivered it?"

Lizzie said, "Sort of. I was by the door when it came through the mail slot, and I opened it and looked out. A young woman was walking away quickly, and she turned toward Denman. I didn't chase after her but stood there and opened the letter."

"Can you describe her?"

"She was a bit taller than me, with long black hair tied back in a ponytail. I saw her face. She turned and glanced at me. She was oriental, probably Chinese. She was wearing black pants and a white shirt with long sleeves."

"Okay, that's a start. I'm going to find her and ask to see the flask. Let me start by taking your picture," I opened a desk drawer and took out the Polaroid camera I had borrowed from Sid.

Lizzie looked surprised, "Why do you need my photo?"

"I'll explain it tomorrow. I want to get going, so let's wrap up here for now."

After I took the photo and checked that it turned out well, Darya and Lizzie said goodbye and left. I had a feeling I had missed something, but I let it go

I brought down the coffee tray, put it on the counter, and then slipped Brenda a twenty-dollar bill. She stood on tiptoe, hugged me, and kissed me lightly on the cheek. I had never seen her so happy.

Note to self: tip the waitress.

Polaroid photo in hand, I set out to find the mysterious woman who delivered the letter. I went into every business on the West side of Denman Street. I figured if she carried it by hand, she either lived or worked in the neighborhood. There were two banks, many restaurants, a movie theater (closed at the time), a self-service laundromat, a dry cleaner, and a few others.

I found two young women of Asian extraction who met the description. The first was a teller at the Bank of Montreal. She didn't react to the photo, and I believed her when she said she didn't know Lizzie.

At the dry cleaner, the second woman, a girl really, smiled when she saw the photo, "I don't know the lady, but I have cleaned that suit. A young woman with red hair brings it in, but I know it isn't hers. Too small for her."

That only told me that Lizzie had help.

When I got to the intersection with Davie Street, near Sid's apartment, I almost turned around to do the East side of Denman. But it was after one o'clock, and I hadn't eaten anything. I remembered that the English Bay Café was just around the corner on Beach Avenue. They had a cheap lunch special. It was there I found her.

The English Bay Café was a nondescript two-story stucco building painted pale yellow with brown trim. The menu was typical for a Chinese-Canadian café. Burgers and Chop Suey. There were booths down one side and a counter with stools on the other. Assorted tears and cigarette burns punctuated the brown vinyl upholstery. At the back of the room was a hallway leading to a single washroom and a flight of stairs. A pair of swinging saloon doors led to the kitchen.

I took a battered mimeographed menu from the counter and sat at the booth nearest the window. There were no other customers. No staff was in sight, but I could hear voices in the kitchen. The swinging door opened, and a young woman came out. She matched Lizzie's description perfectly. She was a real beauty, although she wore no make-up. High cheekbones and black, almond-shaped eyes that glittered set off a trim, athletic body. She was in black slacks and a white shirt with an apron on top.

"Can I take your order?" Her voice was confident, without any accent.

"Coffee, and mushrooms on toast."

"Certainly, sir." She turned and went to the kitchen door where she said something in Cantonese. Then she went behind the counter and poured a cup of coffee into a thick china mug. She grabbed a handful of creamers and brought it over. It was fresher and stronger than Brenda's.

"Can I ask you about something?" I pulled out the photo of Lizzie and put it on the counter. She saw it, blushed, and looked away. I knew I had the right person.

"Do you still have the flask?"

She sat down slowly in the booth opposite me. "How do you know about that?"

"I'm working for Elizabeth Hadley, the woman to whom you delivered the letter. She described you to me."

"Are you a detective?"

"My name is Sean Gray. I'm not a licensed investigator, just helping out. What's your name?"

"Cynthia Lu. And I do have the flask." A bell rang in the kitchen. "I'll show you after you finish eating."

She got up and went to get my plate. There were still no other customers, so she sat down opposite me again. Her voice had a pleasantly chirpy quality.

"My Dad found the flask a long time ago. He used to love beachcombing, and he has a big collection of things he picked up, mostly bottles. He never opened the flask. I was cleaning up and throwing things away when I came across it. I was curious about the contents. The lid was tight, and I had to heat it to get it open. I found the letter."

"Is he…?"

"Dead?" She smiled ruefully, "No, but he had a severe stroke. We had to put him in a nursing home. He won't be coming back."

"I'm sorry."

"Don't be. Dad's been out of it for quite a while. Mom and I have to decide what to do with this place. I have been cleaning up and disposing of some of the stuff."

"Cynthia, this is a valuable location, right on the water. Do you own the building?"

"Call me Cindy. Yes, my parents own the building, but we're thinking of selling it."

We talked a bit more about the ever-rising value of real-estate in Vancouver. I finished my lunch, and Cindy got up and cleared away the dishes. She locked the front door and walked to the back hall. A single bare bulb lit the steps dimly. I couldn't help appreciating her graceful form and the light, easy way she ran up the steps.

At the top, she turned left into a small room. It was a study with a single chair, a TV, and a bookshelf filled with bottles, many encrusted with barnacles. There were soda, whiskey, medicine, and perfume bottles. None looked valuable or rare, just old. She picked up the flask and handed it to me. When our fingers touched, a jolt of electricity ran up my arm, and I almost dropped the container.

I laughed, "Wow. Did you feel that?"

"Yes. Static electricity. It's the nylon carpet up here."

"I was hoping for a less scientific explanation."

"Are you flirting with me?" She grinned and tilted her head in a way that did little to discourage me.

"Absolutely. You are the best thing I have seen in a long time."

"Listen, I'm a waitress. I get it all the time." She did a passable imitation of a deep male voice, "Say, baby, what time do you get off work?"

"I give them this look." She looked me in the eyes with a fierce stare that could vanquish a dragon, "They give up."

Her index finger pointed at me, then drooped. I got the message and laughed.

"I don't give up that easily."

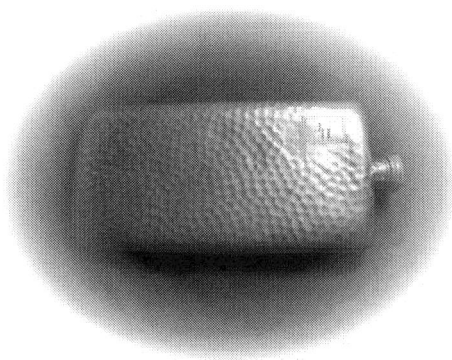

I examined the flask. It wasn't silver as I expected, but pewter, with a dimpled finish. The initials "JH" were engraved on the front. On the bottom was stamped "MacGregor & Smith, Glasgow."

It showed signs of heavy use or perhaps bumping against rocks as it floated around. I unscrewed the lid, which came off smoothly. It appeared empty, but when I held it to the light, I could see something white. I showed it to Cindy. She licked her finger and reached in, coming out with a slip of paper. It was a claim check, the sort a camera shop gave you when you take in a film for developing.

Printed on one side in a curly script was "Front St. Photography, Juneau, Alaska." There was a phone number, but it had only three digits. On the back was written in pencil, "J. Holcomb, 9/15/18."

"Cindy, this is great! Can you meet me at Miss Hadley's tomorrow morning at nine? Bring the flask. She will certainly want to reward you."

She nodded. "I can open the café at ten. Will that be enough time?"

"Should be. Can I take this?" I held up the claim check.

"Sure."

We went back downstairs, where she gave me the bill. It was a dollar and ten cents, but feeling generous, I left a two-dollar note.

I headed around the corner to bring Sid up to date. I asked what kind of camera someone would have been likely to carry in 1918.

"A Kodak for sure. It would probably look a lot like my Dad's old camera."

If it isn't an Eastman, it isn't a Kodak.

The No. 1 Autographic
KODAK, *Special*

Small enough to go in your pocket—*conveniently.*

Good enough to do any work that any hand camera will do—*satisfactorily.*

SPEED. The shutter has a speed of 1/300 of a second and slower controllable speeds to one second—also has the time and bulb actions, *and is large enough to give the full benefit of the anastigmat lenses* with which the camera is listed.

QUALITY. All the way through the No. 1 Autographic Kodak *Special* has that mechanical precision, that nicety of adjustment and finish that gives the distinction of "class".

SIZE. The pictures are 2½ x 3¼ inches; the camera measures but 1¾ x 3¼ x 6½ inches, in spite of the fact that its equipment provides for anastigmat lenses of the highest speed.

AUTOGRAPHIC. It is "autographic", of course. All the folding Kodaks now are. You can date and title the negative easily and permanently at the time you make the exposure.

SIMPLICITY. Effective as it is, the Kodak Idea, Simplicity, has not for one moment been lost sight of, there are no complications. The No. 1 Autographic Kodak, *Special*, has the refinements that appeal to the expert—to the beginner it offers no confusing technicalities.

THE PRICE.

No. 1 Autographic Kodak *Special*, with Zeiss-Kodak Anastigmat lens, *f.*6.3,	$45.00
Do., with Cooke Kodak Anastigmat lens, *f.*6.3,	36.00
Do., with Zeiss-Tessar, Series Ic lens, *f.*4.5,	56.00

All Kodak Dealers'.

EASTMAN KODAK CO., ROCHESTER, N. Y., *The Kodak City.*

The camera he showed me was a folding bellows type with a tiny viewfinder. It was an Autographic, with a feature allowing you to write a note to appear on the margins of the film. Even the latest cameras didn't have that.

"I don't know the year it was made, but there's a list of patents on it, the last one is from 1915, so probably about the right age."

After that, Sid and I took a walk around the West End, and I pointed out Lizzie's home. It was the first time I had seen it myself. Two city lots contained a large house. The surrounding wall and first floor were stone, the upper parts stucco, and wood. Very impressive.

Only a few houses in that style were left, as high-rise apartments were springing up everywhere in the West End. The only other one that came to mind was the old Rogers mansion on Davie. Lizzie's wasn't quite as fancy, but close.

Behind a wrought iron gate was a driveway leading to a single garage. The door was open, and a uniformed driver was polishing an old Rolls-Royce with enormous headlights. It was black with cream flanks.

Sid headed home, and I walked back along Denman, toward the boat. On my way, I passed a tall skinny hippy, wearing nothing but sandals. Hair grew profusely from all parts of his body. He had flowers in his reddish-brown hair. Not that hair—*that* hair. One look at his eyes told me he was a space cadet.

"Hi, Sean." He whispered as he passed. I had no idea who he was.

Welcome to Vancouver. I never saw anything like that in Alberta.

In the afternoon, I took a trolley downtown and joined a few friends at the St. Regis Hotel pub.

We sat at a small round table filled with beer glasses. There was a lot of laughter as we watched the mixed crowd of business people and hippies. I recounted an abbreviated version of the story of *Princess Sophia* and the letter in a flask. I left out all mention of Thomas Bay or the carved box. They weren't that interested. I kept my attraction to Cindy quiet.

About nine, I caught a trolley along Pender and went back to the boat. I didn't have much to drink, maybe five beers. Strange how the dock seemed narrower than usual.

When I climbed into the cockpit of my boat, the companionway was open. The ship's bell rang from below as I started to descend. Brenda, the waitress from the Shipmate, was sitting on the port settee. I was surprised. I certainly wasn't expecting her.

"Hello, sailor," Brenda cooed. She was wearing a yellow cotton bathrobe, which dropped to the floor as she stood up. Always the observant detective, I noticed the absence of anything underneath. I also observed that Brenda looked much better naked than the hippy did.

"Brenda, this isn't a good idea." I stepped closer and picked up the robe, trying to pull it back on. She shrugged it off and put a hand behind my head, pulling my face to hers. I tried to resist, but her tongue snaked into my mouth. Her lips were full and soft. So was the rest of her.

CHAPTER 5 – NOT A DREAM

In the morning, I woke up with a headache. My mind replayed last night's events. In my mental fog, I wasn't certain Brenda had been there. Maybe it was a dream. I was prone to realistic dreams, so it was possible. When I got out of bed, I spotted a pair of lacy red panties on the saloon floor. Not a dream.

I lit the propane stove and made a pot of strong coffee. There were two eggs in the icebox, along with an onion. I diced the onion and scrambled it with the eggs. After eating and doing the dishes, I felt almost human. It was time to head up to Lizzie's place.

Walking up Denman, I thought about Lizzie's reason for sending me to Alaska. The story in the letter didn't seem enough motivation. I decided to confront her.

I was a few minutes late. When I rapped the door knocker—a brass lion head—a young woman in a maid's uniform came to the door. She was about five-six, with flaming red hair, freckles, and maybe a few extra pounds on her hips. She wasn't smiling.

"You must be Sean Gray. You're late. Miss Hadley is expecting you. The parlor is through there." She pointed to the left but didn't lead the way.

The hall was plain, with polished maple floors and cream walls, devoid of decoration. The parlor had a heavy oaken door with a stained glass inset. It was open. Lizzie and Cindy were already seated on an antique Chesterfield of carved mahogany with tufted red velvet upholstery. Lizzie was examining the flask.

They looked up as I came in, and Cindy stood up. Lizzie waved me to a seat opposite.

"Darya will be here in a little while. Cindy and I have been getting acquainted." They both smiled. I imagined they had been talking about me.

"We were just discussing the contents of the letter. Cindy has read it of course." Lizzy said, her British-Canadian accent apparent.

I said, "I have some questions for you, Lizzie. First, I think you should reward Cindy for her help, then let her get back to her work."

I liked Cindy—a lot—but I didn't want her to know too much.

"Already taken care of. Right, Cindy?"

"Yes, Miss Hadley. Two hundred dollars is most generous. I'll be on my way now." She turned to me and winked. "Stop by the café later if you get the chance. We have an offer."

Just after Cindy left, Darya came in. I hadn't started talking yet.

I stood up and exchanged greetings with Darya, and then she sat down. The maid brought in a tray of tea and tiny triangular sandwiches and set them down silently.

I said, "Lizzie, I have a few things I need to know before we get into the logistics of the expedition. First, who have you told about the letter?"

"Nobody except Darya and you, of course. Cindy has seen it too."

"What about your maid?"

"Stella? She might have heard us talking, but I haven't shown it to her. I keep it locked up."

I got up and closed the parlor door.

"Okay, I want to keep this quiet. Our expedition could attract the attention of the press, and we don't want any hangers-on following us."

I changed my tone, trying to sound stern.

"Lizzie, I don't believe you have told me everything. There is at least one previous letter from Jakob, isn't there?"

I wasn't Sherlock Holmes, but my bullshit meter was finely honed. There had to be more to the story.

Lizzie looked at her shoes for a moment. When she raised her face, it was angry.

"How dare you! That's none of your business."

"I'll take that as a 'yes.' I need to see it. I'm not going into something as complex as this without knowing more details."

Darya was looking on with great interest. Obviously, she didn't know about any other letter or *letters*.

"I admit there are several earlier letters. They're of a personal nature." Her anger was gone, replaced by a blush.

"Lizzie, I suspect that the letter in the flask contains coded information which relates to an earlier letter. I think that because there must be more at stake to make this expedition worthwhile. I need to read what you have. You can work with Darya to make a copy without personal information if it embarrasses you."

"Mr. Gray, you are quite presumptuous. I don't need to give you those details. You just do what I pay you to do."

Seeing red, I stood up and said, "Sorry, Miss Hadley. I don't work that way. If I am to lead the expedition, I need to know what this is *really* about. And I want to know a lot more about your relationship with Jakob and your marriage to Captain van Zant. If you aren't prepared to tell me, then please pay for my time so far and get someone else."

Darya finally spoke, "Sean, let me talk with Lizzie. Give me a call after one o'clock, and I'll let you know what we decide."

I went back to my office. The Shipmate was closed, although it was after 10 AM. I had a key because the door to my office was inside. I let myself in quietly. There was a light on in the kitchen, and I went back there. Gus, the chef—if you call someone who can make beans on toast a 'chef'—was slouched in a chair. He was a short, wide man with a completely bald head, big ears, and a large red nose. He looked miserable. A half-empty bottle of whiskey sat on the grill, which was off.

He looked up at me. "We was robbed last night. And Brenda didn't show this morning."

I felt guilty. "What was taken?"

"The money in the cashbox. The float plus the weeks' take. Today's Friday, the day I go to the bank to deposit. I don't know the exact amount. A few hundred, not more than five. The door was locked when I got here, so they had a key."

"Did you call the police?"

"Nah. Brenda's a terrific gal. If she did it, I don't want her arrested."

Neither did I. Then, it occurred to me to check my office. "Gus, I'll be back in a minute. I want to look upstairs."

My office door was ajar. The desk had been moved, and all the drawers were open. The bookshelf, which was hinged like a door, was swung out, revealing the old safe behind. The safe door was open, too. That wasn't a surprise to me, though. Since I'd inherited the safe, but not the combination, I'd glued the knob so it wouldn't accidentally lock. Inside was a half bottle of Cockspur Rum and a nearly full bottle of Crown Royal. The box containing an unopened bottle of Glenlivet— a birthday present from my father—was missing.

However, the thief failed to find the hidden double back in the safe. The copy of the letter Darya left me was still there. I figured he or she was just after money. Then I remembered what happened with Brenda the night before. The bell could have been a signal to someone that I would be occupied for a while. Brenda had heard me talking to Darya. She probably wouldn't be back. I closed the safe and the bookcase and went downstairs.

I told Gus that someone had been in there, but nothing was missing except some booze. I took the opportunity to pay my rent for the week, just to make him feel a bit better. He made me promise to try and find him another waitress. He seemed to think I ran an employment agency.

I got my Mustang from the marina and drove to the Maritime Museum in Kitsilano. I spent an hour or so there and came away with a copy of the crew and passenger list for *Princess Sophia* on her last voyage. It revealed little new information. I didn't find any listed wrecks that could explain a Chinese presence in Thomas Bay.

I stopped at the English Bay Café for lunch. It was busier than the last time, and it was a while before Cindy could sit across from me. When she did, she flashed a big grin.

"A hundred and fifty thousand. That's the offer. It's more than the tax assessment. A developer. They'll knock it down and put up something bigger and more modern."

It was a lot of money, but I was still skeptical. "Don't accept it yet. Let me check them out and make sure they are legit. What's the name of the company?"

She handed me a card. It was a numbered company, and the name given was Irwin Joseph. I copied the information down and gave her back the card. I promised to call her later, and she wrote down the number for the upstairs suite where she lived with her mother.

I used the café phone to call Darya.

CHAPTER 6 – THE LOOK

When Darya came on the line, she told me Lizzie Hadley had decided to recount her story and give me a copy of Jakob's other letter.

"Lizzie has kept diaries since childhood. She has reviewed them and made notes of the main events. Come over to her house tomorrow morning around ten. She'll answer your questions then."

"Thanks, Darya, I have you to thank for this, don't I?"

Darya chuckled, "Definitely. You can repay me by taking me sailing sometime. I've never been on a sailboat."

"Done, but I have one more favor to ask. Do you know anything about real estate and commercial property sales?"

"I guess I do. Most lawyers in Vancouver spend a big part of their time on contracts and conveyancing, and I'm no different."

"Do you know a guy by the name of Irwin Joseph?"

"I've seen his name on a few contracts. He's been buying up properties in the West End, particularly along the beach. He built a couple of high rises near the Burrard Bridge. Legit, but drives a hard bargain."

"He offered Cindy one-fifty for the English Bay Café. I think it might be worth more. Can you check it out for me?"

"Sure. I'll call you tonight if you'll be home."

. "Make it after nine, and I'll be there for certain. We can talk about sailing too."

I sat down at a table and called Cindy over. I told her Darya was checking up on Irwin Joseph and would call me later. Then I added. "Have dinner with me tonight?"

She gave me "the look." I laughed.

Cindy relented and reverted to her usual cheery expression, "Pick me up at six-thirty. I'll be around the corner at the Berkeley Tower. My mother doesn't like me to date *gweilo*."

When I pulled up in front of the Berkeley a minute or two late, I didn't see Cindy. A young woman in a dark red dress and high heels was standing in the shadows of the doorway. She turned toward me and stepped forward. Wow. The waitress had become a movie star. I got out of the car and went around to open the door for her. She threw her arms around me and kissed me on the cheek.

"What did you do to Irwin Joseph? He called and raised the offer to two-fifty. He sounded meek."

"Me? Nothing. But Darya may have spoken to him. Don't accept it yet."

She got in the car. "Where are we going?"

"Well, I was thinking of the White Spot drive-in. But seeing you now, I'm thinking Hy's Steak House."

She turned to me and put a hand on my knee. "I have another suggestion."

"I'm all ears."

"Do you like Japanese food?"

"I've never had it, so I can't say. But I'm willing."

"I'm sure you are, but let's have dinner instead. Aki's is down on Powell Street near Main, in the area that used to be Japantown. Only two or three restaurants are left, and Aki's is the only one with a Japanese owner. You can't get sushi anywhere else."

When we got to Aki's, we were greeted at the door by a woman in a traditional kimono, who led us to a tatami room with a sliding door. I knew what it was because Cindy told me what to expect on the way over. We took off our shoes and left them outside. Inside was a table surrounded by woven reed matting. It looked like we would have to sit on the floor, but there was a recess under the table for our feet. The waitress put two menus on the table and slid the door closed. It was completely private. I wondered if that was why Cindy liked the place.

"I've only been here once before, with my friend Barbara Kitayama. She showed me what to order. I loved it."

"Okay. I have no clue about Japanese food, so you do the ordering. But no raw fish!"

Cindy grinned and stuck out her tongue at me. When the waitress came, she ordered. I didn't pay attention, thinking about other things. The waitress left and came back in a minute with a teapot and two tiny cups. Cindy poured.

"That looks like pretty weak tea."

"It's *Sake*, silly."

I took a sip. It was hot and alcoholic. Not bad.

"Okay, I admit that I like 'sake silly.' Please pour some more."

Cindy took a drink herself, then moved closer to me and filled the cups. I was about to kiss her when the door slid open, and the food arrived. I had never seen sashimi before, but I knew raw fish when I saw it. Cindy showed me how to use the small, pointy Japanese chopsticks, and I didn't do too badly. I liked the raw fish much more than I expected, and the tempura prawns were fabulous. The spicy green stuff called *wasabi* cleaned out my sinuses.

We had a great time. I learned Cindy was born in Hong Kong after her parents fled from China during the Communist revolution. She was brought to Canada as a toddler. Her father was a teacher in China but ended up working as a waiter in Vancouver until he saved enough to buy his own restaurant, with help from his older brother.

Cindy was the only Chinese kid in most of her classes at school, although a few more appeared later. I was the first guy she had been out to dinner with, although she admitted to having walked on the beach with one or two others.

Cindy asked me a few questions about my background, and I told her pretty much what I had told Darya. Then she hit me with a zinger.

"I don't like beards."

I had a full beard, brownish on my chin but tending toward blond on the mustache. Before I could say anything, she continued.

"But I like yours. At least it's well-trimmed."

I said, "I like everything about you so far, but I want to know more. What do you do for fun?"

She looked serious.

"My family isn't big on fun. Working hard has always been the focus. The TV is always on in the evenings after the café is closed, but I prefer reading. My library card is well worn."

I asked, "Who are your favorite authors?"

"Jane Austen and Ernest Hemingway. Han Suyin. I like Agatha Christie and John Steinbeck too."

Only one Asian author, coincidentally one I had read. I was surprised at some of her choices, but I didn't comment.

Cindy slid alongside me. After the dishes were cleared, we drank some more sake. I put my arm around her, and she leaned against me. Then the bill arrived, and I paid in cash. It was pricey (not much change from a twenty) but worth it.

The evening was balmy, and I put the top down for the drive home. We motored slowly through downtown and along Robsonstrasse, where many pedestrians were looking in the shop windows. The Mustang's bucket seats didn't encourage hanky-panky, so I invited Cindy back to my boat.

"I'd love to see it, but Mom worries if I'm out late."

"You could phone her from the boat."

Cindy giggled, "Then she'd *really* worry. Better take me home. I'll call you tomorrow. Don't phone me. You'll get me in trouble."

I stopped the car around the corner from the café and got out to say goodnight. I got a short kiss on the lips and a hug. It was enough to leave me semi-delirious.

CHAPTER 7 – LIZZIE'S STORY

The next morning I had breakfast at the English Bay Café. It was busy, and Cindy had no time to sit with me until I was finished. As she came around with more coffee, her mother came out of the kitchen, took one hard look at me, and went back inside. Cindy winked at me but didn't speak. I took the hint, gave her a little wave, and dropped some money on the table.

Lizzie's house was a five-minute walk from the café, and I arrived almost exactly on time. To my surprise, Lizzie answered the door herself. She was dressed simply, in a plain white dress. On her feet were sensible shoes. Her long blonde hair was tied back. I wondered if it was a wig. She slipped out the door and closed it silently behind her.

"Hi, Sean. I'm so sorry I was rude to you yesterday. I have a bit of a temper sometimes."

She paused for a moment.

"Can we take a walk? The house is being cleaned, and I would like to keep our conversation private."

She seemed to be in a cheerful mood.

I said, "Of course. Any particular destination?"

Lizzie smiled up at me. "Not really, but maybe we could head down Denman to Stanley park? We can talk on the way."

We set off at a leisurely pace. To get things rolling, I asked Lizzie to tell me about her childhood.

"Were you born here?"

"Yes, my birthday is July the first. I won't say what year."

That was Canada's national holiday, celebrated in Vancouver with fireworks at English Bay.

"I was seven or eight before I found out the fireworks weren't for me."

"We lived in a shack where the garage is located now. The house wasn't completed until about 1911. I have never lived anywhere else."

"My father owned a saloon in downtown Vancouver. It must have been profitable, as our house was well built, with furnishings and artworks imported from San Francisco and Europe."

"Mother was much younger than Father. She was born in Sussex, to what she described as a 'quality family.' She was beautiful in her youth, although of short stature. As she got older, she became increasingly stout."

"I remember my girlhood fondly. I was sent to a girl's school—Miss Bishop's Academy—in a house just two blocks from ours. Young ladies were not expected to go to University, so we were given a practical education."

I asked, "What does that mean?"

Lizzie laughed.

"When repairs were needed at the school, Miss Bishop made us do them. I learned to hammer a nail, saw a board, and shovel coal. I didn't mind. The girls made a game of it. We learned how to keep a household ledger and write letters, both personal and business."

I asked, "What did you do for fun?"

"I had a special friend, Anne Stevens, who lived nearby. She was very lively, and we would run through Stanley Park. We turned over rocks to see the worms and beetles underneath. We would serve tea to Mr. Duck and Peter Pig, our stuffed toys."

"On warm summer days, we would go to the beach. Both of us learned to swim from the lifeguard, a huge black man named Joe. He was the kindest, gentlest man I ever met. All the children loved Joe, but I sometimes heard young men say rude things about his color."

We reached Georgia Street, and Lizzie pointed at the remains of the auditorium. She swept her arm to the left.

"There used to be an ice arena beside the auditorium. I learned to skate there. It burned down in the thirties. Big-name entertainers played the auditorium in the fifties. I saw Fats Domino once, and another time Sir John Gielgud gave a Shakespearean recital."

It was fascinating Vancouver history, but I wanted to stay with Lizzie's own life. I asked, "Did you finish High School?"

'Yes, I graduated in 1914, the year the war started. After that, I had no more education except for reading the books in our library."

I said, "Do you remember the war years?"

"Of course! Father was too old to join up, so our life didn't change much at first. Mother began to keep what she called a 'salon' on Saturday evenings. She invited artists, authors, and business people, and sometimes soldiers in uniform. We had an extensive wine cellar, with French and Italian vintages."

Lizzie and I continued on Georgia Street to the small lake known as 'Lost Lagoon.' Lizzie changed the subject.

"When I was young, *Lost Lagoon* actually was a lagoon, which dried out at low tide. When they built the road through Stanley Park, it was cut off and turned into a lake. Pauline Johnson named it."

We sat on a bench by the lagoon for a while. Majestic swans glided by, and a few young couples in rowboats appeared, more interested in each other than the birds.

Lizzie had witnessed the main events that turned Vancouver from a frontier town into a great city. Unfortunately, the history lesson was a side issue for me.

To get her back on track, I asked, "How did you meet Jakob?"

"I first met him at one of Mother's events, when the maid was ill, and I was pressed into service with a canapé tray. I was flirtatious by nature, and he addressed me in a friendly manner. A few weeks later, he was there again, and he asked me to sit with him. My mother did not object. I learned he was a geologist employed by mining companies to survey potential locations. He was a childless widower, his wife having died of cancer a few years previously. He was about fifteen years older than I and had been wounded in the Boer War."

"Jakob became a frequent visitor, although he was sometimes absent for weeks at a time. We became good friends. I never considered him a suitor."

We got up and strolled through the underpass beneath the Stanley Park causeway, past the Vancouver Rowing Club, a large mock-Tudor style building on piles over the water of Coal Harbour. Lizzie looked somber.

"1917 was the year everything fell apart. In February, my father died suddenly from a stroke while out walking. Mother was devastated, and I had to take on the running of the house. Father left us everything, but he had some debts. The only assets were the house and the saloon. The saloon made money, but in October, the provincial government introduced prohibition. The saloon had to close."

"Suddenly, we had no income. Mother realized prohibition created business opportunities. She continued the salon under slightly different terms. Wine was still served but at a dollar a glass. She started calling it a 'private club' and charged a ten-dollar membership fee. We began to open six nights a week. I was put in charge of collecting the money and paying the bills. It was no longer possible to buy wine, and the cellar began to run low."

"Mother found a source of whiskey in Blaine, Washington. It was delivered weekly in a grocery wagon to disguise the rather large quantity we were purchasing."

By then, we were walking past the Royal Vancouver Yacht Club, where *Lady L* was docked. It made me think about Hans.

I said, "How do you meet your husband?"

"I'm getting to that. Once the wine ran out and we had to pay for liquor, we didn't make enough money to manage on. The house had ten bedrooms and two bathrooms. Mother decided to rent out rooms to presentable young ladies. Soon six women occupied the bedrooms upstairs. Mother and I, along with the servants, were on the ground floor. The cook grumbled about extra mouths to feed, but the women, who all seemed to have jobs as secretaries or phone operators, often graced the evenings with their presence. A phonograph and a collection of recordings added some atmosphere."

"Around that time, Jakob stopped visiting, but I received monthly letters from Chile and later Peru. They were quite short, describing life in mining towns, and always ending with increasingly fervent expressions of affection. My replies were even briefer and never mentioned love. This did not deter him."

"Sometimes a young woman would disappear upstairs, followed by one of the gentlemen. I mentioned it to Mother, and she explained to me that she charged additional rent for those wishing to entertain in their rooms."

"One night, a dashing gentleman came to the house. He was dressed in a double-breasted blue uniform with polished brass buttons and wore a white Captain's hat. He was Captain Hans van Zant, owner of a trading steamer."

"I was immediately attracted to him. He was tall, with medium brown hair and a tanned complexion. Hans was about ten years older than I, with courtly manners and an infectious laugh. Although he had a Dutch name, he admitted to a cocktail of Dutch, British, and native blood, common in Batavia. We spent time together in the salon, where I had my first alcoholic drink in his company. He didn't smoke, except for an occasional cheroot after dinner."

"Hans was an astute businessman and sensed our need for a source of liquor. He offered to supply almost any quantity of excellent Arrack rum. Mother accepted and struck a deal."

"Around then, I got my last letter from Jakob, mailed from Alaska, and wrote a reply. Shortly afterward, we received news of the terrible tragedy of

Princess Sophia. I didn't know Jakob was aboard, although I thought it was possible. I was so besotted with Hans, I just put the letter away. I never heard from Jakob again."

Lizzie opened her handbag and handed me an envelope. Assuming it was the letter from Jakob, I slipped it into my pocket to read later.

"Whenever Hans was in port, we would walk together in the streets of the West End, and in Stanley Park, where he gave me my first kiss."

We arrived at Prospect Point, where there was a small navigation light. Lizzie paused.

"It was on a bench near here where Hans asked for my hand in marriage. He explained that he had a wife in Batavia, so it could not be strictly legal. I was in love, so I agreed anyway."

Lizzie blushed visibly and looked down.

"Later, in his room at the Sylvia Hotel…you can guess what happened. Soon we were spending long hours there. One day he presented me with an emerald engagement ring."

"Hans announced that we had married in secret in Victoria, and Mother gave a reception for us at the club. We began to live as man and wife. He moved into the house with us and gradually took charge of the business."

Lizzie laughed, "Prohibition was a total failure! The man in charge was even arrested for smuggling liquor."

Vancouver Daily Sun.

With Which Is Incorporated The Daily News Advertiser

THIRTY-FOURTH YEAR—No. 342   VANCOUVER, B. C., THURSDAY, DECEMBER 12, 1918   12 PAGES

Prohibition Commissioner Findlay Arrested Last Night

Charged with Illegally Importing Liquor Into the Province--Car of Rye Whiskey Missing

"After the war, Vancouver began to boom. Prohibition was repealed in BC, and the need for Arrack rum disappeared."

"Hans sold his ship. About that time, the United States started prohibition, with even more restrictions than BC. Hans saw the opportunity and purchased several small motor fishing boats. Soon he had a thriving business based in the South Arm of the Fraser River. Since alcohol had become legal in BC, supply wasn't a problem. On the US side, demand was high, and there was little water-borne enforcement."

"With the liquor export business booming, we stopped taking in boarders. Mother wanted to be a respectable pillar of society, so she started to host afternoon teas and attended St. Paul's Anglican Church, where she made many friends."

"Hans joined the Royal Vancouver Yacht Club. He moored a small sloop there for a time, in which we sailed on sunny afternoons on English Bay. He was interested in a larger yacht. We were invited out on boats belonging to other members, which was enjoyable. We took excursions to Bowen Island, Gibsons Landing, and up the Indian Arm. It was an idyllic time for us."

This was taking longer than I had anticipated. I glanced at my watch. Lizzie didn't notice. We were near the Totem Poles, which marked a small replica Indian Village. Lizzie sat on a bench.

She shook her head, "When I was a child, a few people were living here in shacks. All gone now."

"In 1929, the stock market crashed. Many of our friends lost everything. Hans was not much affected, as he had no stock investments, and the liquor trade still thrived."

"Hans saw the opportunity to acquire a large yacht. The *Malachite* had been seized by the bailiff. Boats were costly to store and maintain, so they were auctioned off quickly. There were few bidders, and he picked it up for a fraction of its original cost."

"*Malachite* was a splendid craft, 110 feet long, and 21 feet in breadth. There were seven large staterooms and a galley better than the kitchen in our house. It even had central heat, and according to Hans, she had all the latest instruments, including wireless. It was upholstered in tan leather and blue velvet, with lace curtains on the windows. There was hot and cold running water and even a bathtub in the owner's stateroom."

"Hans renamed her the *Lady L* in an elaborate ceremony meant to prevent bad luck. I broke a bottle of champagne on the bow."

"He started to wear his old captain's uniform when he was aboard, and although there was a paid crew, he usually took command of the wheel himself. We made some long voyages in her, including a six-week tour of the BC coast and Alaska."

"In the winter, Hans would take *Lady L* on at least two trips a month to the US, delivering liquor. The voyages were very profitable. Hans never told me exactly where he went to unload, but I handled our banking and saw to the accounts."

"In 1933 the US repealed prohibition. That ended the liquor business for us. Hans was resourceful, and he realized that another war was coming. He invested in a foundry in the industrial area of East Vancouver. It was slow going at first, but soon it thrived, making parts for ships and aircraft. In 1936 Hans bought the Rolls-Royce car I still have. He also modernized the house."

"When the war started in 1939, business boomed. We had a comfortable life, but by the end of the war, Hans was slowing down and moving with some difficulty."

Lizzie stopped. I could see her eyes glistening with tears. She took a handkerchief from her purse and wiped her eyes before continuing.

"Sorry. Just remembering. In 1946 Hans was diagnosed with spinal cancer, which was fatal within a matter of months. It destroyed me. I thought I would never laugh again. Mother stood by me and helped me through, as I did for her when Father died."

"Hans left me a considerable fortune, and I sold the foundry, which yielded a decent amount. I have lived on the proceeds ever since. Mother was taken from me in 1958. She simply did not wake up one morning. Somehow, I carried on. Since then, I have lived a quiet life."

I could see remembering the past had taken a toll on Lizzie. She looked tired. I said, "Thank you, Lizzie, I appreciate this. I'll walk you home now."

It was a fascinating insight into Vancouver's history but did little to solve the mysteries raised by Jakob's letters.

CHAPTER 8 – JAKOB'S LETTER

Sept. 9, 1918
General Delivery,
Juneau, Alaska

Miss Elizabeth Hadley
1618 Barclay St. Vancouver, BC

My Dearest Lizzie,

I think about you every day and hope that after my return, we can become engaged.

I have been in Alaska for some months now. I was initially here on a contract with Consolidated Mining to survey a potential copper mine site. The site quickly proved unsuitable, and my services were terminated. I decided to stay on and explore the area.

The coast directly south of Juneau, the capital, has only two significant towns, Petersburg and Wrangell. Neither has extensive shops or services, so I made Juneau my base. I intended to find a boat to rent but found nothing suitable, so I took a steamer to Skagway.

There I rented a small gas boat of some charm, called Scurry, *with a one-cylinder Easthope engine, a sleeping cabin, and a coal stove for heat and cooking. Behind it, I towed a canoe for shore excursions. I obtained the local charts and what geological surveys were available.*

My purpose was to explore areas where geological conditions indicated the probability of valuable ore deposits. Gold and silver were foremost in my mind, but I also considered zinc and lead. There are many bays and inlets in the area, and glaciers extending down to the water are common.

In one such bay, I found what I thought was suitable terrain for a gold mine and found quartz deposits, which often accompany gold. I found a couple of rocks that seemed to have veins of gold and took them aboard for subsequent assays.

When I tied to raise anchor, I found it firmly snagged, and try as I might, I could not get it loose. The water was cold, and I had no desire to enter it, but I had no other anchor. The water was only about 20 feet deep at low tide. I disrobed and dived in, pulling myself down by the anchor line, which was of heavy hemp. The water was milky with melted glacier water, but the rising tide brought in clear ocean water and gave me some visibility.

The anchor was snagged on a large iron box, about 6 feet on each side. It was heavily encrusted with barnacles. There were several large bolts on the sides. The anchor line was wrapped around two of them and was quickly freed. I dove again to investigate and chipped away some of the barnacles. It was a large ship's safe, apparently intact and closed. There was writing, but I couldn't make it out in the murky water. There were broken and rotted timbers and other debris in the surrounding area, so I was sure it was an old shipwreck.

After I moved my boat to an unobstructed location, I thought at length about the safe. Surely it must have some valuable contents. I determined to raise and open it. But Scurry was too small to carry something that size, and in any case, I lacked the equipment needed to lift it. I marked the spot where it was located by making a cairn of rocks fifty feet inland. The safe was located about eighty feet from shore, at right angles to the cairn. I also marked it by another method, in case the cairn was to be destroyed.

Alaska is full of scoundrels, so I did not record the bay's location in the ship's log or on the chart, in case they were to fall into the wrong hands. I intended to find a larger boat to charter, with a crane capable of lifting several tons and return here to retrieve the safe.

I explored the bay further and had some extraordinary experiences which I will not burden you with. After a short trip to Wrangell to mail this, I will come back to the bay for one last exploration for gold before returning Scurry to her owner. If there is no suitable vessel with lifting capabilities available in Skagway, there is a likelihood of finding such a boat in Juneau or, failing that, Prince Rupert. But winter is near, and I may be forced to wait until spring to complete the mission.

Lizzie, I'm sure that after I retrieve the valuables in that safe, I will be in a strong position to ask for your hand in marriage. Please wait for me, as I expect to be back in Vancouver before Christmas.

With all my love,

Jakob B. Holcomb

CHAPTER 9 – THREATENED

The next morning Darya called me on the boat, and I met her at my office. The Shipmate still hadn't re-opened, so we walked up to a convenience store and got a coffee to go. Then we strolled up Nelson St. toward Stanley Park and found a bench to sit on. Darya asked me about my meeting with Lizzie.

"What do you think of Lizzie's story?"

"I'd say it's a highly sanitized version of events. There had to be a lot more conflicts and intrigue than she indicated. They were operating several businesses outside the law, at least before the war. But for the most part, it rings true, and the parts I was interested in were there. What do you think her finances are like now?"

"Why do you ask?"

"First, I would like to make sure I get paid. Second, I'm trying to understand the motivation. Jakob's letter contains nothing that assures me the safe has value, and it will cost many thousands of dollars to retrieve it if we even find it."

"She's always paid my bills promptly, but I'm her lawyer, not her accountant."

"Okay, I'll ask her about it myself. By the way, thank you for what you did for Cindy. It will make a big difference to her family."

Darya grinned, "Always glad to be of service. It turns out Irwin Joseph owns the vacant lot next to the café, and the two lots together make a great building site for something bigger. Tell her to ask him for three hundred thousand."

"Darya, do you have an office? Your card just gives a phone number, no address."

"No. I have a penthouse apartment near the Burrard bridge, and the second bedroom is my office."

She opened her purse and took out a small plastic box with a red button on the top, "This is a pocket pager. It beeps when my answering service has a message for me, and I call them to pick up the message. It gives me the freedom to move around and never miss a call."

I was impressed. "I better get one of those, I have two phones and still miss quite a few calls."

As we parted, she reminded me of my promise to take her sailing. We decided on 10 AM the following Saturday. I asked her to wear rubber-soled shoes and a windbreaker. She promised to bring lunch.

I walked up to the English Bay Café to get something to eat and talk to Cindy. She didn't look happy to see me, which was a surprise. The place was busy, but when she got to me, she sat down, looking frightened.

"Sean, what's going on. Are you mixed up in something bad?"

I answered with alarm, "What's happened?"

"After you dropped me off last night, some guy grabbed me from behind and threatened me. He put his arm across my throat. He said I should stay away from you—he called you the tall beard—or I could get hurt. Then he pushed me away and ran off along Denman."

I was upset and worried about her. "Are you okay? Did he hurt you? Did you call the police?"

Cindy's voice cracked.

"Yes, no, and yes. I called you too, but you didn't answer. The police sent a car. A cop took a statement, but I don't think they'll do anything. His radio was busy with more urgent crimes. My mother blames you."

I had no idea why someone would threaten Cindy.

"I'm sorry I wasn't there. I'm going to get a pager right away, so I won't miss any more calls. Did you see the attacker's face? Can you describe him?"

"I didn't see his face at all. I saw his back. He was wearing jeans and a black sweatshirt. Short combed hair. It was dark, so I couldn't tell the color. He was a few inches shorter than you and sturdy, not fat. He had an accent, maybe Polish or Russian."

She was gradually getting back to her usual cheerful self, but she had a bad scare. I tried to reassure her.

"I don't have any enemies that I can think of. The only debts I have are with the Royal Bank and Wright Mariner, and they wouldn't threaten you. It must have something to do with the Alaska Job."

Cindy was still nervous, "Well, anyway, better stay away from here for now. We can talk on the phone. Call me tonight. I'll tell Mom to back off. I'm an adult and can talk to anyone I want."

I forgot to tell her what Darya said about the offer on the café,

After I left, I wondered who could have harassed Cindy. It might have had nothing to do with me, maybe a jealous suitor, or perhaps her mother hired someone. There were many drifters around who would do something like that for just a few dollars. I decided to let it lie. I took the bus downtown to the phone service Darya had recommended and signed up. When I walked out, I had a pager and answering service attached to my office phone. They would answer "Gray & Associates."

I went back to my office and called Lizzie. Stella fetched Lizzie to the phone without more than a grunt aimed at me.

"Elizabeth Hadley."

"Hello Lizzie, this is Sean. I thought about our talk and read Jakob's letter. I understand better now. Before we start organizing the expedition, I have one question. Can you afford it?"

"I can, but I suppose you have guessed that my funds are beginning to run short. I must admit that is the case, but for now, I'm still solvent."

"That's what I wanted to hear. Thanks for being candid. We'll get along fine if I'm kept informed. Now can we meet at your boat, so I can do an inventory and meet the crew?"

We agreed to meet at the RVYC docks at 4 PM. Lizzie suggested we could dine aboard, and Darya could join us. I agreed.

At a quarter to four, I used the halyard winch to lift the dinghy off the cabin top of *Tangled Moon* and launch it. It was a lovely lapstrake pram but on the heavy side.

I dug around in the cockpit locker and found the oars, noting that they needed re-varnishing. Then I rowed the short distance over to the Yacht Club and tied up at the end of the float where *Lady L* was moored. I strolled down the dock. *Lady L* was gleaming with fresh paint and varnish and looked almost new, although she was forty years old. A foldable teak stairway extended down from her high bulwark. I climbed up and knocked on the wheelhouse door, which was closed.

After a brief wait, the door slid open. The man who answered wore a captain's uniform of a slightly old-fashioned style, white, with gold epaulets. He wasn't wearing a hat, but a captain's cap was lying on the boat's dashboard.

I stuck out my hand, "Sean Gray."

He looked at my hand for a beat, then shook it once. "André LaPalme."

"Is it okay to call you *The Hand*?"

"Sure, as long as you don't expect to live past sunset." He grinned in a friendly way, and I could see that we'd get along fine.

"How about Skipper?"

"I had a dog by that name once, so no. Lizzie said you were a smartass. Call me André."

André was several inches shorter than I, with a mop of brown hair and a goatee. Apart from the uniform, he looked so little like my notion of a yacht captain that I felt a certain mental disconnect. He saw me eyeing the outfit.

"Lizzie called and told me to put on the uniform. I guess she wanted to impress you. How'm I doin' so far?" He had a slight French accent.

"I'm impressed by how young you seem to be. How did you get the job?"

"I was the deckhand—don't bother with the joke— paid the bare minimum. Captain Stewart was in charge and had been since the end of the war. He used to come into the marina pretty fast, with total confidence, then give it full power in reverse, stopping perfectly where we are now. It was dazzling to watch but scary from onboard."

He continued, "This boat has a single Atlas Imperial diesel engine. There is no gearbox. The engine can run in either direction. To get reverse, you ring the engine room telegraph. The engineer stops the engine, pulls a big lever to change the valve timing, and starts it up in reverse. The starter isn't electric. It uses compressed air. There is only enough stored air for two starts."

LaPalme narrated the story with hand gestures and sound effects.

"Anyway, a few months ago, Captain Stewart was coming in here, fast as usual. When he was a couple of hundred yards out, he rang for neutral. Ding. And the engine stopped. Then he rang for full astern. Chuffa, chuffa, chuff…and it didn't start. I was on deck with the spring line ready to drop over a cleat. He tried again. Ding.Ding. Chuff. Chuff. No go. As we headed into the slip, still moving quite fast, I dropped the loop of the spring line over the first cleat on the dock and yelled as I jumped away to the other side of the boat. The spring line grabbed and stretched. And stretched. The bolts holding the cleat to the dock snapped off with two loud bangs, and the cleat became a missile."

"We were barely moving when we hit the dock. *Lady L* weighs over a hundred tons, so there was still plenty of momentum. The dock splintered, and we continued almost all the way through it before grinding to a halt. By then, I had another line on and ran around getting it tied up. The captain was staring straight ahead like a zombie. After a few minutes, he took off his cap and dropped it on the floor. Then he went into his cabin and slammed the door."

"He retired the next day. Lizzie asked me if I could handle his job, and I said I could. So here I am." He bowed theatrically, sweeping off an imaginary hat.

I was about to applaud when Lizzie and Darya appeared on the dock. A loud wolf whistle came from inside the wheelhouse, and a big red and blue macaw flew out and alighted on the rail.

"Hey baby, how about it?" The parrot said to Darya. His diction was perfect, his baritone voice sounded utterly human.

"Quiet Ajax. Go inside." Lizzie spoke with authority, and the parrot disappeared back into the wheelhouse, grumbling to himself in a language I didn't recognize.

CHAPTER 10 – *LADY L*

Lizzie and Darya came aboard. Lizzie was wearing wide-leg pants. Not bell-bottoms, which were in fashion, these went straight from the waist. Her blouse was white with a blue collar and a small scarf at the neck. She looked like a 1930s movie star out for a day on the water. Darya wore her usual business suit and carried a briefcase. Both had on white tennis shoes.

Captain LaPalme rang the ship's bell, and two other people appeared from below decks. A short, bald, grizzled man of indeterminate age was the ship's engineer. LaPalme introduced him as Jock MacGillivray. He wore blue overalls and held an unlit pipe.

A thin man with short dark hair and brown skin was introduced as the steward/deckhand, Juan Gomez. I thought he looked Filipino, but he could have been Mexican. He nodded but didn't speak.

Lizzie suggested we move to the aft deck, which was covered and furnished with rattan chairs and a large central table. The crew sat around the table, and Lizzie introduced me.

"This is Sean Gray, he'll be leading an expedition to Alaska onboard the *Lady L*. The mission is a secret for now. You'll be fully informed when you arrive. Your pay will be increased by twenty percent for the duration of the trip. Captain LaPalme will remain in charge of the ship's operations, but Sean will set the agenda. He may bring additional people with him. The expedition should leave by mid-June to take advantage of the long daylight hours."

She asked that any questions be addressed to her personally after the meeting. Jock shrugged and went back to the engine room, but Juan wanted to speak to Lizzie privately. They went into the saloon for a minute, and Lizzie came back alone.

"Juan has resigned. He doesn't want to go to Alaska. He didn't say why, just that he prefers to remain in BC. We'll need to find a replacement."

I said, "I can do deckhand work, and I'm good at fixing things. But we'll need someone for cooking and housekeeping. Lizzie, you haven't said whether you plan to come with us."

"No. I might send Darya up there by plane if there are legal issues that need sorting out. Otherwise, you are fully in charge."

I was flattered by her trust, but then I reminded myself that LaPalme was younger than me, and his job was arguably more important. Lizzie and Darya took their leave. Darya pointed at the pager on my belt and said, "I'll call you later."

I stayed around so André could give me a tour of the ship. The gleaming clean engine room with the massive white-painted diesel was most impressive. Brass pipes and gauges were all polished. Jock, pipe puffing away, pointed out the functions of the various levers and valves. There were three auxiliary motors for generating power and compressed air to start the main engine. The smallest, a Lister, could be hand started. Everything appeared to be in tip-top shape, just old.

The wheelhouse had an array of modern instruments amid the antique-looking controls. There was a depth sounder, radar, and a VHF radio at the helm. There was an ancient wireless transmitter in a small room behind the wheelhouse, complete with a telegraph key. A more modern SSB radio was above it, and a Loran A navigation system was to one side. The Loran had a round CRT display and many dials and switches. I counted 54 in total. The user manual was the size of a city phone book.

"You better learn how to use all this stuff." André said, "I'm appointing you navigator for the trip."

I pointed to the chart table, where there were dividers and protractors. "I know how to use those. The trip to Alaska won't be out of sight of land."

André chuckled, "Yes, it will. Ever hear of fog? It's guaranteed on the North Coast this time of year. Pretty much any time."

I took another look at the Loran, "Mind if I take the user manual home? I'm good at learning things from books. Learned to sail from a book."

We went downstairs and sat down in the saloon. Ajax flew in and perched on the back of a chair. He cocked his head and said to me, "What's your name, or should I just call you fuckwit?"

It took me a moment to respond. I wasn't used to talking to a bird, although I had dealt with plenty of birdbrains.

"Call me Sean, or I'll wring your scrawny neck."

The parrot spread his wings and hooted like an owl. He jumped two chairs down, then turned to me and said, "Sean. Sean, the fuckwit."

. Then he flew up the staircase to the wheelhouse.

We made a list of things to do. It was a long list. André got a bottle of red from a locker and poured us each a glass. We drank as I wrote the list in my notebook. When we finished, I remembered Lizzie had promised dinner on board.

André explained, "The steward quit, Lizzie paid him off. So, no dinner. Sorry."

"Okay, let me treat you to dinner. How about Trader Vic's? We can row over in my dinghy." Trader Vic's was a steep-roofed Polynesian restaurant alongside the Bayshore Inn.

André agreed. He changed into khaki pants and a collared shirt, almost precisely what I was wearing. We got into the dinghy, which was just big enough for two, and I rowed across to my mooring spot. It was a short walk from there to Vic's. André took a moment to admire *Tangled Moon*, and then we went to dinner.

Many stories were swapped over Mai Tai cocktails, complete with little umbrellas and a pupu platter. The main dishes were just like Chinese food—because all the cooks were Chinese.

I asked how Ajax joined the crew and how he got his name.

"He belongs to Lizzie, but he refuses to live in a house. The boat is his home. Ajax is a brand of strong powdered cleanser. Apparently, Lizzie threatened to wash his beak out with it every time he swore. She used the word so often he thinks it's his name. I don't know where she got him, but he is way older than us."

By the end of the meal, André and I were fast friends. And maybe a little tipsy. He took a cab home, and I stumbled back to my boat alone. It was just after 9 PM.

I called Cindy first. She answered on the first ring, "Sean?"

" 'Tis I, oh Sweet Rose of English Bay."

"Are you drunk?"

"Maybe a bit. Trader Vic's with the Captain."

"Captain of what? Oh, I guess you mean Miss Hadley's yacht."

"Got it in one."

"Alright, sober up for a moment. I have news."

"I'm all ears and rubbery knees." Maybe not so sober.

"We sold the restaurant."

I suddenly felt guilty. I hadn't passed on Darya's message about asking for three hundred thousand. "Ah, how much?"

"Three twenty-five. I asked for three-fifty, and we compromised. He was willing to lease it back to us until the re-development permits are approved, but Mom said no. She has already closed the restaurant. I'm going to apply to UBC for the fall. Mom plans to get an apartment near Chinatown and retire."

My guilt subsided. Cindy didn't need my help. But I got an idea.

"Cindy, can you cook?"

I could hear a smile in her voice.

"Is this a trick question? Will you ask about laundry next?"

"Maybe. The steward on *Lady L* quit, and we need to hire a replacement. University won't start until fall, and we'll be back from Alaska by then. It would be cooking and light housekeeping for five or six people."

"Wow. I was worried you were going to propose or something. I'll get Mom to give me some lessons. I'd love to go to Alaska. Do I get a private cabin?"

I wondered why women were afraid I might ask them to marry me. I was under the impression that all young women were eager for marriage. I almost forgot to answer.

"Your own cabin? If you insist. I was prepared to offer you the top bunk in mine."

I didn't even know if there were top bunks, but then, I'd been drinking.

Cindy said, "Thanks, but no. What about pay?"

"I'll check with Lizzie, but I'm sure it will be enough, and you won't have any expenses, so you can save it all."

"It would be great to have some money of my own. Mom has only been giving me fifteen dollars a week." She sounded excited.

"One more thing. Tomorrow I promised to take Darya sailing. I'd like you to come along too."

Cindy snickered, "You need a chaperone to protect your virtue?"

I laughed. I liked this woman a lot. "How do you know it isn't to protect Darya? Or maybe I'm planning something kinky?"

"Good luck with that. What time?"

I gave her the details, and we said goodbye. It wasn't really a romantic conversation, but I felt a connection growing.

Then I called Darya. I told her about the sale of the English Bay Café and thanked her on Cindy's behalf. I didn't admit to not passing on her message. Why rock the dinghy?

I added, "I asked Cindy to join us tomorrow. I hope that's okay."

"It's your boat, you can choose the crew." Her voice was flat.

"Thanks. I'll provide food for lunch, just bring yourself. Wear soft shoes. We'll anchor and have lunch before sailing back."

And so, to bed. I fell asleep immediately.

CHAPTER 11 – SAILING

Stormy seas marched toward the ship in rows. Whitecaps were breaking, and spume blew off the tops. A driving, icy rain hit me in the face. I was bow lookout on a ship, steaming into the waves at full speed. Ahead and to port, a taller wave rose up above the others. With horror, I realized it was breaking over a group of rocks. I waved a signal flag and pointed in the direction of the reef. The ship began a slow turn to starboard. I looked out again, and the rocks were foaming dead ahead. I fell forward as we hit with an explosive bang, followed by the grinding scrape of iron on rock.

I woke up bathed in sweat. The sun was shining through the ports, and I could hear seagulls. I was in my own bunk on *Tangled Moon*. The shipwreck was just a bad dream. I slid out of bed, dressed in yesterday's dirty clothes, put clean ones in a bag, and walked myself up to Sid's to use his shower. I used my key to let myself in quietly.

He was still in bed when I finished, so I left him a note and slipped out quietly. On the way home, I stopped at Sam's Deli and bought Freybe salami, sliced havarti, and a container of potato salad. Then I went into the Sterling Bakery and got a couple of fresh baguettes. Lunch for Darya and Cindy.

The Shipmate was open, so I went in and sat down. Gus had hired a new waitress without my help. She was tall and skinny, with reddish-blonde hair in a ponytail and many freckles. I introduced myself.

"Hi, I'm Sean Gray."

"Do Canadians always introduce themselves to the waitress?" I recognized an Aussie accent.

I laughed, "Only if they have an office above the café."

"Ah! Gus warned me about you. I'm Gwenda. What can I get you?"

"Coffee. Toast with Vegemite."

She laughed, "Nice try, but not on. I'll bring peanut butter."

After breakfast, I went back to the boat. As I was taking off the sail cover, the pager started beeping. For a moment, I wondered what the noise was. After a few seconds, I pushed the red button to stop it. Then I called the answering service. The message was to call Darya, and I did.

She told me that she wouldn't be able to go sailing with me as "something had come up." It didn't surprise me. I had found almost everybody was eager to sail on a yacht until the time came to show up, then about half would bow out for one reason or another.

I had the boat ready to go when Cindy arrived. She was wearing jeans, sneakers, a red t-shirt, and a light blue windbreaker. Her long black hair was tied in a high ponytail. She looked terrific, and her smile was bright. I took her bag and showed her how to step over the lifelines. She was far more graceful than I was. Once onboard, she gave me a warm hug.

I put her bag down below and showed her around *Tangled Moon*.

"Wow! This is a beautiful boat. I don't know much about boats, but it's easy to see how well made everything is. Are there many like this?

"Only one exactly like this, it was custom made for someone back in the 1930s. Wooden boats like this are not being made in any quantity now, most of them are fiberglass, like that one." I pointed at a Coronado moored nearby.

"That looks okay, but nowhere near as beautiful as yours. All this lovely wood. Is that deck teak?"

"Yes, it's teak. Keeping it leak-free is a challenge, but right now, it's dry. Come inside, and I'll show you how to use the head."

Cindy was agile and had no trouble with the steep ladder. I showed her the interior and explained the intricacies of the marine toilet.

"Where does that pump to?" I pointed downward. She wrinkled her nose but made no other comment. I showed her the propane stove, which I had recently installed, replacing a diabolical pressure kerosene contraption.

"Let's get going. I'll start the engine."

"Can I do anything to help?" she asked.

"In a minute, you can help me untie and back out."

The Graymarine gas engine started after a couple of tries and smoothed out as it warmed up. I showed Cindy how to untie the lines and push off while climbing aboard. Soon we were underway, heading past the Esso, Chevron, and Shell fuel barges. The harbor was calm, and we motored along at about six knots. I showed Cindy how to steer and warned her to watch for logs.

The tide was favorable under the Lions Gate bridge, and it spat us out into English Bay. The wind was light, so we kept motoring until we got near the beach and gave Cindy a view of her home.

"It looks so small from out here, with the big buildings behind and the change rooms in front. I wish I had a camera."

I went below and got my Canon FX and attached the telephoto lens. "Here you go. Or would you like me to take the photo?"

Cindy gave me a look of disdain and took the camera. She set the f-stop and held the camera to her right eye, quickly taking three shots while adjusting the shutter speed. Bracketing the exposure. She knew her stuff. I abandoned some illusions.

"Thanks. At least one of those will be good."

She handed me back the camera, and I put it safely in the cabin. The typical English Bay thermal breeze was starting to stir, and I got Cindy to steer into the wind while I raised the mainsail, then the jib. Soon we were heeled to the wind, beating out toward Point Atkinson. Cindy sat beside me in the cockpit, and I put my arm around her shoulders. All was right with the world.

Suddenly Cindy sat up straight and pointed behind us, "Is that boat going to hit us?"

I turned my head. A modern fiberglass motor yacht of about 50 feet was catching up on us fast. "We have the right of way…but it's always better to be safe."

I turned the wheel to fall off the wind a few degrees, which should have given him ample space to pass without changing course. But he did change course...toward us. I could hear the rush of his wake and the roar of two big diesels. There was no way I could get out of the way in time. I grabbed Cindy and hung on to the wheel. At the last second, the motorboat veered away, missing us by inches and soaking us both with spray.

I shook my fist and yelled some choice words. I couldn't see the faces of the people on the flybridge. There was a dinghy tipped up on the swim grid, which blocked the name.

"I'm soaked. What an asshole. Did he do that on purpose?" Cindy was angry, wiping her face with her sleeve.

"I'm sure he did. Some people get their jollies in strange ways, although I have never had a close call like that before. That was a pretty new Hatteras 50. There can't be many in Vancouver. I guess I could find him. But what then? We aren't hurt, just wet."

I paused for a moment, then said, "I have dry clothes down below. I'll get some out for you. You'll warm up as soon as you're dry."

Cindy looked at me like I was a moron. "I'm half your size. How do you think they'll fit?"

"Ah. I used to have a girlfriend named Suzy. She was close to your size. She left a few things behind when she moved to Toronto."

I went below and got Cindy a towel. Then I rooted around and found a blouse and a pair of khaki shorts, which I handed out to her.

"Thanks, smart guy. You think I'm going to change out here? Trade places."

She went below, went into the head, and closed the door. In a couple of minutes, she returned in Suzy's clothes, which were a little loose, but not bad. I noticed that she wasn't wearing a bra. I suppose it got wet.

I gave her the wheel, and I went below to change my own clothes. The rest of the day was great. We dropped anchor in Coward's Cove and had a nice picnic lunch with wine in the cockpit. Then Cindy snuggled up, and we necked for a while, but she stopped me from going further. It dawned on me that she was probably a virgin. I would have to treat her gently.

We sailed back in a dying breeze, motoring the last half of the distance. We talked about the trip to Alaska. I had been as far north as Campbell River, but no further. It would be all new to me past there. Cindy was enthusiastic. With our lack of experience, it seemed to me that we could use a least one hardened, experienced crew member. I decided to ask Brice for advice since he seemed to know everyone. André might know someone too.

Once we were tied up, I took Cindy over to meet Brice and Eva. They got on well, and while Eva was showing Cindy their immaculate floating home, I told Brice about the planned trip to Alaska, without mentioning the safe.

"I'd love to go with you, but there is no way I could afford the time off work. I'll ask around about someone else for your crew."

I thanked him and said, "There is something you can do from here to help."

On a shelf above the saloon bunk, Brice had an old-fashioned AM marine radio.

"We'll need to keep in touch daily, and your radio is just the thing. We can call you on 2182 kilocycles daily. I'd suggest 10 PM, just to check in and let you know our position. If we have a phone available, I'll call you on that instead. That way, if something goes wrong, you'll have a rough idea of where to send the Coast Guard."

"Okay, but I'll have to get the radio fixed. It isn't working right now."

"Let me take it. Sid will have fun fixing it, and I'll take care of any costs."

After a glass of wine, we left with the radio under my arm. I locked it in the trunk of the Mustang, then walked Cindy home. I kissed her at the door of the café, and she let herself in.

CHAPTER 12 – FINGERS

On Sunday, I took Brice's radio to Sid for repair. We got in the Mustang and went to the White Spot on Georgia for breakfast. They had car service, but we went inside to a booth. I showed him the pager, and we talked about the latest technology, computers in particular.

"One day soon, computers will be small enough to fit on a desk," Sid opined.

"Seems obvious, but what will we use them for?"

Unable to come up with an answer to that question, we moved on to other topics. Later I dropped Sid home and parked the car at the marina. I walked up to the Shipmate and went in. Gwenda looked surprised to see me.

"I thought you were already up there." She looked at the stairs. The light was on.

I took the stairs to my office two at a time. The door was ajar. The safe was open, and the bottles were on the floor, but the intruder had missed the false back again. All my books were on the floor too, but nobody was there.

I went back downstairs.

"Gwenda, did you see anybody come out of my office?"

"Yes, somebody came down the stairs about five minutes ago. I didn't notice until I heard the front door open as they left. All I saw was one foot. He—or maybe she—was wearing jeans with white socks and blue sneakers."

"That doesn't help much. Half the people in the West End are in jeans and sneakers."

"Sorry. Maybe we need a better lock. I'll tell Gus. He isn't in yet."

I had a sudden thought. I bolted for the door and ran up the street, heading for Lizzie's place. It was only a few blocks, and I'd be fastest on foot. When I got to the house, I went up to the front door. Before I could knock, I heard heated voices from within. The door was unlocked, so I let myself in as quietly as possible, then walked softly toward the sounds coming from the kitchen.

"Where is it? No more bullshit. I want it now, or she dies!" It was a man's voice yelling. I could hear someone sobbing.

As I came through the kitchen door, I saw a man's back. He had his left arm around Stella's neck and a knife in his right hand. Stella was crying. Facing him stood Lizzie, holding a small revolver. She turned her head toward me as I came in. She didn't look frightened. I grabbed the man's right arm by the wrist and twisted while I kicked at his legs. He dropped the knife and yelled in pain. In a moment, I had him on the ground, arms pinned behind him.

"Call the police, then get me something to tie him up with!"

Stella was sitting on the floor by the fridge, face in her hands, crying softly. Lizzie started walking toward the phone in the saloon.

"Police! What's going on here?" The voice was loud, masculine, and deep with a noticeable Welsh accent. I turned my head and saw a uniformed officer coming toward me, gun in hand.

I yelled, "I caught an intruder. Please handcuff him, and I'll explain."

I didn't want him to think I was the criminal, but he didn't argue. He holstered his gun and took a set of handcuffs from his belt.

After the suspect was cuffed, the officer stood him up and turned him towards me. "I'm Constable Jones, this is my beat. I just happened to be passing. This here is Fingers Finnegan. He's a thief for hire. Now tell me what happened."

Lizzie took charge and explained the events.

"What was Finnegan after?" asked the cop.

"He kept yelling about a letter. I have no idea what he was talking about."

I spoke up.

"Officer Jones, I'm Sean Gray. I followed this man here from my office on Denman, where he broke in and rifled my safe. I don't think he took anything. Could you have someone go over there and dust for prints? I'd like to press charges."

Jones used Lizzie's phone to call the station and arranged for someone to meet me at my office. Soon a police van arrived and took Fingers away for questioning. He hadn't said a word since I tackled him, just moaned a bit.

After the police were gone, I took Lizzie aside for a serious talk.

"Where is the letter?"

A slight smile crossed her face. "I hid it in Hans' favorite hiding spot."

She walked me over to a huge moose head on the wall in the study and pointed into his mouth. It was too high for her to reach without a stool, so I reached in and fished out an envelope.

"Can I take this now? I'll put it and my copy where nobody will find them. I'm assuming whoever is after this already has a copy of Jakob's letter about the safe. Without the letter from the flask, they would know what we're looking for but not where. I want to make sure they don't find out. And the sooner the expedition gets going, the better."

"Okay. I'll feel safer if it's gone. I didn't tell you before, but last week I had a feeling someone had been in the house when we were out shopping. Nothing definite, but it seemed like a lot of small items weren't quite where they were before."

It made sense. Someone knew about the letter and my connection to Lizzie and sent Fingers Finnegan to get them. I hoped the police would find out who.

The rest of the day was spent with the police, swearing a complaint, and signing statements. I was promised they would call me if they found out who sent Finnegan.

Finally, I got done about dinner time and called André. He and I decided to meet at Olympic Pizza, so I could fill him in. I called Cindy, and she agreed to meet us there.

When I got to the Olympic, Sid Engelman was in a corner by himself. I went over and suggested we move to a bigger table to make room for Cindy and André.

They arrived within a few minutes, and I made introductions. Sid was my oldest friend, Cindy and André were the newest, but I trusted all three. We ordered drinks and a large "everything but anchovies" pizza to share. I spent about ten minutes, filling them in on the day's events until the food arrived.

We ate in silence for a while, then the questions started.

André asked, "Who could possibly be after the safe? It would have to be someone with the resources to get it if they found out where it is. That means someone with money and connections, certainly not Fingers Finnegan, who sounds like a petty criminal."

"I have no idea. I'm hoping the police turn up something. I'll talk to them tomorrow. Sid, is there any way someone could track our boat on a map, like in a James Bond film?"

Sid thought for a moment, "The short answer is no, the screen in James Bond's Aston-Martin is a fake, just like the rocket launcher. Frank Baker just bought the car for the Attic restaurant if you want to take a look."

"Back on topic, the only way I know of is with direction-finding equipment that picks up your radio transmissions. It would take three fixes from three different locations for the DF operator to establish an accurate position for you."

André said, "If I wanted to steal a treasure, I'd just sit back and let us find it first, then take it away from us. That way, we do all the hard work."

"Makes sense. But maybe whoever is after it has superior technology, and therefore a better chance than us. We might fail."

André smiled and shrugged, "Better than us? How is THAT possible?"

He continued, "They are seriously after the letter. Why not give it to them?"

"But, it gives away the location!"

"Exactly. You forge a letter which alters or disguises the location and release it to the Vancouver Sun. I can picture the headline: 'Lost Letter from Doomed Lover Delivered 50 years Later.'"

"Brilliant. I can write a letter. But I'm assuming the crooks have a copy of Jakob's earlier letter, so we should match the handwriting and paper."

Sid had an idea, "My friend Levi can forge it. He can forge anything. Don't worry about the paper, just give the Sun a photocopy."

We debated what to put in the fake letter. André had the chart of the Thomas Bay area with him, and we looked for similar bays. We picked one and then debated the wording of the letter for a bit.

As we were leaving, I said to Cindy, "Now that it looks like we are up against an organization of some sort, it might be a good idea to move aboard the boat with me until we leave for Alaska."

"I'll think about it… Okay, I thought about it. No. But you can walk me home."

CHAPTER 13 – A BODY

I wrote the letter the next morning, based heavily on Jakob's original. The location was changed to Farragut Bay, just a few miles north of Thomas Bay, with somewhat similar geography. Some of the scary details from the original remained.

Later I took the letter with me to Sid's apartment, where I met Levi. He was ex-Israeli military, a compact man a few years older than I was. He wore a tight black tee-shirt and black shorts, sandals with black socks, and a black baseball cap, which he took off revealing close-cropped dark hair, bushy eyebrows, and intense brown eyes. His skin was copper, and his body was hard, with no sign of fat. I suddenly felt out of shape.

Sid introduced us, and Levi nodded. "Good to meet you, Sean."

The accent sounded Russian to me, but maybe not. I had never met an Israeli before.

He didn't crush my hand, but it was like shaking hands with a living granite statue. This wasn't a man to mess with.

We settled a price for the forgery, and he left silently, letter in hand.

"He'll bring the finished copy tomorrow morning. You can give me the money now, so I can pay him."

"Okay, but one question. Is Levi as tough as he looks?"

"From what I hear, tougher. He knows a gazillion ways to kill you or make you wish you were dead." Sid smiled, but his voice was grave.

I said, "When you see him ask him if he'd be willing to sail to Alaska with us as a security consultant. Well paid, of course."

Sid replied, "I'm pretty sure he would. He's been working as a short-order cook while waiting to qualify for a job with the police."

I left some money with Sid and went back to my office. Then I called the VPD to talk about Finnegan. They found his prints in my office, so he was charged with breaking and entering, plus assault with a weapon.

To my surprise, the desk sergeant told me Finnegan had been released on bail of $25,000, paid by a lawyer named Tod Wackner. The name sounded familiar. I asked about him, and the sergeant just told me he was "connected."

I didn't know what that meant. Further research was needed. I called Darya.

She had heard about Finnegan from Lizzie, and I gave her my version. Then I asked what "connected" meant.

"It usually means mob ties. There are at least three organized crime groups in Vancouver: Italian Mafia, Bikers, and Chinese Triads, usually with Hong Kong connections. Also, there are individuals and corporations involved in white-collar crimes such as money laundering and stock fraud. Then, of course, there is the Port, which is a hotbed of crime, some related to the unions."

I thought for a moment, "So being connected tells us very little?"

"Not much. I'll try to find out who Wackner's main clients are and get back to you. The bail money will have come from one of them."

I thanked her and hung up. I got the car, picked up Cindy, and drove down to Chinatown, where we ate at an underground restaurant called the Orange Door. It was in an alleyway, and the only indication it was there was the door's color. Down in the basement, it was loud and smoky. The menu was in Chinese on long strips of paper tacked to the walls.

Cindy pushed ahead and found us a table, which we shared with another couple.

"I can't read Chinese, but I can speak it, so I'll order, okay?"

"I'm putty in your hands. Order away."

Sometimes I love a woman who takes charge. This was one of those times.

We had an excellent meal for about three bucks. I have no idea what some of the dishes were, but they were delicious; salty, and bitter, and nothing like the Chinese takeout we used to get in Alberta.

Cindy and I were pretty comfortable by then. The place was so loud we couldn't really converse, so we held hands and enjoyed each other's company. Then we went up the theater row on Granville to see what was playing.

Jane Fonda looked good to me in Barbarella, but Cindy preferred Romeo and Juliet, so that's what we saw. I knew the story since our drama department did the play in high school. Still, the Hollywood movie treatment added some glamor, and we enjoyed it.

After I took Cindy home, I parked the car and went back to the marina. Someone was sitting in the cockpit of my boat. It was Fingers Finnegan, and he was staring without blinking. Or breathing. He was dead. One of the jib sheets was around his neck, the end cleated off to keep him upright. It was not the first time I had ever seen a dead body, but it was still a shock.

I went inside and called the police. I had to go up and meet them at the marina entrance because there was no easy way to find my boat.

Two police cars and an ambulance showed up. They put me in a black-and-white while they investigated the scene. After the body was taken away, I was taken to the VPD station on Main Street to give a statement. I was fingerprinted and had to account for my movements for the day. I gave them Cindy's phone number as well as Sid's.

Then a detective in a grey suit came into the room and dismissed the uniformed cops.

"I'm Detective Simpson, Homicide."

"Sean Gray, Innocent Bystander."

"Well, 'Sean'—if that's really your name—I'm not sure that's true. Finnegan broke into your office. You caught him at Elizabeth Hadley's. He got out on bail, and now he's dead. That makes you a suspect."

"How did he die?"

"He was strangled by somebody bigger and stronger than him. You meet that description."

"A lot of people do. You seriously believe I'd kill a guy then leave his body on my own boat? Can I call a lawyer?"

Before he could answer, a uniformed cop came in and gave him a note. Simpson looked up after reading it.

"You won't need a lawyer. Your alibi checks out. Apparently, you were at the movies with a Miss Lu when he was killed. You're free to go."

I was relieved. "Thanks. Do you have any other suspects?"

"I can't tell you that, but be careful. Somebody was trying to send you a message."

"You think? I got the message, but I'm having trouble reading it."

His eyes twinkled, "I'd say whoever killed Finnegan doesn't like you. Now skedaddle."

It was so late the buses had stopped running, so I had to grab a cab back to the marina. The police were gone by then. I climbed aboard and sat down, feeling shell-shocked. After a bit, I dug out a bottle of rum and poured myself two fingers.

CHAPTER 14 – CREW

I looked out into a fog-shrouded bay. Behind me, rain dripped off misshapen cedar and arbutus clinging to a steep shore. A rickety dock extended from the tip of a rocky outcropping. Something was tied alongside. As I approached, I could see it was a small dugout canoe. The rocks were slippery, and I gingerly picked my way over them to the dock. I looked down at the body in the boat.

It was a woman, shrouded in a long black dress that covered her feet. Her hands were folded neatly in her lap, and strands of long hair fanned out around her head. Her face was unnaturally white, and I realized she was wearing a mask, carved of bleached driftwood. The nose was hawk-like, and the mouth was a round O. There were no eyes.

I seemed to know who she was. For some reason, I thought the dugout wasn't secure there. I should haul it up on the island. Leaning down, I untied the single frayed painter and dragged the canoe over to a gap in the rocks. As I tried to haul it up, it overturned, and the body spilled out. The arms spread out, and it slowly sank, face-up, into the clear water. The mask floated off, and I could see the face, distorted by the rippled ocean.

Without hesitation, I dived in.

I woke up when I hit the floor of the boat, twisted up in my quilt. In the dream, I recognized the woman, but now I couldn't remember who she was.

It was morning anyway, so I went up to my office. Rather than tell the story over and over, I called the *Lady L* team to meet me at the Shipmate for breakfast. Lizzie declined but said Darya would fill her in later.

By 10 AM, Cindy, Darya, André, Sid, and Levi were there. And me.

I introduced Levi. He gave me an envelope. We ordered coffee and food before I started talking.

"Last night, I found a dead body on my boat."

This caused expressions of horror and concern from everybody but Levi. When they settled down, I continued.

"It was Fingers Finnegan, the guy who broke into my office and assaulted Stella. He was strangled and then posed in the cockpit of my boat. The police won't say if they have any suspects."

André said, "Don't you think a pattern is emerging? Two break-ins at your office, Cindy threatened, attempted theft from Lizzie, and now the guy who did it killed. Any idea why?"

Cindy said, "The guy who threatened me was working for my Mom, so discount that one. It won't happen again."

That was news to me, but I continued. "It seems that someone wants to discourage our expedition by scaring us off."

Sid interrupted, "Not everybody, if Cindy is correct, it's just you, Sean. I think Fingers was killed because he knew who employed him, and they thought he might snitch."

"Makes sense. It also means we are dealing with ruthless people. Darya, did you find out anything about Finnegan's lawyer, Tod Wackner?"

Darya said, "I did. He mainly defends white-collar criminals, and as far as I know, has never defended a murder case. I'm guessing, in this case, he was used just to post bail for Finnegan. The client will probably never employ him again."

Levi spoke for the first time. "I can find out who the client is. Just say the word."

I found that a little scary.

"Levi, we haven't agreed on a contract yet. Are you coming with us to Alaska?"

"I'll go."

"Okay, stay behind, and we'll discuss terms. You too, Darya. Back to business. I want to get going on the trip as soon as possible. Cindy, can you take charge of provisioning, assuming a crew of six for a month? André will give you an idea of the size of the fridge and freezer on board."

"Okay, who are the six crew?" asked Cindy.

"Me, Captain LaPalme, Jock the engineer, you, Levi, and one other to be determined. There are six guest cabins and the master. The captain and the engineer both have their own quarters, so we have room for one or two more people if needed."

André spoke again, "Do you want to run night and day to get up there as fast as possible? If so, there should be at least one other person who can steer the boat, besides you and me."

Levi said, "I can run a boat, but I suggest one more person anyway, in case anyone gets ill."

I said, "Is it safe to run at night? I wouldn't do it in my boat, too many logs floating around."

André chuckled, "When *Lady L* hit the dock, she went right through it without damage—to the boat that is. There is a massive iron cutwater on the bow, which makes her nearly log proof. Still, we would run slower after dark."

"Good, It's about a thousand miles to our destination. I'm estimating six to seven days travel, allowing for stops for fuel and water."

"I'll be giving the forged letter to Lizzie, and she'll call the Vancouver Sun. Cindy, if you could be there too, it will make a hell of a story, and our pursuer will —I hope —believe he has the letter and stop trying to steal it."

After Sid, Cindy, and André left, Levi and Darya agreed on a salary, and I asked him to find out what he could about Tod Wackner's client. I didn't ask how he would do it.

The story was pushed off the front page by the assassination of Robert F. Kennedy.

CHAPTER 15 – VANCOUVER SUN

Letter Delivered 50 Years Late
Dropped Overboard from Doomed Ship in 1918

VANCOUVER — Longtime West End resident Elizabeth Hadley has revealed that she recently received a letter written to her on board a doomed CP liner in 1918.

The SS *Princess Sophia* foundered on Vanderbilt reef in Alaska en route from Skagway to Vancouver. She was stranded for two days before finally breaking up and sinking. All 343 people aboard perished. The only survivor was an oil-soaked dog rescued later from a nearby island.

One of those aboard was Jakob Holcomb, a friend of Miss Hadley's. Realizing he was almost certain to die, he penned a final letter and sealed it in a metal flask, which he threw overboard.

The flask floated an unknown path for decades until it was finally found a few years ago at Second Beach, by Wai Chang Lu. He was a collector of beach artifacts and never opened the flask.

Lu's daughter tidied up his effects after he moved to a nursing home. She found the flask and opened it. The letter inside was addressed to a house just blocks away, so she hand-delivered it to Miss Hadley. The two are now fast friends.

"I was very glad to receive Jakob's letter, even 50 years later. And I'm so grateful to Miss Lu for delivering it. I will add it to the small treasures I have collected in my lifetime," Miss Hadley said.

A reproduction of the letter followed. There was also a photo of Lizzie and Cindy standing close together but not embracing.

CHAPTER 16 – ARMED

A few days later, *Lady L* was ready to go. I still had not found another suitable crew member. I asked André for a recommendation. As it turned out, he had a friend named Charlie Quant, who had just graduated from UBC Engineering and planned to take the summer off.

According to André, Charlie was the kind of guy who could build or fix anything mechanical, the way Sid was with electronics. That seemed like an asset, so I asked André to sign him on. We set our departure date for Monday, June 10.

I didn't have much time to spend with Cindy while getting ready to leave. She was organizing the provisions, bedding, and many other things I would never have thought of.

I met with André onboard the *Lady L* to go over the checklist and ask a few questions. I was worried about security.

"Do we have any weapons on board?"

"There is a gun case just behind the wheelhouse. There are a couple of Remington hunting rifles, one with a scope. There is also a Purdey 12 bore double-barrel shotgun. We have plenty of ammunition."

"Okay. Anything else?"

"A couple of spearguns. Oh, and a fifty-caliber machine gun."

"What? Is that legal?" Canadian gun laws were pretty strict.

"Who knows? The Coast Guard commandeered the *Lady L* during the war, and it was on board when they gave her back. They just returned the boat exactly as they had used her, gray paint and all. The gun is dismantled and stored with the engine spares. Jock knows how it goes together."

So, we were armed to the teeth. I could shoot, having lived in northern Alberta as a youth, but I had only used a Single-shot 22 and a small-bore shotgun. I never killed anything bigger than a grouse.

I asked André about diving gear.

"I'm a diver, and I have a set of scuba and tanks. Levi brought a set on board too. I think he has weapons of his own as well."

"What about lifting gear? That safe is very heavy." I had forgotten that detail earlier.

"Charlie has an idea about that. Talk to him."

"Okay." Something else hit my mind, "What ID do we need to enter Alaska customs?"

"Driver's license or citizenship card. Passport is only required for non-Canadians. I already asked everyone. Charlie, Jock, and I all have passports. Cindy has no driver's license, but she has a Canadian Citizenship Card. Levi has four or five passports from different countries, including Canada. I suggested he use that one. What about you?"

"I don't have a passport, but I do have a driver's license and other ID. Technically I'm not a Canadian Citizen. I'm a landed immigrant, although I was born in the West Indies. I have driven across into the US several times and never had a problem."

I introduced myself to Charlie, a thin but fit looking guy with short brown hair and gray eyes. I asked him how we would handle the safe.

"I brought several air bladders. There is a compressor in the engine room, but I have a portable one just in case. We'll float the safe with the bladders and then drag it ashore for opening."

"How will you open it?"

He twirled his right hand. "Magic fingers?"

"Seriously?"

"Not a chance. I also brought an oxy-acetylene cutting torch and a power drill."

"No dynamite?"

"Too noisy. It might wake the neighbors."

"What neighbors? That bay is uninhabited."

"Says you. I read *The Strangest Story Ever Told*. André lent it to me."

That night we had a farewell dinner on board. In addition to our six-person crew, we invited Darya, Sid, Brice, Eva, and, of course, Lizzie. Sid planned to bring a date, a girl called Katrin.

The weather was good, so I helped Cindy set the large table on the back deck. It could seat as many as sixteen, so plenty of room for twelve of us. It was the first time she had to cook for a big group, so I helped in the kitchen by cutting up vegetables. Then she shooed me out.

At about 6:30 PM, the guests began arriving, and I served drinks; a choice of red or white wine, or fruit juice. Sid was alone. Katrin had begged off. Everyone was in shorts and tee-shirts except Levi, who wore long black trousers. Lizzie—who arrived last—was another exception, in an expensive-looking cream-colored pantsuit.

At 7:30, Cindy rang the dinner bell, and everyone except André and I sat around the table. The two of us helped Cindy. I insisted she sit down and eat with everybody else, and André and I brought in the food.

It was a five-course gourmet feast, beginning with Vichyssoise and an apple salad in aspic. The main course was Chicken Kyiv. I squirted butter on my shirt with that one, and everyone laughed. The conversation was light and mostly between people seated next to each other.

André had chosen a wine pairing for each course, which was a success, but Cindy's face started to turn red after two glasses, and she declined any more.

The dessert was something called a Tunnel of Fudge, which I had never encountered before. It was pretty rich, but everybody except Lizzie finished theirs. I noted Lizzie ate exactly half of each course. Darya ate about 75%, as did Cindy. The men ate everything, but nobody asked for seconds. That was good because there weren't any.

I proposed a toast.

"I'd us like to show our appreciation for Chef Cindy. I have eaten Chow Mein at the English Bay Café many times, so my expectations were modest. Cindy told me she would get some tips from her Mom, but I think something else is going on here. To the Chef!"

Glasses clinked, and then everyone applauded. Someone asked Cindy where she learned how to cook like that. She stood up and pointed to the bookshelf.

"This is all stuff I liked the sound of but never tried before. André and Jock helped by trying my test samples. Don't expect a meal like this every day!"

André showed off the slight tummy he developed from eating the samples. The crew applauded. Ajax flew in, wolf-whistled, and spoke to Cindy, "Hiya dollface. How about having dinner with me?"

She looked startled at the talking bird. Lizzie introduced him.

"This is Ajax. He has a foul mouth, but he never swears at the cook. He might end up in the stew."

After the dishes were cleared away, Lizzie took the floor to give us a send-off.

"I want to thank you all for coming together as a team to help me clear up a mystery that has haunted me since 1918. I refer to the sunken safe and what is in it. The letter Cindy delivered brought it all back to me and revealed another mystery. What was it in Thomas Bay that so frightened Jakob? Perhaps this expedition will solve both mysteries."

"I'm certain that Sean and André will prove able leaders, and they will be reporting to me as often as possible. May you all have the best of luck."

Ajax made clacking sounds with his beak.

As the party broke up, I mused that we might need that luck. Somebody with power and money was trying to stop us or beat us to the treasure. We had no clue who.

I grabbed Brice as he left and suggested we change to another radio frequency for our nightly check-ins. If someone was trying to track us, they would listen to the standard calling frequency. We chose a channel used by logging crew boats, which would likely be unused at 10 PM. I also told him I would use the yacht's original name—*Malachite*—rather than *Lady L*.

The team all slept aboard that night, to get an early start and catch high slack at the Lion's Gate.

After everyone was in bed, I knocked on Cindy's door. She opened it a crack to see who it was. She opened it a bit wider and let me in. She was wearing fuzzy flannel pajamas with bunnies. We cuddled for a while and talked about the trip. She was excited because she had never been north of Vancouver before. I was excited because I was with her.

She pushed me out to go sleep in my own bunk.

CHAPTER 17 – DEPARTURE

At 6 AM, an alarm went off in the cabin ahead of mine—Levi's. I got up and threw on some clothes. The dawn was gray. I could hear activity in the engine room, and gradually we all came to life. An urn of coffee was waiting in the dining room, along with fresh croissants. Cindy looked bright and cheerful. Nobody else did, but by 6:45, we were ready to go.

Jock started the engine and let it warm up in reverse while still tied up. The lines strained but held. Then he shut it down. André came up into the wheelhouse and slid the door open.

Levi and I untied the lines and stood on the dock until André rang the bell for reverse. When the diesel started, we threw the lines aboard and climbed on. We backed straight out a hundred yards or so, then André rang for standby. The engine stopped. The boat coasted backward for a while, then André rang for forward. The engine chuffed twice, started, then sped up. André spun the wheel, and soon, we were underway heading past the four fuel barges and around Brockton Point.

We were all on deck as we passed under the Lion's Gate at nine knots, with Canada's new Maple Leaf flag flying on the stern staff. A group of hippies camping near the north foot of the bridge dropped their pants and mooned us. Another new experience!

It was still early, and the wind was calm. English Bay was almost glassy. When we got near Point Atkinson, a swell caused by the outgoing tide started to rise. Cindy and Levi looked a bit green as the *Lady L* rolled from side to side. Near Passage Island, the swell subsided, and good cheer returned.

André started giving steering lessons to Charlie and Levi. I went into the chartroom and began plotting our course and marking it in pencil on the chart. I switched on the Loran and started figuring out how to use it while I could easily verify the accuracy of our position.

Just after noon, we slid through Welcome Pass. I took the helm for a while so André could eat lunch with the others. Cindy had put out soup and sandwiches on the back deck. She brought me a coffee and a sandwich and stood beside me at the wheel. Steering *Lady L* wasn't difficult—at least in the smooth waters behind Texada Island. I let Cindy take a turn at the helm. For someone who had never driven a car or even ridden a bicycle, she was a natural. I showed her how to read the compass, then sat back and ate my lunch.

When lunch was over, André took over again. We passed Pender Harbour and continued up Malaspina Strait beyond Nelson Island and the entrance to Jervis Inlet. I helped Cindy with the dishes and told her about wondrous Princess Louisa Inlet, which was at the top of Jervis. I promised to take her up there in *Tangled Moon* sometime.

At about 5 PM, we were just north of Savary, a low crescent-shaped island that—at first glance—resembled a tropical atoll. Beyond that, the snow-capped peaks of Vancouver Island glistened in the distance. There came a grinding, crunching noise from somewhere aft, then the engine slowed and stalled. I ran forward to the wheelhouse.

André looked worried.

"What happened?" I asked.

"I'm not sure. I'll go below and see what Jock thinks. I hope it isn't a seized bearing. Take the wheel."

The boat was still coasting along at a fair speed. I held the course until it came to a complete halt, then went below to see what was happening. André came up, shrugging his shoulders.

"Jock says whatever it was, it's outside the hull."

Everyone else was on deck, discussing what could be wrong. Charlie spotted a frayed rope trailing astern. It was a thick hawser made of synthetic floating line.

"The other end must be wrapped around the prop. Starting the engine in reverse might get it off."

I relayed that information to André, and Jock tried starting the engine in reverse. It wouldn't turn over. The rope had jammed the prop tight.

Levi offered, "I could put on my dive gear and go down to cut it free."

The boat was rolling and pitching in a rising northwest swell. André said, "It's too dangerous. We'll have to call for a tow."

Lady L had two lapstrake rowing boats and a 16-foot center console Boston Whaler on the cabin top. The Whaler had a 40-horsepower outboard.

I suggested we use the Whaler as a tug and bring *Lady L* into the calm waters of Finn Bay, just north of Lund, which was a couple of miles ahead on the mainland.

"It's worth a try," André said.

We lowered the boat with the electric crane. I jumped in, and Charlie accompanied me for safety. The outboard had an electric starter. I got it running and idled up to the bow of *Lady L*, where André threw us the bow-line. There was no towing bitt on the Whaler, but Charlie made a bridle off the stern cleats. Then I gave the motor part throttle to take up the slack. At first, pulling *Lady L* felt as if we were tied to a dock, but eventually, she started moving and finally got up to about three knots.

After an hour, we were entering Finn Bay, and I cut the motor. Then Charlie let go of the bow line, and we motored back to the stern. Levi threw us another line, and we used that to slow the *Lady L* as we came in. André dropped anchor, and we pulled back with the Whaler to set it. Charlie and I climbed back aboard, leaving the dinghy tied astern.

Levi came on deck in a wet suit, carrying a scuba tank. He put his gear on and jumped in backward. It took him half an hour to cut and untangle the rope around the prop. There didn't seem to be any other damage.

André announced that we would spend the night there, and I proposed we go to the Lund Hotel for dinner. The Whaler was ready, so we piled in and headed for Lund, a five-minute ride away.

The Lund Hotel was a slightly ramshackle place at the end of the road from Powell River. It was as far as you could go by car on the mainland coast north of Vancouver. We ascended a narrow wooden staircase to the second floor. The pub served hearty food and was frequented by lumberjacks and fishermen. The two groups occupied separate sides of the bar. All turned and stared at five yachtsmen and a pretty girl. Okay, maybe they only stared at Cindy.

After a few seconds of silence, the loud conversation resumed. We ordered fish and chips and fried chicken, which was about all they offered. And of course, beer. Cindy had apple juice.

An old fisherman with a bushy white beard came over and sat with us as we finished eating.

"Name's Fred. You off the *Lady L*?"

"We are. I'm the Captain." André said. They shook hands.

"Pretty young, ain'tcha? I used to work on her back in the thirties, running booze to Poulsbo and Anacortes."

André introduced the rest of us, first names only.

"Where ya headin' after this?"

André answered in general terms, "North. Desolation Sound, maybe the Broughtons."

"Watch them Yewclataws, they's treacherous."

André nodded but said nothing.

For an hour, Fred regaled us with tales of outfoxing the US Coast Guard and sabotaging rival smugglers. I asked for the names of their rivals, but he claimed not to remember any. Then he changed the subject.

"Hotel's haunted, ya know. Old Thulin, who built the place, paces the hallways to keep an eye on things. I seen him a few times, wearing a brown suit and a top hat. And there's a lady in a white dress who comes out of room 207 without opening the door."

Having thrown a scare into the city folk and scored several free drinks, Fred went back to his gang. I paid the bill. Before we went back to *Lady L*, I found a payphone and called Brice to bring him up to date. He would let Lizzie know how we were doing.

Back aboard, we turned in, planning an early start. As I drifted off to sleep, I wondered who the Yewclataws were.

CHAPTER 18 – DESOLATION

A loud banging on my door woke me. Surfacing from a deep sleep, I realized it was daylight. I struggled out of bed and opened the door. It was Charlie.

"You missed breakfast, we're ready to go. Cindy rang the bell, but you never showed. Put on some clothes." Charlie shielded his eyes.

I grunted, "That's no way to greet your fearless leader."

It was too late. He was gone. I got dressed and went to the head to wash up. Then I went to the galley to give Cindy a morning hug. She handed me a cup of coffee and a bowl of cold porridge.

I could hear the generator running and the anchor chain rattling up through the hawse pipe. Then the engine started, and we were moving. I made my way up to the wheelhouse and logged our departure time.

André was at the wheel. I had a question.

"Who are the Yewclataws old Fred mentioned? An Indian tribe?"

He laughed.

"Not a tribe. A place! That's the local pronunciation of Yuculta. It's a set of rapids at the north end of Desolation Sound, a narrow pass where the tide rushes through at tremendous speed."

I found it on a chart. There were a series of rapids through Cordero Channel (named by the Spanish in 1792) on our route north. Gillard, Dent, and Greene

Point rapids followed in quick succession. The chart indicated tides up to 14 knots.

I went back into the wheelhouse to talk to André.

"Do you know how to traverse the rapids?"

"Yes. It's tricky, and you have to time it right. The alternative is to go through Seymour Narrows over by Campbell River."

Just as we were about to enter Thulin Passage, I noticed a motor yacht passing astern on a more westerly course. It was a Hatteras 50, similar to the boat that almost hit me in English Bay. I got the binoculars and tried to read the name. It was flying a large US flag off the stern, so I assumed it wasn't the same boat.

I went to the chart table and got out the tide book to calculate the optimum time for the Yucultas. Ideally, we would arrive shortly before high slack tide, fight the current through the first rapids, then, as the tide turned, ride it through Gillard and Dent. High slack tide was about 3 PM, so we would be early. I asked André to slow down, but he decided to continue at eight knots with a plan to anchor at the Rendezvous Islands for lunch and wait for the tide.

The trip up there through Desolation revealed beautiful blue-tinged mountains in the east as we threaded our way between steep-sided islands with sparse settlements. We passed a few other boats. Some sailboats were beating toward Squirrel Cove as we went by. At the top of Cortes Island, we encountered a massive log boom with a tug on each end, and we had to idle down until they cleared the channel.

Charlie took the helm for a while as André grabbed a catnap. He had put in more than his share of time at the wheel since we left Vancouver. We planned to continue all night up Johnstone Strait. It would be easy navigation after the rapids.

As we approached the Rendezvous Islands, I could see that the anchorage I chose on the chart was too tight to accommodate the *Lady L.* We continued on to the south end of Stuart Island, where André took command to drop the anchor in a small nook. It wasn't sheltered enough for overnight, but it would do for lunch. Cindy produced a buffet with a mix of hot and cold dishes, including an Irish stew and a Chinese stir-fry. She had become a major asset and received many compliments.

Several of the crew retired to nap in preparation for the night watch later. I helped Cindy with the cleanup. A big pot of the stew remained on the stove for later.

About 2:40, André came on deck. Charlie hoisted the anchor. I joined André in the wheelhouse for the trip through the rapids. As we approached the Yuculta Rapids, the boat slowed as we fought the strong tide. André rang for full ahead, and the speed through the water increased to about eleven knots.

The water was boiling and curling in small whirlpools. There was a definite feeling of climbing uphill. As we approached the narrowest point, the current gradually subsided and was almost gone as we exited the rapids.

The next mile or so was calmer, but ahead we could see rougher waters and white peaks and spray. André rang the bell three times, our pre-arranged signal for all hands on deck. As the crew assembled, I saw what André already knew. The spray was coming from a pod of killer whales disporting themselves in the salmon-filled waters. Large fins would appear suddenly then disappear again. One show-off whale jumped completely clear of the water and landed with a big splash.

We were catching up on them and were soon quite close. André rang for slow ahead, so we were moving at the same speed as the pod. I had never seen an orca outside of an aquarium, and Cindy had never seen one at all. There were a couple of mothers with babies, which probably explained why they were slower than us.

Cameras appeared as the crew tried to take pictures of the glorious sight. I didn't bother because I could see that timing it right would be tricky. A movie camera would have been better.

The current began to pick up in our favor as we approached Jimmy Judd Island, where we had to make a sharp turn to port. André timed it correctly, but the *Lady L* leaned quite far to starboard, and I could hear things sliding and falling inside. Cindy ran back to the galley.

The whales changed direction and headed for the Arran rapids, and we soon lost sight of them. The water was calm, but we were being swept along at a good clip. As we approached Dent Island, small whirlpools began to appear. The water was hundreds of feet deep but still moving fast. André rang for more speed to give him greater control. We seem to be flying along, the boat leaning first one way and then the other.

"Yeehah!"

Charlie gave a cowboy yell, and everybody was excited by the wild ride. Ahead of us, a large whirlpool appeared, looking big enough to swallow a small boat. We skirted the edge and shot through into calmer waters.

After that, it was smooth going for an hour or so. When Greene Point rapids came in view, the water was wild with big whirlpools and upwelling waves.

"Are you sure we want to go through there right now?" I was a little scared.

André said, "No, I'm not sure. I have never been this way before, I always went through Seymour Narrows and up Johnstone Strait."

"Now you tell me!" I looked at the chart.

"There is a bay to port marked as Crawford Anchorage. It's behind that island." I pointed out Erasmus Island. "Let's wait for the next tide."

I got Charlie back on deck, as André turned into the quiet bay. He cut the engine, and we dropped anchor in 60 feet of water, with almost perfect shelter.

I checked the tide table and saw that the next high was at 4:15 AM. A 3:30 AM start would be needed.

Cindy produced a dinner of Shepherd's pie and a green salad, followed by fresh-baked apple pie with ice cream. We were allowed one glass of wine each.

After dinner, we played poker for matchsticks. There was a lot of laughter. Levi won, and Jock was a close second. I was the big loser. Cindy didn't play, and after I ran out of matches, I joined her in the galley.

Cindy gave me a hug and smiled. "Can I sleep in your cabin tonight?"

"How could I say no? What brought that on?"

"Levi suggested I come to his cabin. I told him I was with you. He took no for an answer, but I'd like to reinforce it by letting him see me go into your cabin."

"Sure, join me in the saloon later, and we'll head off at the same time he does."

I went to the radio room and tried to get through to Brice without success. There were many bursts of static, indicating a thunderstorm in the area, which interfered with reception. I called the Coast Guard and asked them to relay an "all's well" message to Brice by telephone. Then I went back to the saloon and found Cindy.

In my room, I turned my back as she undressed and slipped into one of my shirts, which came down to her knees.

We cuddled and whispered sweet nothings in the narrow bed, then drifted off. When the ship's bell rang, I woke up. Cindy was already up making coffee for the crew. There was just a hint of dawn in the sky when we got going. I turned on the radar and conned André through the rapids, which almost flat. The weather had turned misty and damp and much colder than it had been. Jock started up the furnace.

We had a couple of hours of smooth running, and then we joined the main shipping channel of Johnstone Strait at Eden Point. Visibility was poor in fog and light rain. There was more traffic, including fishing boats and log booms. A few tense moments followed as I learned how to interpret what I saw on the radar screen. It wasn't easy to tell the difference between a small island and a barge.

Charlie took the helm while André discussed the next leg of the voyage. It was not yet 6 AM. Port McNeill was about 50 miles ahead, and I estimated we would arrive about noon. We decided to stop there for fuel and water even though we still had plenty of both. Insurance, André called it.

The wind was increasing from the northwest, but the ride was still pretty smooth, with only a slight roll. André thought the breeze would drop in the late afternoon. After Port McNeill, it was about a 60-mile run in the open ocean past Cape Caution until we were in sheltered water again.

We planned to run all night, so we arranged two-person four-hour watch schedules. Charlie and I first, then André and Levi. Jock would not take a watch, but he was always on call if the engine bell rang. His cabin was right beside the engine room. Cindy would fill a thermos of hot coffee at the start of each watch. Otherwise, she was free.

I showed Levi how to read the radar screen. By eleven, the fog was lifting, and visibility improved. Shortly before noon, we pulled up to the fuel dock at Port McNeill. As we pulled in, the same Hatteras 50 we had seen off Lund pulled out. It was no longer flying a flag, and the name was still not visible. I was beginning to suspect their presence wasn't a coincidence.

I found a payphone and called Brice at work to let him know we were okay. I promised to try the radio again but told him not to worry if it failed again. Then

I called my answering service. There was only one message, just a number to call. I didn't bother with it.

While we waited for the tanks to fill, I remembered to ask Levi if he found out who employed the lawyer that bailed out Fingers Finnegan.

"Wackner said it was Lorne Greene. Not the TV star, but someone who resembles him. He didn't know the guy's real name. Paid in cash, no receipt."

"I hope you didn't hurt him."

"Not even a tiny bit. But Wackner did pee his pants with fear, so I may have embarrassed him. I didn't show him my face."

Levi chuckled and cracked his knuckles, "Most people are cowards. It's rarely necessary to hurt someone."

The way he said it scared me enough that I would probably have told him anything he asked.

I knew Lorne Greene as the star of an American TV series called *Bonanza*. I imagined it was a nickname based on a physical resemblance.

As he left the room, Levi said, "By the way, did you know Lorne Greene's real name was *Chaim* Green?"

So now I knew Levi was a trivia buff. I added it to the case notes.

When the tanks were full, we headed out. In the shelter of Malcolm Island, Cindy served lunch. I was on the helm. The big yacht was very easy to steer in a straight line. It was even easier when I figured out how to switch on the autopilot, which André had omitted to mention. All we really had to do was watch for logs and other boats.

Two hours later, we were leaving the shelter of Vancouver Island. Although the wind was light, swells were rolling in from the open Pacific. Out to the west, the next land was Kamchatka, over 5000 miles away. In the next hour, the swells grew more significant, and *Lady L* began to roll. I got Jock to slow down to ease the motion. André felt the change and came up to the wheelhouse to report that Cindy and Levi were both seasick and out of commission. We decided to stop for the night in Miles Inlet, which was just south of Cape Caution, a very sheltered anchorage, shaped like a cross.

Half an hour later, we nosed into the inlet. It was narrow, with trees growing right down to the water. About a mile in, there was a tee shaped intersection with a shallow cross channel. There was just enough space to turn around and anchor the *Lady L* facing out. We launched the Whaler, and Charlie used it to tie a stern line around a tree. The water was glassy, and although we could see blue sky above, huge trees filtered most of the sunshine.

The seasick crew enjoyed a miraculous recovery as soon as we were in smooth water. Cindy produced a feast with lamb kebabs, roast potatoes, and a Greek salad. After dinner, everybody except Cindy and I played cards. We went into the kitchen and cleaned up. She made cinnamon buns to be baked in the morning and put them in the fridge. Then we sat out on the foredeck and enjoyed the orange and purple sunset.

CHAPTER 19 – CAUTION

In the morning, my eyes opened before the bell rang. Cindy was nestled in my arms, sleeping peacefully. It seemed life could not be more perfect, and I wanted the moment to last forever.

What seemed just seconds later, the bell rang. Cindy woke up and kissed me lightly on the cheek.

"There is something I'd like to talk about, but I don't have time right now. Can we find time later?" She sounded serious, but not worried.

"I'm sure, once past Cape Caution, we can sneak off together. I suggest you and Levi avoid solid food until we're in smoother water. It will be rough for a couple of hours, and it would be a shame to waste those fabulous buns."

Half an hour later, we were all drinking coffee. The cinnamon buns were perfect. Cindy put the icing on the side so you could add it yourself—or not. I chose not. As advised, Cindy saved hers for later. Levi took his out on deck.

The morning was misty and cool, with water dripping off the low hanging trees. It was so silent that we all talked in whispers. Charlie paddled the Whaler over to let go of the stern line, then we hoisted it aboard. The sound of the engine starting was shocking in that silent place. We raised anchor and idled out of the inlet. As we approached the entrance, the bow began to rise to the swell.

The swells were even bigger than the day before, but Levi seemed to have gained his sea legs. André took the helm, and I manned the radar as visibility was poor. Ahead of us, a log boom was being towed by a large tug. The tug showed well on the radar, but the boom faded in and out. It was heading south and passed outside of us, sheltering us from the swells for a while.

Once past the boom, I spotted a faster boat coming up behind us. It proved to be a large aluminum crew boat carrying loggers to work in one of the inlets. After that, we didn't see any more traffic.

Two hours later, we were inside Cape Calvert, and the water was getting flatter. By noon the mist was gone, and we were cruising in bright sunlight under blue skies with a few fluffy clouds. The landscape consisted of treed islands backed by tall snow-covered mountains to the east. It wouldn't change in character for the next 800 miles.

André handed the helm over to Charlie, and Levi took over the radar. I went back to the galley and helped Cindy make lunch. After everybody was fed, we went out on the back deck and relaxed in the lounge chairs. I pushed two together so we could hold hands.

"What did you want to talk about?"

"Our relationship. I think I'm in love with you."

"I know I'm in love with you."

Cindy blushed and looked at her feet. When she looked back up at me, she said, "I want to take it to the next level."

Sex at last! Or maybe I had it wrong. I wanted to make sure I understood correctly.

"Umm, what exactly is the next level?"

"Marriage."

I gulped. I had been thinking the same but was waiting for the time to be right—a few months at least. I made a quick decision. I got up out of the chair, got down on one knee, and opened an imaginary ring box.

"Cindy, will you make me the happiest man alive?"

"Yes, as long as we can get married first."

I slid the imaginary ring onto her real finger.

"I'll get you a real ring as soon as possible."

"Can you get André to perform the ceremony?"

There was a plaque in the wheelhouse which read:

Marriages performed
by the Captain
are valid only for the
duration of the voyage.

I assumed Cindy had seen it, but I reminded her what it said.

"That's okay. I expect a real wedding as soon as we get to Prince Rupert."

"A church wedding?"

"Technically, I'm a Buddhist, so no."

I told her I would make the announcement after dinner. I was willing to bet André had never before performed such a ceremony.

Late in the afternoon, we saw many fishing boats all heading the same way. Soon we passed a large cannery called Namu, where they were unloading. A small freighter was alongside, probably to take the canned salmon to Vancouver. It was an industrial operation. Charlie steered in close but didn't stop. We had plenty of canned fish in the larder.

CHAPTER 20 – WE DO

We anchored near Bella Bella at about 6 PM. Charlie, Jock, and André took the Whaler ashore to check out the local nightlife. They were back within half an hour, so I guess there wasn't any.

Perhaps in honor of passing Namu, Cindy produced salmon steaks she had thawed earlier, and I barbecued them while she made scalloped potatoes and green beans. After dinner, Cindy showed me a round layer cake with white icing.

"Is that dessert?"

"It's our wedding cake, you dolt!"

"Sorry. I'll make the announcement immediately."

"Wait until I change my clothes."

She was wearing jeans and a tee-shirt. She went to her cabin, and I went past to my own, where I took out a clean blue shirt and khaki pants. I even found a blue blazer. No tie, though.

A few minutes after I went back to the saloon, Cindy came out in a simple white dress I hadn't seen before. She had her long hair up in a chignon. White sandals with chunky heels adorned her feet. Lipstick and makeup had transformed her into the movie star seen only once before. There never was a more beautiful bride.

I motioned the ship's company to gather.

"We have an announcement to make. Cindy and I are getting married."

There was a general buzz of congratulations. Charlie asked, "When will this event take place?"

"Right now! André, can you perform the ceremony? I've written it out for you. I'll let Cindy look it over first and add anything she wants."

I handed Cindy the two 3 x 5 cards I had written the ceremony on. While she was reading it and correcting a few things, I borrowed a ring from Charlie, the iron ring of an engineer. Levi went to the kitchen and came back in a few minutes with a bouquet. There were no flowers available, but he had carved carrots and broccoli into a bouquet, surrounded with lettuce leaves. He was very handy with a knife.

André disappeared and came back in his captain's uniform, even the hat. He handed me a navy-blue tie with crossed red signal flags, which I put on. Ajax was wearing a parrot sized bow tie.

Jock offered to give away the bride since he was the only crew member old enough to be Cindy's father.

André read the ceremony silently a couple of times, then put the cards aside. Levi skillfully whistled a wedding march, with Ajax humming along. Jock solemnly marched Cindy to my side. Charlie acted as best man.

"Friends and crew members, we are gathered here today to celebrate the union of Cynthia Lu and Sean Gray in unholy matrimony. If anyone objects to this ceremony, please send a letter of complaint care of general delivery, Nowhere, Alaska."

"Marriage is a serious lifelong commitment between two souls. Love and respect are the mooring lines of a successful marriage, and commitment is the anchor. Cindy and Sean are undertaking an epic voyage into the uncharted waters of a long-term relationship, fearlessly and with great hopes for a future together."

"Do you Sean, take this woman to be your unlawfully wedded wife, to sail with her through rough seas and smooth, avoiding shoal waters and reefs, as long as there is wind in your sails?"

"I do."

"Do you Cynthia, take this man to be your unlawfully wedded husband, to be the keel that keeps him upright in the storm, the rudder that steers him true when the way is misty, and the safe harbor where he moors his tired ship, as long you can stand him?"

"I do."

I placed the ring on Cindy's finger. It was very loose.

"By the power vested in me by nobody in particular, I now pronounce you shipmates for life. You may kiss the bride."

I took Cindy in my arms and leaned her back in a kiss that lasted so long André had time to find a bottle of Dom Perignon and pop the cork. The kiss ended when the cork hit my left ear.

"Ow!"

Charlie laughed. "Appropriate first word for a newly married man. You'll be saying it again and often!"

Cindy tossed the bouquet. I think she was throwing it to André, but he stepped aside gracefully, and it hit Charlie in the eye.

"So not sorry." She giggled.

"Fuck you, Charlie," Offered Ajax.

I got the cake out from the galley, and we cut the first piece together. After we ate cake and drank champagne, André put a record on the wind-up phonograph. It was Frank Sinatra singing "Young at Heart." I slow-danced with Cindy. I didn't really know how to dance, but it felt great all the same.

When the record ended, André put on the only other record he had, Glen Miller playing "Begin the Beguine."

Levi went back to his cabin and came out with a Philips cassette player and a stack of tapes. The sound quality was only marginally better than the Victrola, but the music was more modern. The first song was Bill Haley's "Rock Around the Clock."

After one glass of champagne, Cindy's face was flushed bright red, so she switched to apple juice. The rest of us moved to beer because the champagne bottle was empty.

Everyone danced with Cindy, even Jock. I kept a sharp eye on Levi, but he behaved himself. By the time the evening ended, the music was up to the Beach Boys' "Good Vibrations."

André made an announcement.

"The newlyweds will now occupy the master suite for the duration of the voyage."

Cindy ran over and kissed him on the cheek. This was great news because the master suite had its own head, bathtub, shower, and, more importantly, a double bed! I was flabbergasted.

"Thank you, André. That was unexpected. You and the crew have treated us unbelievably well."

"You're an asshole, Sean, but we all love Cindy. We want her to be happy. If that makes you happy too, it's the price we have to pay."

Ajax added, "Sean, the fuckwit!"

Cindy kissed the crew in turn. When my turn came, I grabbed her waist and hustled her off amid tipsy goodnights.

We quickly moved our things into the master suite, which was only slightly bigger than the other cabins, but more luxurious. The bed had a proper mattress, unlike the slabs of foam on the other bunks.

Cindy sat on the bed, still dressed.

"Sean, I'm scared. I've never done this before. Made love, I mean."

"I'm not all that experienced myself, just two before you." That would be Suzy and Brenda, but I thought it better not to name them.

I whispered, "I'll be gentle."

I turned off the ceiling light and just left on a small desk lamp. We undressed each other slowly and lovingly. We draped our clothes over a chair. Cindy's underwear was white and plain, but on her, it looked sensational. I fumbled with the bra snaps until she helped.

She looked as good naked as I had imagined. Perfection! I hoped she wasn't too disappointed in me. I lifted the sheet, and she slid into bed. I slipped in beside her, then a thought struck me like an ax blade between the eyes.

"Are you on the pill?"

"What pill?"

"Birth control pills. I thought most women used them these days."

"Not me. I wasn't planning this until yesterday."

"Okay, I'll see what I can find."

I got up, slipped on my boxers, and rifled through all the drawers and shelves in the room looking for condoms. Nothing.

Then I went out to the saloon where the four remaining crew were playing cards. Charlie looked up and said, "That was fast!"

I blushed and asked, "Do any of you have a box of condoms?"

Everyone laughed, but I didn't see the humor.

Jock said, "You were the only one likely to need them, so it was your job to bring them!"

Ajax chimed in, "None for you, Sean!"

More laughter. I headed back to bed disconsolately.

Cindy was understanding. I taught her everything I knew about oral. We both had a good time, but she fell asleep, still technically a virgin.

CHAPTER 21 – BELLA BELLA

A dark shadow moved across the full moon, glistening on the rippled surface of a small lake. I was swimming near the beach, in warm water. A few yards away, Cindy was facing toward me, smiling. Then her eyes went wide, and her mouth opened in a scream, but no sound came out. She disappeared under the water as though dragged down from behind. I called her name and swam to the spot where she had been. Everything went black, and I fell into the void.

My eyes popped open. Cindy was looking into my face and holding my shoulders.

"Sean, are you alright? You called out my name."

It took me a few moments to answer.

"I'm fine. I was dreaming about you. Stay in bed for a while. I'll make breakfast."

I got out of bed and pulled on some clothes. When I got to the galley, André had made coffee and was breaking eggs. Together we made scrambled eggs, bacon, and buttered BP biscuits. I set the table, laid out jams and jellies, then went to fetch Cindy while André rang the breakfast bell.

Cindy was up and dressed in shorts and a tee-shirt. I took her hand and led her to breakfast.

Charlie, Levi, and Jock all looked a bit hungover, but André was cheerful. After breakfast, we resumed our normal duties.

Jock asked Cindy, "So where is Sean taking you on your honeymoon?"

Cindy giggled, "I suggested a week in Hawaii, but he talked me into an Alaska cruise instead. It's a long honeymoon, but apparently, I have to earn my keep."

I told André that I wanted to go ashore for a few minutes before we left. The Whaler was still in the water, so I jumped in and motored over to the Bella Bella public dock. I walked into the one street town and found a small pharmacy, where I was able to purchase a box of Trojans from a disapproving older woman.

Then I remembered our mission. I walked down to the fuel dock. There were no customers, and the attendant was jigging for cod off the end of the float. He turned around when he heard my footsteps. He was native, a bit shorter than me, with a large gut that prevented his black tee-shirt from reaching his pants. The shirt had a gorgeous painting of an eagle on it in style I didn't recognize.

He looked at me sullenly.

"You off that big yacht?"

"Yes. I'm Sean Gray."

"You the owner?"

"No, just the deckhand."

"Pretty well dressed for a deckhand."

I was dressed almost exactly the same as he was, except my clothes had fewer grease stains.

"I'm off duty. The owner makes us wear sailor suits when we're working."

He guffawed and stuck out his hand.

"Jessie Humchitt."

"What band?"

"I'm partial to the Rolling Stones… Oh. You mean clan? Heiltsuk. This is our land."

He swept his arm widely in a way that could have meant the town, the island, all of British Columbia or all of Canada. I didn't ask.

I did ask a few questions about the town, and soon we were chatting and joking like buddies. He even managed a bit of a smile.

"Did a Hatteras 50 come in here for fuel in the last few days?"

"Maybe. Can you describe it?"

"50-foot motor yacht, white hull, wide blue stripe along the gunwale, flying bridge, dinghy tipped up on the transom."

"I might have seen it."

His fingers were twitching. I fished in my pocket and found a ten-dollar bill, which I took out and presented to him with both hands, bowing from the waist. That was how Cindy had taught me to present a gift.

He looked thoughtful then spoke.

"A boat like that was in here yesterday, bought a couple of hundred gallons of diesel. Paid cash."

"What did the Captain look like?"

"Big guy, reminded me of a guy I saw in a TV western."

"Lorne Greene?"

"Nah, wasn't he in Robin Hood?"

"That was Richard Green."

"Oh, right. English pansy. No, this guy reminded me of Ben…Ben Cartwright. That's the guy."

Ben Cartwright was the character Lorne Greene played on *Bonanza*. The man in the Hatteras was our villain—maybe. Certainly, he was the man who bailed out Fingers Finnegan, and he was heading in the same direction we were.

"Was there anyone else with him?"

"You bet. A blonde girl, maybe twenty years younger than him. A real looker." He held his hands well out in front of his chest to indicate what he'd been looking at.

"No other crew?"

"None that I saw. Oh, there was a dog. White with a black patch over one eye. They called him 'Pirate.' Not very big but sturdy."

I thanked my new friend and headed back to *Lady L.* We hoisted the dinghy on board and got ready to leave. Before we did, I called a quick meeting of the crew and told them what I learned in Bella Bella.

Jock said, "So it was a spy mission. I thought you were looking for somewhere to buy rubbers."

Cindy and I both blushed. I had slipped the box to her when I came aboard.

André remarked, "An old guy with a young woman and a dog for crew doesn't sound too threatening."

He was right. But it was too much of a coincidence that they were heading the same way as us.

"Maybe they have accomplices waiting in Alaska or traveling separately?"

We left it at that and got the ship moving northward. I took the helm. As we left Bella Bella, the *Northland Prince,* a sizable passenger and freight ship passed us. She was traveling a few knots faster and left us rolling in her wake.

CHAPTER 22 – UGLY ROCK

Just north of Bella Bella, we had to pass through an open area of the Pacific, and larger swells were present. As seemed to be the pattern, the morning was misty and cool, but that day it was drizzling as well. The wind was strong from the south, which would have been great sailing if we had a sailboat.

The crew all seemed to have sea-legs by then, and nobody was sick. After a few twists and turns, we were back in the narrow channel behind Princess Royal Island. Cindy served lunch. Charlie was standing beside me, eating a sandwich when he dropped it and pointed.

"What's that?"

Directly in front of us, perhaps a hundred feet away, a large rugged boulder was breaking the surface of the water. I rang the engine bell for full astern. Nothing happened.

"Who's in the engine room?" I yelled.

Charlie whipped around and ran below. He was supposed to be on engine duty.

I threw the wheel hard over to port. Seconds later, we hit the rock with the starboard bow. It made less noise than I expected, but you could hear it. André was on deck in a flash, as the engine stopped and restarted in reverse. I rang the bell to stop the engine again.

André was laughing hysterically. I went out on deck to see what was funny.

"You hit a floating Styrofoam rock. You know in the movies when cavemen are throwing boulders? This is one of those. My dad had one in the front yard of our house. He kept the spare key under it."

The helm was still hard over, and the yacht circled around the rock. André hooked it with a pike pole and tossed it on deck. It was about three feet across but not more than ten pounds in weight. A flat bottom made it look like there was a lot more beneath the water.

"It might come in handy at some point. Must have been lost from a movie shoot."

Levi lashed the boulder on the upper deck between the two rowboats. I rang for ahead and steered back on course.

A few hours later, we came upon an abandoned cannery. The chart labeled it Butedale. The buildings were wood, painted white, with brown trim and red roofs. They looked in good shape, but you could see peeling paint and rotting pilings when we came in close. There was no apparent vandalism. A small store and a fuel dock were open, and several crew boats were tied up. We passed nearby but didn't stop.

The trip continued up the long narrow Grenville Passage. We cruised for miles in glassy waters surrounded by glorious vistas. The snowcapped mountains and waterfalls were becoming more extensive.

The only further excitement was passing a large tug coming the other way with two barges in tow. We had to squeeze right over close to shore to make room for them. Near the top of the passage, Kumealon Inlet branched off. The inner basin was perfectly sheltered, and it was there we stopped for the night. We anchored in the narrowest part of the entrance in 60 feet of water. It was only about 40 miles from Prince Rupert, so we would be there by noon the next day.

With the prospect of fresh supplies, Cindy made room in the freezer by taking out a large roast of beef. Jock taught her how to make Yorkshire pudding. For dessert, there were the remains of the wedding cake. We had an early night. Cindy and I were eager to get the honeymoon started properly. And we did.

CHAPTER 23 – BOOM

The thrashing of a propeller and a rumbling diesel engine close by woke me. An air horn blew a long blast. Bright lights shone through the ports. It was 2:38 AM.

The all-hands bell rang. When I got to the wheelhouse, André and Charlie were already there. Ajax had one eye open and was mumbling about scurvy bastards.

"What's going on?" I asked André.

"It's a tug towing a log boom. It must have been tied up around the corner out of our sight. Now they want to leave, and we're blocking the entrance."

André turned on the running lights, so the tug crew would know we were awake. I went up on the foredeck to help Charlie raise the anchor. Jock got the engine ready. Levi was in the wheelhouse with André. We got going and moved out of the way. We had to go right out into Grenville Channel to make room for the boom.

"This is normal?" Levi sounded annoyed.

André shrugged, "It happens. Pleasure boats are just a nuisance to commercial boats."

"But why they are leaving at 2 AM?"

"It's high tide. They need to catch the falling tide down the channel."

Levi seemed satisfied and went back to bed. André and Charlie decided to keep going until morning since the way was lit by a bright moon. I climbed back in with Cindy, who had somehow slept through the commotion.

CHAPTER 24 – RUPERT

I woke up to the sound of rain on the cabin top. Cindy was already getting dressed. I admired the process for a while, then got out of bed and went to the head. We were settling into life in a shared space. Neither of us had much in the way of possessions. To me, this was an ideal way to start the marriage. Whatever we needed—I hoped it wasn't a lot—would be a mutual choice. People who live on a small boat can't accumulate too much.

The engine was still running, but I heard it slow down. I put on some clothes and went up to the wheelhouse. We were just entering Prince Rupert harbor. I went up to the wheelhouse and called the local Yacht Club on VHF to see if they had room for us. *Lady L* was too big for their docks, so they directed us to the commercial terminal, which did have room. I booked us in for two nights.

The commercial dock was a bit run down, but serviceable, and we tied up with an array of fishing boats and tugs, plus a few small freighters. The *Northland Prince* was there at another dock. Once we were secured, we sat down to breakfast in the dining room. As usual, Cindy had done wonders with freshly baked croissants, scrambled eggs, and bacon.

"We're out of fresh fruit," she announced.

After breakfast, Cindy and I planned a big shopping trip to Safeway, the closest grocery store. Cindy suggested I ask each crew member if they had any favorite dishes she could try to cook. I talked to everyone in turn and came up with a list.

Angus: Haggis, neeps, and tatties (I think he was kidding about the haggis), second choice bangers and mash.

Charlie: Macaroni and Cheese, Boston Cream Pie

André: Confit de Canard, Tourtière

Levi: Couscous and Lamb Tajine

Sean: Callaloo soup, Kedgeree

I didn't put Cindy on the list as I figured she could handle that herself. Before we left for the shopping trip, she consulted her cookbooks to determine what ingredients she would need. What were "neeps" anyway? According to Cindy, rutabagas. I still didn't know what those were.

I told her "callaloo" was dasheen leaf. Maybe that helped.

The rain had let up, so we risked walking to town without wet gear. It was a fair distance up a hill, but it was good to get our legs moving after days on the boat. On the way, we saw more bald eagles than I had ever seen in my life. They were sitting in rows like crows on a wire. We had seen some on the way up the coast, but they were far off, flying or nesting in trees. These were urban eagle gangs. Maybe "Hell's Eagles?" "The Wild Birds?"

The Safeway store was big, modern, and had a decent selection of fresh and frozen food. I let Cindy shop while I went looking for city hall to apply for a marriage license. It was only a couple of blocks away. The nice lady at the counter there told me I should go to the registrar next door. I would need Cindy's ID as well as mine. I went back to Safeway.

Cindy didn't have her ID with her, so we concentrated on getting the shopping done. The cart was pretty full, and some of it was frozen, so we took a cab back to the dock.

While we loaded the groceries aboard, the crew was cleaning the boat. André always kept *Lady L* immaculate. Cindy made a simple lunch, and then we gathered our documents and went to the city hall.

The registrar, an older man with a bald head and little round glasses, examined our documents. He asked Cindy where she was born and her nationality even though she had a Canadian citizenship certificate. He didn't ask me, even though I was born in Grenada. Anyway, we paid a small fee and got a license. I got a list of ministers who could perform a ceremony. I asked him if there was a non-religious alternative. He looked puzzled but gave me two names of retired justices who could do the job.

I found a payphone and called the first one on the list, William McKenzie. He didn't answer. The second one, Oliver Engstrom, picked up on the first ring. He sounded pleasant, with a slight Scandinavian accent. I gave him the details and asked if he could marry us the following morning at 10 AM, onboard *Lady L.* He agreed, the fee would be twenty-five dollars. That done, Cindy and I walked around town to explore. The locals were mostly friendly. We identified two hotels with dining rooms, one a bit rough looking, and a Chinese restaurant called the West End.

I said, "You haven't had any Chinese food since we left Vancouver. Why don't we go there for dinner?"

Cindy smiled and squeezed my hand, "I'd like that, but we should bring the whole crew. Chinese food is always better when shared."

We stopped for an ice cream cone at Smiles near Cow Bay. They had a few flavors. It turned out Cindy and I both liked rum raisin, so we shared a large one.

Between licks, Cindy asked the lady at the counter how Cow Bay got its name.

"Some guy unloaded some cows here in 1908 by pushing them into the water and letting them swim ashore. Before that, it was Cameron Cove."

"So, the name sticks until the next big event?" Cindy asked.

The clerk didn't smile.

Back at the boat, we told everybody about our plans for dinner and the "official" wedding the next day. The rest of the crew went to explore the town. Cindy and I retired for an afternoon "nap."

At about 6 PM, we all gathered in the saloon before going up to the restaurant. André gave the crew a little pep talk.

"We've got a fine team here. The boat is in tip-top shape, and we're equipped for salvage. I expect great things ahead. I'm sure you are all wondering how we plan to accomplish the recovery. Over to you, Sean."

André had caught me off guard. I didn't have a plan. My usual approach was to think ahead only as far as the next step. I figured that would save a lot of wasted time planning for things that didn't happen.

"This could take a while. Let's have dinner first, and then I'll outline the plan."

Fortunately, everyone was hungry, so I got away with the diversion. We walked up together, with Cindy in the lead, since she knew where the restaurant was. Again, we passed many eagles and a couple of stray cats. The restaurant was a plain building of a reasonable size. It was busy, but they had a big round table that worked for six and could hold several more.

The waitress, who looked like a kindly grandmother, asked if we wanted to order off the menu.

"What's the alternative?" Cindy asked.

"I can ask the chef to make a Chinese banquet for six people and let him choose the dishes. If you have no allergies, you will get the best food that way."

Cindy scanned the crew for objections. There were none. She nodded her assent.

"Better bring chopsticks AND forks," I said, unsure of the general level of competence in that area. Most Vancouverites can use chopsticks, but you never know.

There was no booze, but we were served a large pot of green tea. When the food came, I could see we would have leftovers. There was hot and sour soup, ginger chicken, beef with wild mushrooms, garlic prawns, whole rock cod, and steamed rice.

Cindy gave me some chopstick lessons, although I already had the basics. Charlie just used a fork, but I think it was because he was hungry, not incompetent. Not much talking went on around the table, except about the food. When we were done, we had two boxes in a paper bag to go. The bill was reasonable.

Fortune cookies were provided, and we read them aloud for fun.

> André: "You are talented in many unknown ways."

> Charlie: "You missed your bus, but there will be another."

> Jock: "Your shoes will make you happy today."

> Levi: "Help! I'm being held prisoner in a fortune cookie factory."

> Cindy: "The voices in your head say watch out."

> Sean: "A dream you have will come true."

Laughter and speculation on the meanings were rampant. We all agreed that Levi's was the best. I didn't believe in that stuff, but mine did make me nervous. My dreams tended toward disaster.

André reminded me about the plan.

"Let's stop at the pub on the way back to the boat, and I'll explain there."

There was a hotel pub nearby. The entrances were marked "Men" and "Ladies and Escorts." We all went into the "Ladies and Escorts" door. A barrier separated the two sides, but it was only waist-high. It was Saturday night, and the place was nearly full.

There was a preponderance of male customers on both sides. Most looked like lumberjacks or fishermen. Everyone looked at Cindy. She was the only woman in the place wearing a skirt, although it was a modest pale-yellow shirt dress, buttoned right up to the top. The tables were small. Cindy and I sat at one, and the other four sat at the next.

Before we even got served, a rough-looking character in a red plaid shirt, grubby jeans, and muddy boots stood up and came over to our table.

"How much for the Chink Bitch?" His voice was loud and rude.

I'm not a violent man, but for the first time in my life, I wanted to kill someone. Not just kill him, but rip his throat out, gouge his eyes and tear off his limbs. I started to stand up but was hampered by the table.

Cindy shot to her feet, half-turned toward me, and said sternly, "Sit down, Sean."

She jumped up on her chair and pointed at the oaf. I sat back down. All conversation stopped, and everyone looked her way. The waiter was frozen in his tracks with a tray of beer in the air.

"Ladies and Escorts, allow me to introduce this fine example of manhood. I'll call him 'Bozo' since he hasn't seen fit to introduce himself."

"In just six words, Bozo has efficiently managed to insult at least 80% of the world's population. All women, anybody who has even a trace of non-white blood, and of course everybody of decent character."

The whole place was staring at Bozo, whose face was turning several shades of purple. His fists were clenched by his side, his knees slightly bent as if preparing to attack. Cindy showed no fear. There were a few claps from some of the women in the place, but nobody said a word.

"Bozo thinks he can raise himself up by putting other people down. So, let's have a serious look at him. He's well dressed. Who knew Brooks Brothers had a store in Prince Rupert? He's a fine physical specimen if you ignore the beer-gut hanging down over his tiny limp dick."

Laughter erupted, and a few shouts of encouragement were aimed at Cindy. She was having fun now. Even Bozo's buddies seemed to be enjoying the show. Cindy continued.

"He is obviously a man of substance—or maybe substance abuse. Look at that haircut. Did you do that yourself, or did a buddy do it with a chainsaw? And the manicure—amazing how they get the black polish under the nails like that."

"What woman wouldn't be impressed? If we met under different circumstances, I would seriously consider mating with Bozo. What circumstances? Umm—you got me. None come to mind. Anyway, Bozo, feel free to offer a rebuttal. By the way, my name is Cindy Lu. 'Chink Bitch' is my occupation!"

Cindy sat down and took my hand. Before I could say anything, the whole place erupted in laughter and applause. Bozo seemed to shrink in stature, and he slowly slunk toward the exit, muttering to himself. Levi quietly followed him out.

I realized that I didn't know Cindy very well. I was married to somebody of far greater courage and wit than expected. I was proud and more in love than ever.

The regular din of a busy pub resumed. Several women came over and introduced themselves to Cindy, and hugs were exchanged. She was suddenly the most popular person in the place. Our table was filled with drinks, all paid for by other tables.

The band came back from a break and started playing "Hello Mary Lou," but they sang it as "Hello Cindy Lu, goodbye heart." The crowd sang along.

Levi came back a few minutes later. He dropped a handful of shotgun shells in my pocket and whispered in my ear. "Shotgun in his truck. I took the ammunition and tied him to the steering wheel. I also explained to him what an orchidectomy is and how it could be performed without anesthetic."

André said, "That was fun. I was sure we'd have a bar fight on our hands, but instead, they buy us drinks. Cindy is the bravest person I have ever seen."

We raised a toast to Cindy. Then Charlie spoke up.

"Now you see why the 'Ladies and Escorts' law was passed. Bozo wouldn't have been allowed on the Ladies' side in those days."

Jock said, "Yeah, but then guys like him would never get to meet someone like Cindy."

I said, "There is nobody else like Cindy. In fact, until now, I didn't even know Cindy was like Cindy!"

Cindy turned on me. Her blood was up. "Don't you start getting all proud of little wifey, Sean. Who I am has nothing to do with you!"

I shut up. Nobody asked about my great plan for Alaska. We left soon afterward. In the parking lot, we passed Bozo's rusty blue Ford pickup. He seemed to be sleeping peacefully with his head on the wheel.

After we got to our cabin, Cindy put her arms around me and whispered. "I'm sorry, Sean. You didn't really do anything wrong. I love you."

We made a long, slow, gentle, and passionate love, then drifted away in each other's arms.

CHAPTER 25 – WE STILL DO

I was falling naked through space. Above me was a tall blue mountain with a waterfall cascading off a rocky slope into a curiously pastel blue lake. I twisted in the air until I was in a diving position as the lake came up to meet me. There was a tremendous splash as I hit the icy water, and I knew I would drown. My limbs were paralyzed by the cold, so I couldn't swim. My lungs filled, and I felt peace descend on my soul. The world turned black.

Cindy giggled as my eyes popped open.

"Wake up, Sean. You were so sound asleep that I had to throw cold water in your face to wake you."

I was groggy. "What time is it?"

"Nine. The wedding is at ten, better get up. There's coffee in the galley."

I left Cindy to change into her wedding clothes and went to get breakfast. It was a sunny day, with just a few patches of mist in the harbor. André and Charlie were in the saloon drinking coffee and eating donuts. I joined them. We planned to do the wedding precisely as before, except André would be the ring bearer. I showed him the simple gold ring I bought in a jewelry store uptown while Cindy was grocery shopping.

Cindy and I had decided to let the J.P. use the official wedding ceremony, just replacing the word "obey" with "cherish."

After several cups of coffee, I went to the cabin to clean up and put on a shirt, tie, and blazer. I didn't have a suit. Cindy had gone back to her original cabin to change.

Just before 10 AM, there was a knock on the hull, and Charlie welcomed Mr. Engstrom on board. The weather was excellent, so we had decided to hold the ceremony on the fantail.

Engstrom was a tall, slim man in his sixties, with piercing blue eyes and a shock of silver hair. He wore a grey suit of impeccable cut, somewhat worn and very old fashioned.

He got set up, with a portable lectern, at the front of the deck. I stood up and took my position. Levi activated the cassette deck, which played Brahms' "Wedding March."

Jock walked Cindy up the aisle, but my eyes were on the bride. When she got to the front, Ajax wolf-whistled and croaked, "Hot stuff!"

Cindy was wearing a lacy white cheongsam with a high collar. It was almost floor-length but had a thigh-high slit up one side. I wondered where she got it. There were matching shoes with medium heels. She held a bouquet of wildflowers. For the second time, she was the most beautiful bride I could imagine.

The ceremony was simple, and we played it straight. At last, Engstrom said, "I now pronounce you man and wife. You may kiss the bride."

I kissed Cindy, but not as dramatically as the first ceremony. Champagne popped again, but I ducked, and André missed my head.

We signed the register, and André and Charlie witnessed our signatures. We were officially married! I paid Engstrom, and he took his leave.

We didn't have a reception, having decided to do that when we got home to Vancouver and could invite a larger group of friends. Everybody changed back into work clothes, and I walked Cindy up to the payphone so she could call her mother. There were a lot of strong words in Chinese, and Cindy hung up abruptly.

"She's delighted I'm married, but not so delighted with the groom. She'll come around."

No more was said about it. I phoned Lizzie collect, told her Cindy and I were married. She offered sincere congratulations. Then I brought her up to date on Lorne Greene. She said she had no idea who he was or what he wanted.

I phoned my answering service. There was one message. Brenda. She wanted me to call right away. It was a 403 area code. Alberta. Good thing I brought a few rolls of quarters. I returned the call, but there was no answer. I couldn't think of a reason for Brenda to call me, especially after what seemed to be her role in the break-in. I kept the number in my notebook.

Then I called Brice at home. It was Sunday morning, so I figured he would still be there. It took a couple of rings before Eva answered.

"Congratulations, Sean. I hear Cindy has made an honest man of you. Tell me all about the wedding."

I told her about the ceremony. Eva wanted to know about Cindy's dress, shoes, and bouquet. I did my best to describe them.

"Thanks, Sean. I'll see the pictures when you get back. I'll put Brice on now."

We hadn't taken any pictures. Brice came on, and I told him to turn on his radio. I promised to try another transmission when I got back to *Lady L*.

I turned to Cindy. "Eva asked about wedding pictures. I guess we better get some."

"There must be a photographer in town." Cindy was thinking of professional photos.

"I'm sure, but it's Sunday. In a place like this, nothing will be open. We can get pictures done in Alaska. I have to see the photo store in Juneau anyway."

Back at the *Lady L*, I tried the radio again.

I keyed the mike, "*Mersey, Mersey*, this is *Malachite, Malachite*. Come in, *Mersey*, over."

When I took my finger off the button, all I got was static. I waited a while, but there was still no response. I decided our radio might be faulty. I walked down the docks until I found a fisherman on his boat and introduced myself.

Ted was a friendly older native guy. His troller had a dugout hull about thirty feet long carved from a single log, with a couple of planks added to raise the freeboard. The wheelhouse was the size and shape of a phone booth, and the single-cylinder Easthope engine sat exposed in the middle. The fish hold was a picnic cooler filled with ice. One large salmon and several beer bottles were visible.

"I'm looking for a radio repair guy. Do you know anyone who can help?"

"Maybe, what make is it?"

"Spilsbury & Tindall. It looks pretty old."

"They're the best, made in Vancouver. My son Jeff is the guy who fixes all the radios around here. He'll be down here in the morning. I'll send him over."

"Thanks! I really appreciate it."

"Hey Sean, I heard about the show your cook put on at the pub last night. Gordy had it coming, but he's a mean bastard. You all better watch your backs."

"Thanks. I appreciate the warning. We'll be careful."

Ted sold me a thirty-pound "smiley" as he called the big salmon, and I took it back to the galley for Cindy.

I told André about the radio, and we decided to delay our departure until after it was looked at. We also planned to keep a watch on the dock in case Gordy showed up.

Since everything was closed on Sunday, we had dinner on board that night. We filleted the salmon, put half in the freezer, and the other half on the barbecue, skin down. Sprinkled with lemon juice and soy sauce, we let it cook without turning it. Cindy made a Caesar salad and boiled some veggies. Maple sugar pie was served for dessert.

After the dishes were done, we decided to walk up to town and see what was showing at the movies. *2001, a Space Odyssey* was written by one of my favorite authors, Arthur C. Clarke. We bought tickets and went in. It was surprisingly full, considering the streets of Prince Rupert seemed empty.

We all enjoyed the film. On the way back to the *Lady L*, Charlie kept saying, "Just what do you think you're doing, Sean?" in a good imitation of the computer.

It was still light when we got back, but the sun was waning. We all sat on the back deck with a glass of wine to watch the sunset. André raised a toast to the newlyweds then said, "Okay, Sean, now would be a good time to tell us the plan."

Caught. Fortunately, I had given it some thought and was able to outline a general plan of action. I laid it out in point form:

1. Check-in at customs in Juneau, bypassing Ketchikan.

2. See if I can get the photos Jakob took.

3. Stop at Farragut Bay on the way back, see if anyone is there looking for the treasure.

4. If all clear, continue to Thomas Bay. If not, make a new plan.

Immediately André pointed out a flaw.

"Juneau is over 150 miles north of Petersburg, the closest town to Thomas Bay. It would be a waste of time and fuel for us to take Lady L all the way up there for some photos which might not even be there."

He was right. "What do you suggest?"

"You fly up to Juneau from here, get the photos, then meet us in Petersburg."

That made sense, and would save at least two days of travel and a lot of fuel. Even so, I was reluctant to leave Cindy.

"Could we send somebody else? I don't want to leave Cindy alone."

"She won't be alone, she'll be safe with us. This is your responsibility, and the photos could be important."

Cindy spoke up, "Sean, I have managed fine without you for most of my life. I can handle a couple of more days."

That was the end of the discussion. Levi and Charlie agreed to watch out for intruders. Cindy and I went to bed. It was another wedding night, and we were starting to get good at celebrating them.

CHAPTER 26 – FLIGHT

There was a sudden thump on the dock.

"Jesus fucking Christ!" The voice was loud and angry.

I was lying awake imagining what could go wrong if I left Cindy on the *Lady L* while I flew to Juneau. After that single shouted curse, Levi's voice rang out, "Don't move!"

I jumped up and pulled on my pants. When I went out on deck, I could see Levi standing over a prone figure. Charlie was on the dock too. I jumped down just as Levi turned the guy over and shone a light on his face. It wasn't Bozo. It was a smaller guy with almost white-blond hair, shoulder-length, tied back in a ponytail. He had a shaggy mustache and little round glasses.

Levi stood him on his feet, and the guy brushed himself off. Levi kept a hand on his shoulder.

"Who are you? And what are you doing here?" Levi demanded in a harsh voice.

The intruder took a few moments to answer. "Johnny Bishop. I'm just a tourist. I was taking a stroll down the dock to look at the boats when I tripped."

I could see Levi had tied a thin rope across the dock at ankle level. It was an effective way to stop an intruder. He untied it while I questioned Johnny Bishop.

"Where are you staying?"

"The Crest Hotel."

"Can I see some ID?"

"Sorry, I left it back in my room." He looked scared and innocent, so we let him go.

I went back to bed. Levi reset the booby trap, but there were no more incidents.

As we were eating breakfast, there was a knock on the hull. It was Jeff, the radio guy, a young native kid in jeans and a sweatshirt. He had a canvas bag full of tools. I showed him the radio and left him to it while I went up to town to see about flying to Juneau.

As I walked up the dock, I saw two fishing boats whose names looked oddly familiar. One was *Johnny B Good*. The other was *Ellen Bishop*. Johnny Bishop got his name from them.

I stopped at the Crest Hotel. Johnny Bishop was not registered. Nor was anybody answering his description. We'd been duped.

The Apollo travel agency was run by a middle-aged Polish lady with big blonde hair. No, I mean BIG hair. You could hide a waffle iron in it. She also had alarming gravity-defying cleavage. It was impossible not to look since she kept adjusting them for maximum effect.

"I'd like to fly to Juneau as soon as possible."

The answer was instant—no need to consult a schedule.

"That's simple. There are no scheduled flights from here to Juneau. You can fly to Sandspit or Vancouver."

"Any other suggestions?"

"You can go by ship or charter a floatplane. It isn't as expensive as you might think."

She gave me a card. It read:

Slim Peterson
Air Skeena
Prince Rupert, BC

There was no phone number, but there was a plane registration number.

"How do I get in touch with him?"

"Go down to the seaplane dock. If that plane is there, look in the nearest pub. If the plane isn't there, ask around, there are other planes available sometimes."

I thanked her and walked down to the dock, which wasn't far from the marina where *Lady L* was moored. There were two planes there, one a tiny red two-seater made of wood and stretched canvas. The other one was more substantial, a Beaver, which I recognized because they flew in and out of Coal Harbour, where my boat was kept. Neither matched the registration number on Slim's card.

A guy was checking the engine on the small red plane. I introduced myself and told him I was looking for Slim Peterson.

"I'm Fatty Gordon. Slim is over in Masset with a fishing group. He won't be back for a few days. Where d'ya wanna go?"

"Juneau."

"I can take you. It's a two-hour flight, fifty bucks an hour. You have to pay for the return trip too."

"I want you to wait a couple of hours there, then drop me in Petersburg on the way back."

"No problem. Come back in an hour. Don't bring too much luggage."

As I walked up the dock, I mused on the fact that Fatty was about the skinniest individual I had ever seen. He was only a little shorter than I was, but not more than half the weight. Keeping with the naming convention, I imagined Slim Peterson was massive.

Back at the boat, I told André the plan. *Lady L* would head to Ketchikan to clear customs. They wouldn't arrive in Petersburg until the following day, so I would stay in a hotel overnight and look out for their arrival. I told Levi and André about the fake Johnny Bishop. We figured he was working for Lorne Greene. He didn't get aboard, so no harm done, or so we thought.

I packed a small bag and kissed Cindy goodbye. She was a good sport about being left behind so soon after the wedding. As I was going, the radio kid came out.

"Radio's fine, but the connection to the antenna was corroded. All fixed now. I tested it by calling the Spilsbury & Tindall base in Vancouver. They read me five-by-five. That'll be twenty bucks."

I paid him and got a receipt, which I put in the chart drawer with others I had collected. Lizzie had given me a thousand-dollar advance on expenses before we sailed. I was running through it. I left a hundred with Cindy and took the rest.

Fatty was ready when I got back. I held the plane while he swung the prop. It started on the first swing, which gave me some confidence. The two seats were one behind the other. I climbed in the back.

"Put on the headset so we can talk. It's too loud otherwise. Fasten your seatbelt."

The seatbelt was the military-style that went over both shoulders and buckled in front. I found the headset in a side pocket and plugged it into the only socket. Fatty gave the plane a shove away from the dock and clambered aboard. He opened the throttle a little, and we taxied out into the harbor. The wind was from the south, and he headed into it. The engine roared, the plane lifted off in quite a short distance, circled out over the harbor, and headed north.

Fatty said something into the radio, and somebody replied. It was just indistinct buzzing to me. The plane stayed low as we headed into Alaska. Fatty kept up a running commentary.

"That's Metlakatla on the left. It's a Tsimshian Village. A group of them left and moved to Alaska in 1887. There's another Metlakatla up there on Annette Island. That's where the Ketchikan Airport is. You have to take a ferry."

Soon we passed Ketchikan on our left. It was a busy looking place, with ships and boats coming and going and seaplanes taking off and landing. The town was long and narrow, stretched along the west coast of Revillagigedo Island. The island had a steep backbone ridge, and we flew above that. On our right, tall snow-capped peaks stretched off into infinity. It was a glorious sight.

"Uh-oh. Fog ahead." Fatty's voice crackled in the headset. I could see a low cloud filling the horizon in front of us. We climbed higher for a better view. The fog bank extended as far as the eye could see. Hills and mountains stuck up above the fog, but no water was visible.

"We'll have to land. With luck the fog will burn off in a couple of hours. I can only fly VFR."

"What does that mean?"

"Visual Flight Rules. No instrument flying allowed. I don't have any instruments anyway."

He turned the plane, and we glided downward to Ketchikan harbor. After a couple of radio transmissions, we landed in among the traffic. Fatty was a skilled pilot, and the landing was smooth.

"We'll go to the customs dock and clear in."

The US customs guys were efficient and displayed no interest in where we were going or why. They knew Fatty, so they exchanged gossip about other pilots. I offered to buy lunch. We went up to town and found a bar called the Arctic, which claimed to be the oldest around.

They had sandwiches and beer. I had two of each. Fatty had only one beer then switched to Coke. They took my Canadian money at a lousy exchange rate.

We sat out on the deck for a couple of hours and swapped sailing stories for flying stories. The fog did thin out, and we could see for at least a couple of miles. Fatty reckoned it was safe to take off again.

Once in the air, we flew low, maybe a couple of hundred feet up, and followed the channels like a boat. If it got too thick, we could just land. The rest of the flight was uneventful, although we might have scared a few sailboats as we flew low over their masts. We couldn't see the scenery.

We landed in Juneau at about 3 PM. Fatty dropped me off and went to refuel. I looked for Front Street Photo. It didn't take long. The street was lined with false fronted stores in Old West style, plus a few modern brick buildings. The camera shop was in one of the older ones. I went in and casually put the ticket on the glass counter. The guy who picked it up was about forty, with a receding hairline, glasses, and a small paunch. He turned and went into the back without saying a word.

In about five minutes, he came back with a smile on his face.

"I found the film. It'll be ready next Tuesday."

Before I could react, he produced an envelope from behind his back.

He said, "Sorry, old joke. Here they are. Lucky for you, my Dad never threw anything away. That'll be $2.75 plus another dollar for storage."

There were eight black and white prints and three strips of negatives. The first picture showed a foot in a laced boot.

The rest of the photos showed various views of what I took to be Thomas Bay. One showed a small old-fashioned gas boat at anchor. Another showed a canoe pulled up on the beach. The one that interested me most had a white float in the water, some distance from the beach. It might mark the location of the safe.

I asked if they made enlargements. They did, but it would take a week. I decided not to wait and went to find Fatty. The plane was refueled and ready to go. The fog had lifted completely.

On the way to Petersburg, I asked Fatty to fly over Farragut Bay and Thomas Bay. There was a sizable black tug anchored in Farragut Bay. I couldn't see a flag, but the name was *Teacher's Pet*. Thomas Bay was empty.

Petersburg came into view. It was a fair-sized town with extensive docks, mainly occupied by fishing boats. Fatty said it was called "Little Norway", despite the Russian name. Almost everybody was of Norwegian descent.

Fatty landed the plane just outside the harbor and taxied into an empty spot on the dock. I paid him, jumped out, and he took off again for home. I hiked up the dock looking for a hotel and stopped at the first one I came to, Oslo House. It was more of a rooming house than a hotel, with small bedrooms and bathrooms down the hall. The price was low, and it was spotless. The charming young blonde behind the counter was named Inge.

I left my bag in the room, used the bathroom, and took a shower. Then I got dressed and went out to find a place to eat dinner. The main street was Nordic Drive, and most businesses were along there, in wooden buildings of antique style. There wasn't much choice. A pizza place, a bar which might or might not have served food, and a somewhat surprising Mexican restaurant. No seafood joint was in evidence. I opted for Mexican.

The guy behind the counter had tan skin and black hair and looked like he could be Mexican. But he greeted the customer in front of me in Norwegian. Everybody else in the place had blonde hair and blue eyes. I didn't look too out of place, although my hair was light brown, and my eyes were hazel.

The menu was unfamiliar to me, as I never had Mexican food before. I had a chicken enchilada, which was tasty enough, washed down with a couple of Coronas.

Back at the hotel, I picked up a local paper: the Petersburg Press. It was a year of turmoil in the US with student protests against the Vietnam war, the assassination of Martin Luther King Jr., and many other chaotic events. But reading the local paper gave few hints of all that. Instead, it was about fishing, logging, hunting, and the oil riches which were soon to come to Alaska.

Lady L could be expected to arrive by noon the next day, and I was anxious to get back aboard. I fell asleep thinking about Cindy.

CHAPTER 27 – PETERSBURG

The next morning Inge served coffee and pastries in the lobby of the hotel. Then I walked the town, killing time by stopping in the hardware store, the library, and a few other stores. People in Petersburg were friendly, and I engaged in several inconsequential conversations.

Noon came, and there was still no sign of the *Lady L*. I had lunch at the Harbor Bar. As I was leaving, I spotted Johnny Bishop—or the guy who called himself that—on the street heading toward the waterfront. I followed him at a distance. He was carrying a couple of paper bags. When he got to the dock, he went down the ramp to the dinghy float, jumped in a Whaler like the one on *Lady L*, cast off, and headed out quickly, northward up the channel. I was too far away to be sure it was the same guy, but I would have bet on it.

I was beginning to worry about *Lady L*. Although there was no coast guard station in Petersburg, there was a Harbor Master's office.

I went up to the office, manned by a young blond kid called Gunnar, according to his name tag. I asked him if he had heard any VHF radio traffic from *Malachite* or *Lady L*.

"Negatory."

I assumed that meant no.

"Can you radio *Lady L* on channel 16 and see if you can get a response?"

"Affirmatory."

He turned to the radio on the shelf and took down the microphone.

"*Lady L, Lady L*, this is Petersburg Harbor, Petersburg Harbor calling on Channel 16. Respond, please."

There was no response. After a minute or so, he tried again—still nothing.

"Sorry. They aren't answering. They might not have their ears on." He shrugged.

"Thanks for trying."

I stepped outside and went down the dock to look down toward Wrangell Narrows for *Lady L*. A light rain was falling, and visibility was probably less than a mile. There was no sign of her.

I began to imagine all the things that could have gone wrong. I had a vision of *Lady L* stranded on Vanderbilt Reef, sinking with all hands. It wasn't possible, of course. That reef was many miles north of Petersburg. But there were other hazards around.

Then I imagined Johnny Bishop and a gang of pirates capturing the *Lady L* and torturing the crew, Cindy, in particular. My active imagination filled in horrifying details.

I wasn't good at waiting, preferring to err on the side of action. I decided to rent a boat and go looking for my friends.

Back at the office, I asked if there were any rental boats around. Gunnar wasn't much help, but he did say that some of the boats on the dock had signs on them, maybe some were rentals.

Petersburg docks were extensive, and I spent half an hour walking them. I saw a few "For Sale" signs but no rentals. As I walked the last dock, I spotted a derelict looking boat that resembled Jakob's photo of *Scurry*. It was indeed the same boat, but in considerably worse shape than it looked in 1918. The paint was peeling, windows were caulked sloppily, and there were some patches of plywood nailed on the deck. But she was floating, and the bottom was clean. The name "Scurry" was painted on the bow and recently touched up.

I shook my head in amazement that the old boat had somehow survived, but looking around the docks, I saw wooden boats of all ages, some in worse shape. Petersburg had not yet joined the disposable society.

There was a small paper sign in the window. I leaned over the rail to read it. It was handwritten in felt pen: "For sale cheep, newer engine, runs good. $100"

There was a phone number below. As I was copying it down, a guy on the dock came up to me.

"Interested in buying her?"

He had red hair and a bushy beard, oilskin pants, and Petersburg sneakers —the brown gumboots which were standard footwear in that wet place.

"Maybe. Is she yours?"

"My brother's. I'm Lars. Let me show you aboard."

The boat was very basic. Below were a couple of bunks with grubby cotton cushions, a bucket for a toilet, and a one-burner kerosene stove.

The wheelhouse—barely big enough for two people —had a non-functioning depth sounder, wheel, and engine controls. Under the floorboards was the "newer" engine, a Chrysler Crown dating from about 1950. It was the cleanest part of the whole boat.

Lars started it up for me. It was a smooth-running motor, and I tested the gearbox at the dock. It seemed fine. The battery and engine alone were worth more than $100. I offered him $50. He wrote me a receipt in my notebook, and I became the owner of an unregistered motorboat. The fuel tank was half full, enough for about a hundred miles, according to Lars.

I asked Lars about the boat's history, but he didn't know much except that she was very old.

There were a couple of local charts on board, stained and torn, but mostly legible. There was also an anchor with a rusty chain and two worn lifejackets— nothing else. The interior was surprisingly dry, and the bilge held only a few cups of water.

I went back to the hotel, got my bag, said goodbye to Inge, and headed for my boat. On the way, I bought a life jacket and a sleeping bag in case I had to spend the night aboard. I also bought a loaf of bread, some salami and cheese, a bag of chips, and a gallon jug of drinking water.

Lars was still around. He untied the lines for me and gave me a shove off the dock. *Scurry* backed strongly to port, and I had to kick off a couple of fishing boats to get clear. Once in the channel, I engaged forward gear and gave it some throttle. The little ship jumped ahead. The motor had a lot of power.

I turned south toward Wrangell Narrows searching for the *Lady L*. After about forty minutes, I approached the Narrows, which lived up to its name. Although good size ships can pass through, they do so one at a time.

The fog had thickened. *Scurry* had no foghorn. I cut the motor and let her drift and went up on the bow to listen. Ahead I could hear the low thrum of a big diesel and the hiss of a bow wave. I ran back to the wheelhouse, started the motor, and turned toward shore just as the *Lady L*'s high prow appeared out of the mist.

I stepped outside as she passed, yelled, and waved. At first, nothing happened, then her engine slowed and stopped as she was about fifty yards past. I fell in behind and followed until she came to a complete stop. Cindy came out on the after deck and called my name, waving both arms.

Levi and Charlie joined Cindy and held *Scurry* off as I climbed on board *Lady L*. We took *Scurry* in tow.

I hugged Cindy, then went up to the wheelhouse to talk to André.

"Sorry we were late. We had to wait for the tide at the narrows. Then, a log boom obstructed us for a while. But you didn't have to buy a boat and come looking for us!"

"I might have been a bit impulsive. But that's *Scurry*, the boat Jakob rented in 1918. I took it as a good omen when I found her."

"How much did you pay?"

"Fifty dollars."

"You got robbed!"

We decided to stop for the night so we could catch up on the news. Halfway from the Narrows to Petersburg, we dropped anchor off the Beachcomber Inn, a converted cannery. We pulled *Scurry* alongside and secured her, then took the Whaler to shore to eat dinner. We shared the dining room with a group the waitress identified as the Republican Women's Club. They were all wearing dresses, mostly with flowered patterns that reminded me of my grandmother's sofa. They looked at us with utter distaste. Cindy stuck her tongue out at them, and they turned away.

Dinner was standard North American fare, a choice of pasta or various meat dishes. We each had a glass of California wine. There was baked Alaska for dessert, and we all had to try that.

At *Lady L*, I showed the photos and related the story of my flight to Juneau and Petersburg. André told me about the trip up. Cindy and I went to bed to catch up on the honeymoon. I was glad I didn't have to sleep on *Scurry*.

Before the action started, Cindy had a question.

"Let me get this straight. You bought another boat because you were worried about me? Is this how our marriage is going to go?"

I didn't have an answer, so I grabbed her and wrestled her into bed. There were no more questions.

At 10 PM, I got up again and called Brice on the radio. This time I got through loud and clear. I realized that the opposition might also hear us, although we were on a fisherman's channel.

"Hi, Brice. I just wanted to let you know we arrived safely in Area One. We'll start fishing soon. There is at least one other fishing boat nearby."

He got it.

"So, I guess you got the nets repaired?"

"Yes. Nets are now in fine shape. I'll call again tomorrow."

I went back to bed.

CHAPTER 28 – THOMAS BAY

In the morning, Cindy produced a hearty breakfast with blue cheese and bacon frittatas, pan-fried potatoes, and grilled mushrooms. The weather was completely socked in, with fog so thick we couldn't see the shore at all. We sat tight, waiting for it to lift. By 11 AM, it had thinned enough so that it was safe to leave. We let *Scurry* trail behind us like a dinghy.

Petersburg came and went. We didn't need to stop. Across Frederick Sound was Farragut Bay, where we had misdirected our pursuers. We bypassed that and headed for Thomas Bay. I remembered the tug in Farragut and told André, who was steering.

"There was a big black tug anchored in Farragut Bay. The name was *Teacher's Pet*."

"That doesn't sound like a pirate ship," André remarked.

Levi, who was standing behind us, said, "It does to me. Blackbeard's real name was Edward Teach, and his first mate was nicknamed 'Teacher's Pet.'"

Still a fount of trivia. He could have been making it up, as we had no way of checking, but it was a good story.

From the water we couldn't see into Farragut Bay at all, which meant anyone anchored there couldn't see us either. That's how I wanted it. When we got close to Thomas Bay, we started looking for a suitable anchorage. Based on Jakob's letters, I thought we should be toward the north side of the bay. It was an extensive area, but we had to start somewhere.

The center part of Thomas Bay is over 500 feet deep. There are a few coves where anchorage is possible, but *Lady L* was too big for many of them. Also, we didn't want to be visible to boats passing in the main channel. We settled on Porter Cove and dropped anchor in 65 feet. We moved *Scurry* alongside and used the Whaler to take a line around a tree on the shore.

The bay was glassy smooth, and there were no signs of animal or bird life at all. Despite the tendency of Alaskans to shoot anything that moves, most places teemed with life. Eagles, whales, seals, and more were everywhere. But not in Thomas Bay.

It was still early in the morning, and we had many hours of daylight ahead of us. Charlie and I took the Whaler out to see if we could match the landscape to Jakob's photos. We followed the north shore of Thomas Bay eastward from our anchorage. Two hours later, we had not matched a single photo. Thomas Bay was huge. We went back to *Lady L* for lunch.

As usual, Cindy fed us well. After lunch, I suggested we use two boats, *Scurry* and the Whaler, to widen the search. André pointed out that we only had one copy of each photo. Levi got up, went to his cabin, and came back with a folding Polaroid camera. He made copies of all the shots except the one of a shoe.

We split into two teams, Levi and André in the Whaler, and Charlie and I in *Scurry*. The Whaler went west, we went east, skipping over the area we had already covered.

After three hours of holding each photo up against the landscape, moving fifty feet, and trying again, we still hadn't matched anything.

Charlie pointed out into the bay. The Whaler was coming towards us at high speed. Levi waved both arms, and I steered our boat in their direction. When we met in the middle of the bay, André called out.

"Pay dirt! We found a match to the place where *Scurry* is anchored in the photo. Follow us back."

We followed and arrived at what was labeled "Spurt Point" on the chart. There was a small cove north of the point. At the head of the bay was a tiny cabin with a sign on it. It was a shelter for hikers provided by the Alaska Parks Department.

On the shore of the point was a huge fallen tree, covered in moss. It was rotting and collapsing into the soil, but still recognizable. It had one thick branch sticking up near one end. The same branch was identifiable in Jakob's photo.

The photo was taken from shore. We moved *Scurry* to the location where she had been anchored in 1918, and Levi took a Polaroid from the same spot. The mountains on the other side of Thomas Bay were a match. The water was a milky blue-grey color, glacier melt from the Baird Glacier at the head of Thomas Bay.

"What do we do next?" André asked.

"Is there a lead line on the Whaler?" I wanted to check the depth.

"No. We have an echo sounder."

"Even better. Survey the bottom of that cove and see if you can find any high spots. If the safe is still there, it should make a lump. That's a technical term for a shallow bit. I'll go get a marker in case we find something."

Levi said, "I should get my diving gear. Maybe Charlie can stay with André, and I'll come with you?"

We made the swap. As we were leaving, André called out.

"Get Jock to lend you the retrieval magnet."

Back at *Lady L*, Levi loaded his diving gear, and I went to the engine room where Jock was puttering, checking valve clearances or some other amusing pastime.

"André said you have a retrieval magnet?"

"Aye, it's used to retrieve dropped tools or nuts and bolts from the bilge under the engine."

He opened a locker and took out a big horseshoe-shaped magnet attached to a line about six feet long. I held it about six inches from the engine, and it jerked out of my hand with a clang. It was amazingly powerful.

"I'll need a longer line."

Jock rooted around in another locker and found a piece of braided line about thirty feet long.

"This should do nicely." He handed it to me, and I tied it to the magnet. It took both of us to separate it from the engine.

"Thanks, Jock, I'll bring it back soon."

He didn't ask what I needed it for, just went back to puttering. I put the magnet onboard *Scurry*, then on impulse, retrieved the fake boulder from the cabin top, and took it with us.

When we got back to the cove, André and Charlie had nearly finished the survey. I asked what they found.

"Nothing much. The bottom here is pretty flat, getting shallower toward the beach. There are a couple of small bumps, less than a foot high. I'd expect that safe to be bigger."

We looked at the photos again. Charlie noticed that the photo with the white marker buoy partly matched the background across the bay. Between us, we decided that it was closer to the mouth of the small cove than the area we had been surveying and more toward the eastern side. A few passes with the Whaler over that area showed that there was a bigger lump there. I took *Scurry* over and dropped the magnet. I was hoping for a clank like it did on the engine block. It didn't happen. However, the line swung to one side as I dropped it, but before hitting bottom. *There was something magnetic down there.*

I didn't want to get too excited. There were a lot of things it could have been: Old logging gear, a lost anchor, the Titanic. We couldn't be sure. Then I remembered the cairn Jakob placed inland. I went ashore and looked for it. I found some round rocks closely scattered, which could have been it, but again I wasn't sure.

It was dinner time, and although the sun was still high, we could see a fog bank rolling in from the south. I suggested we mark the spot and quit for the day. We tied the fake boulder to the magnet and lowered it down until it tugged at the line. We left plenty of slack to allow for the tide to rise.

From fifty feet off, the fake rock looked like a partly submerged reef, perfect for discouraging boats from coming too close. We headed back to *Lady L.* Within an hour, the bay was entirely shrouded with fog, visibility less than a hundred feet.

There was nothing more we could do except enjoy dinner. Cindy had started working her way through the crew's favorite recipes. I guess it was André's turn, as Cindy produced ourtière and several side dishes. André pronounced it très bon, just like his mother's. Having never had it before, I had no basis for comparison. It had some spices that made it different from the Scottish meat pies I was used to.

"What spices did you use?" I asked Cindy.

"Garlic, cinnamon, clove, allspice, and nutmeg. I also put in a bit of fresh basil, which wasn't in the recipe."

"It's delicious." Charlie said, "I'm really looking forward to your take on mac and cheese."

We drank a toast to Cindy's cooking prowess. As had become a pattern, I helped clear the dishes and serve dessert, which was a *crème brûlée* somehow produced with canned milk! I used Jock's blowtorch to melt the sugar.

The crew played cards after dinner, and Cindy and I retired. At 10 PM, I went up to the radio room and called Brice. Again, he answered with a clear signal.

"This is *Malachite*. We have reached Area 2 and did some preliminary fishing with lines. There are fish around, but we didn't catch any yet. Tomorrow we will try the net."

"Understood. Same time tomorrow?"

"Sure, but could you see if you can find someone who speaks Cantonese? The cook wants to send a message to her mother, and she doesn't speak English."

"I'll try. Let's make it 9 PM tomorrow."

"Agreed. *Malachite* out."

I went back to the room and told Cindy about my plan. I figured the opposition wouldn't have a Cantonese speaking person on board. If Brice could find one, we could communicate our situation without fear of being overheard.

"It's a clever idea. I hope it works. My Cantonese is mainly kitchen terms."

I looked out the window. It was almost sunset, but there was a glow in the sky behind the mountains. The fog had lifted, and I could see a sliver of moon. I went back to the main saloon, where the gang was still playing cards.

"The weather has cleared up. I'm interested in an expedition to investigate other boats in Farragut Bay, particularly Lorne Greene's Hatteras. Any volunteers?"

André looked at me the way you look at someone freshly escaped from the asylum.

"Logically, if you do this, it should be you and Levi because you're big, and he's strong."

Everybody laughed.

"If I take Levi with me, who will protect you wimps in the event of an attack?"

"You make a compelling argument. Take Charlie, he's expendable."

"Hey! Watch it, Captain. I know where you park your Porsche." Charlie yelled.

"Only kidding."

In the end, Charlie and I went. We used *Scurry* for several reasons. Although slower than the Whaler, she was also quieter and had an enclosed cabin. The nights were cold, even in June. Also, it was unlikely the opposition would recognize it as ours.

We put on sweaters and jackets, along with sea boots. I borrowed binoculars, a powerful flashlight, and a flare pistol from *Lady L.*

"Should we take weapons?" I asked.

Levi said, "I'd take a shotgun if I were you and try not to get in a situation where you need it."

I took the Purdey double-barrel 12-gauge and a box of 25 shells, loaded two in the breech, and stowed it under a bunk cushion.

Charley said, "You know that Purdey is worth as much as a small house?"

"I didn't, but it's likely to be more useful than a house right now."

We stuck close to shore and followed the coast all the way. We saw the lights of several boats heading the other way, but they were all far across the channel.

Thomas Bay had a rather narrow entrance marked with a red light and a couple of buoys, but Farragut Bay was more open and completely unmarked. Fortunately, the chart showed it was deep enough for *Scurry* pretty much everywhere. About an hour and a half later, we entered Farragut Bay.

Teacher's Pet had been anchored in a sheltered cove inside a hook on the east side of the bay. As the spot came into sight, I cut the engine to idle speed. There was a boat anchored where I had seen the big black tug, but it was white. As we got closer, I identified it as the Hatteras 50. A Boston Whaler similar to ours was tied astern, and the transom was visible. "Ponderosa" was written in big gold letters.

"That sounds like it could belong to Lorne Greene. Isn't that the name of the ranch on *Bonanza*?" Charlie asked.

"I don't have a TV, so not sure. Maybe."

There was an anchor light showing, the main saloon was brightly lit. We could hear music playing. It sounded like Sinatra. I didn't want to get too close, so I picked up the binoculars. A blonde woman was seated at the counter with a glass of wine, swaying slightly to the music. She met the description supplied by the gas dock attendant in Bella Bella. I handed the binoculars to Charlie.

"How do you like them apples?"

"More like honeydew melons."

"I think she's alone."

"It seems a shame. Maybe we should take her hostage?" Charlie suggested.

"Umm…they haven't done a single aggressive thing towards us. I don't want to be the one to start a war."

"Just kidding. Where do you think *Teacher's Pet* has gone? Maybe to get supplies?"

"I don't think so. Petersburg is just a short way from here. You could easily go there and back during the day."

"Maybe they broke down."

"She doesn't look worried, so I am guessing they aren't expected back for a while. Where would they be going in the middle of the night?"

"If they think like us, they might be checking out Thomas Bay."

He was right. I turned the boat around, and as soon as we were past the point, I opened the throttle wide.

CHAPTER 29 – WHAT?

About an hour later, we were coming up on the entrance to Thomas Bay. We couldn't see Porter Cove, where *Lady L* was anchored until we passed Spurt Point a few minutes later.

As we came around the point, we could see *Lady L*'s lights. There was a large black shadow partly obscuring the view. It had to be *Teacher's Pet*.

I cut the throttle, and we idled in quietly. As we got closer, I could hear *Lady L*'s generator running. The black tug was directly in front of her, blocking her exit from the cove.

We didn't know what was going on, but it couldn't be good. I stopped the engine and let the boat drift. The sky was clouding over, and the stars were disappearing. Although we could see the water, it was impossible to make out details of the tug.

Charlie whispered, "We have no idea how many people they have, and how they're armed. On the other hand, maybe they don't know about us. *Lady L*'s tenders are all there, so they may think they have the whole crew."

"I saw Johnny Bishop in Petersburg. He might have seen me. He certainly saw me in Prince Rupert, but maybe not you. I think we should approach *Lady L* noisily. I'll step on deck and tie us up. You hide here and come to the rescue later."

Charlie chuckled, but without smiling, "That isn't a plan. How do I come to the rescue? Come out shooting? At what?"

"Okay, I didn't think it through. Before we do anything, we should try and find out what we're up against."

The wind was picking up, blowing off the glacier at the top of the bay. We were drifting downwind, away from the big boats. I started the engine, just to keep us in place.

There was the sound of wings flapping, and Ajax landed on the cabin top. He looked at me and said in a deep voice, "Don't move, or I'll shoot!"

The effect was chilling. The parrot had to be repeating something he had overheard.

"Who said that, Ajax?" I asked.

"Sean the fuckwit. Sean the fuckup."

That didn't help. I tried again.

"Was it Lorne Greene?"

"Scurvy bastard!"

I took that as a yes. It didn't help much, except we knew somebody was being threatened with a gun. An icy gust of wind blew down the bay kicking up whitecaps. Our little boat heeled over like a sailboat. Ajax hopped down into the cockpit and went inside.

Flakes of snow began coming at us horizontally. Instantly visibility was down to a few feet. That's Alaska. The next day would be the first day of summer.

The big black tug began to turn broadside to the wind, a sign of a dragging anchor. The engine started, and some lights came on. I used the cover of the snowfall and strong wind to slide *Scurry* in behind *Lady L* and tie her up alongside the Whaler.

Teacher's Pet was pulling away to reset her anchor, which would keep them busy for a bit.

I told Charlie to wait. I grabbed the gun, quietly climbed up the boarding ladder, and rolled onto the side deck below the saloon windows. I could hear a voice inside. I popped my head up for a second and saw André facing me, tied to a chair. Cindy was behind him, sitting on another chair with her hands out of sight. She was looking at the floor. I wondered where Levi and Jock were.

A man with grey hair wearing a black anorak was seated at the saloon table with his back to me. There was a handgun on the table by his hand, but his finger wasn't on the trigger.

I ducked back down and crawled forward to the door on the side opposite Cindy. I was worried that if André or Cindy saw me, they might react and reveal my location. The sliding door was open a crack, and I could hear what was being said.

The voice was sonorous and firm, and matched the voice Ajax had mimicked. "Where is the stuff?"

"As I told you before, we haven't found anything. We have some idea where it might be, but the weather prevented us from searching further."

"You aren't much help Captain LaPalme. Give me one good reason why I shouldn't just shoot you right now!"

André shrugged and cocked his head to one side. "I have a serious lead allergy. It's even worse than cat hair.

It might even be fatal, and my mother would never forgive me if I die."

The man we called Lorne Greene was laughing so hard I took the opportunity to step in the doorway and point the shotgun at him.

"Freeze! Move your hand away from the gun."

He did so and smiled at me. "You must be Sean. I was wondering where you were. Welcome aboard."

There was a sound behind me, and I started to turn when something hard hit me behind the ear.

When I woke up, I was in a chair beside André. My hands were tied behind me, and my ankles were bound to the legs. Cindy was loose and applying a wet cloth to my face. I couldn't have been out long.

"Are you okay, Sean?" Cindy sounded concerned but not frightened.

"I'm okay. Bit of a headache." I looked around the room. The man we knew as Johnny Bishop was standing just inside the door. My shotgun was leaning against the wall beside him.

The gunman said, "Cuff her again."

Johnny pushed Cindy over to the chair she had been sitting in before. She sat down and put her hands through the rungs. He fastened them together with a pair of police handcuffs.

"Introductions are in order. I'm Peter Lorngren, and this is my associate. You'll meet the rest of my crew soon. I've met Cindy and André, but they haven't told me anything useful. Maybe you can do better."

Lorngren. Lorne Greene. It made sense. There was a superficial resemblance, and the voice was uncannily similar. I decided to check him out.

"You seem to have missed one of my crew members. Are you sure you searched the ship?"

"Ah, you must be referring to the gentleman known as Levi. He suffered some minor injuries and is recuperating on board the tug. He'll be alright. We also found your gun cabinet. We left the guns alone but threw all the ammunition overboard."

No mention of Jock or Charlie. That was good. Lorngren kept talking.

"Before I start questioning you, maybe some background will help with negotiations. I am the rightful owner of the safe Jakob found back in 1918. My family has been in the shipping business in BC since the 1880s. One of our ships, the Galiano, was lost in this general area in 1898. Some of the crew escaped in a lifeboat and found their way back to Vancouver."

"The Galiano operated as a personnel carrier on her way north, and as a gold buyer and transporter on the way south. She was a wooden paddle-wheeler used initially in the Fraser River. There was a large safe on board which was used to carry gold dust and nuggets. The ship hit a rock and was holed. She got off but was taking on water rapidly. The captain tried to beach her, but she went down. It was night, and they were navigating without Alaska charts, so the location was uncertain. My family mounted a salvage expedition the next season but failed to find the wreck."

"Now you know the history, I hope you understand why I'm here. I'm not a violent man, and I'd like to settle this peacefully."

I felt anger rising and interrupted before he could say more. "Not violent? I just heard you threaten to shoot André. And what about Fingers Finnegan?"

"That was Lizzie."

"Lizzie?" I was shocked.

"You have no idea who you are working for! Lizzie Hadley is an incredibly successful and ruthless mobster and has been for at least forty years. She has dirt on every important man in the province, and many women too. She had Finnegan killed. I can't prove it, of course, but I know it wasn't me."

If I hadn't already been sitting down, I would have sat hard.

"Alright, tell me what you want." Stalling while I came up with a plan of action.

"I just want the safe and its contents."

"We don't have it."

"For a start, you can give me the real letter. When you didn't show up in Farragut Bay, I figured the published letter was a fake."

"Actually, we did show up in Farragut Bay. I just came back from there."

For a fraction of a second, something like worry passed across Lorngren's face. That gave me an opening.

"I found the *Ponderosa* at anchor. There was a young blonde lady in the saloon drinking wine and listening to Sinatra. I went aboard and requested that she come with me. I didn't ask her name."

"Bambi?" He said it as if unsure.

"Seriously? She was surprised but cooperative. I took her ashore to a cabin I know and locked her in, along with food, water, and the bottle of wine. She's unharmed. Someone will find her eventually."

"You bastard! Bambi has nothing to do with this."

"She said that. That's why I didn't bring her here. Now you know where we stand, what happens next?"

"I kill you and torture your wife until she tells me where the letter is."

My fake hostage gambit had failed.

"She doesn't know. Only I do."

Cindy had been quiet, but she looked up. "Give him the damn letter Sean. It won't tell him anything except that the safe is somewhere in Thomas Bay."

She was right. André nodded his head at me. I agreed.

"Cindy's right. It won't help you much, but I'll get it for you. It's in the wheelhouse."

"Al will go with you."

I looked around the room for Al.

"You mean Johnny Bishop?"

Lorngren looked confused. Al said, "That's the false name I gave them in Prince Rupert."

Lorngren picked up his gun and aimed it at Cindy. "Get the letter. Al can handle you, but if anything happens, I'll kill Cindy."

"If you hurt Cindy, you won't find Bambi."

"I'll take my chances. I was getting tired of her anyway. Al, unload that shotgun and throw the shells overboard."

After that, Al untied me. I led the way to the wheelhouse, which was down the hall and up a flight of stairs. Al walked behind me, not too close, and he kept a small gun aimed at my back.

When we got to the wheelhouse, I was surprised to find a light on. It had been dark when we approached in *Scurry*. I didn't say anything, but lifted the helm cushion, unzipped the cover, and removed the letter which I held out to Al. He didn't take it.

"You carry it. Go out first."

As I stepped out the door, I thought I saw movement to my left, but I continued to the first step. There was a loud thump behind me. I turned in time to see Al crumple to the deck. Jock held up a large pipe wrench, blood dripping off it. He quickly checked Al for a pulse, found one, and dragged him into the wheelhouse where I helped tie him up. Jock had on a blue jacket with many pockets containing thin coils of rope and tools.

I whispered, "Let's go to the gun room."

"They threw the bullets overboard. I saw them fall by my window," Jock said in a murmur.

"I have some shotgun shells in my cabin, the ones Levi took from Bozo in Prince Rupert. Charlie is still onboard *Scurry*. You go find him and bring him here. He's about the same size as Al. Charlie can put on Al's clothes. I'll get them off him."

Jock crawled aft on the upper deck to find Charlie. Al was wearing jeans, and so was Charlie, so I just took off his shirt and windbreaker. To get them off, I had to untie one hand at a time. In the process, I found a switchblade knife, so I searched him thoroughly but didn't find any other weapons. By the time I was finished, Charlie was there, having crawled along the deck and entered by another door.

While he put on Al's shirt and jacket, I whispered to Jock, "Never mind the shells. We have Al's gun."

"Here is my plan. Charlie will follow me back into the saloon, being careful to stay behind me, so Lorngren doesn't see his face. Jock will go down the other side and throw a wrench at Lorngren. Charlie, when he's distracted, you shoot him."

"I've never fired a pistol in my life. Odds of hitting him are slim."

"Okay, I'll grab the gun from you and do it."

I went down the stairs and walked back to the saloon along the starboard side. Charlie followed close behind. Jock went down the port side. We made plenty of noise, and Jock was stealthy, so Lorngren looked at me when I opened the door.

From where Cindy was sitting, she could see Charlie behind me. In a single fluid motion, she dropped the handcuffs on the floor, stood up, and threw the chair at Lorngren. He fired his pistol before Jock's pipe wrench hit the side of his head, and he fell to the floor.

I had Al's gun by then, but I never fired it. Jock stood over Lorngren. I turned to thank Cindy, but she wasn't there. I looked at Charlie. He had a horrified expression on his face. He pointed to the floor behind me, and my whole world fell apart.

CHAPTER 30 – CRASH

Cindy was lying face down, long hair spread across her back. Her arms were above her head. One leg was straight, the other was bent at the hip and the knee.

I stood stunned for a few seconds. Among the strands of black hair, a dark red stain was spreading across her pajama top. I fell to my knees beside Cindy and held her small wrist, looking for a pulse. I found none. I cradled her in my arms and gently turned her over onto her back. The bullet had entered her chest on her right side. I listened for breathing but heard none.

Then she let out a long sigh, her eyelids fluttered and opened halfway.

She whispered, "You bastard Sean! If I die, I'll never forgive you."

I was incapable of speech, but tears of joy fell on her face. Her eyes closed again, and she seemed to fall asleep.

While Jock was tying up Lorngren, Charlie freed André.

Jock said, "We have to get her to a hospital. There's one in Petersburg. Do any of you know first aid?"

Charlie said, "I took a course, but we didn't deal with bullet wounds. There's a first aid kit in the wheelhouse."

I regained the power of speech.

"André, you and Jock get us moving. Ram the tug if you must. I don't think we can take Cindy there in a dinghy. Charlie, get the first aid kit."

I was holding my hand over Cindy's bullet wound, trying to stop the bleeding, but blood was leaking out her back.

Her eyes were closed, and her breathing was ragged. I heard the engine room telegraph ring. Moments later, the main engine started, and the boat lurched forward then stopped with a jerk. I lowered Cindy gently, jumped up, and ran out to the back deck. The stern line was tied to a tree, and it was stretched taught. I looked for something sharp. Then I remembered Al's switchblade in my pocket. As soon as the edge touched the rope, it parted explosively. I fell against the railing as the big yacht began to move forward, prop-wash boiling out behind her.

I went back inside to tend Cindy. When I got there, Charlie had her shirt off and was cleaning the wounds with alcohol. He then taped large pieces of gauze front and back. The bandage was quickly becoming saturated with blood. We didn't know what to do.

There was a godawful crash up forward, and *Lady L* ground to a halt, although the engine was still thrashing away. Then it stopped, and the silence held for a few moments. The engine started in reverse, ran for about 15 seconds, then stopped again. I could hear the rudder turning hard to one side.

I heard running feet on deck. The engine started again, and the boat began to move forward. The port side door opened, and Levi came in carrying a tiny gun. He looked around the room, taking in the scene. He handed me the gun and dropped to his knees by Cindy. He tore the gauze off her chest and examined the wound.

"This needs cauterizing to stop the bleeding. Charlie, go to the engine room and ask Jock for a soldering iron, I'm sure he must have one."

I wondered what was going on. Leaving Cindy with Levi, I stepped out onto the side deck. *Teacher's Pet* was falling astern on our port side. She had a huge vee-shaped gash in her side about 30 feet ahead of the stern. Planks were splintered, and she was taking on water. I didn't see anyone on deck, but she was facing away from us. *Lady L* was moving fast toward the exit channel from Thomas Bay. I went back inside.

Charlie had a clumsy-looking electric soldering iron in his hand. Levi instructed him to clean it thoroughly with alcohol and plug it in to heat up.

"Sean, you better get on the radio. Are we heading to Petersburg?" Levi asked.

"Yes."

"Call the US Coast Guard and have them call the police in Petersburg and get an ambulance down to the dock. Tell them Sergeant Levine of the RCMP is bringing in a suspect and a wounded girl."

My mouth fell open. "Sergeant Levine?"

"That's me. Now get going."

I got up to the radio room as quickly as I could. It took a few minutes for the radio to warm up. It was still dark, and I wasn't sure anybody was listening.

"Mayday, Mayday, US Coast Guard, US Coast Guard, this is the Canadian vessel *Lady L* near Thomas Bay, Alaska."

When I took my finger off the mike, there was just static on the radio. I waited a minute or so, then just as I was about to try again, a laconic American voice crackled over the air.

"Mayday vessel, Mayday vessel, this is US Coast Guard station Sitka. Please state your vessel name and the nature of your emergency."

I spent about fifteen minutes explaining, as best I could, what happened in Thomas Bay. I had to repeat myself several times as Lester—the Coast Guard guy —had trouble following the story. I left out the safe and a few other details which I deemed private.

He indicated that they had a cutter on the way, but it was coming from Sitka. They offered to send a chopper, but it couldn't land on *Lady L*. Our best bet was to get to Petersburg on our own. I went into the wheelhouse.

"André, where did Levi come from?"

"He jumped over from *Teacher's Pet* when we rammed her. He said her crew is incapacitated. They'll need rescuing. I told him Cindy was shot."

"The Coast Guard will get them. Did you know Levi was a cop?"

"Are you kidding? No. What kind.?"

"RCMP."

"He must have been undercover, after Lorne Greene."

"Maybe, but why sign on with us?"

We were steaming at maximum speed, about 13 knots. At that rate, we'd be in Petersburg in less than an hour. I went aft to check on Cindy.

Cindy was lying face down, and Levi was wielding the soldering iron, cauterizing the damaged blood vessels. It would have hurt like hell, but she was unconscious. The bleeding was all but stopped. As I got there, he finished up and applied gauze bandages, taping them around front and back.

I went to our room and got two blankets. We wrapped Cindy up as she was shivering. Levi stood up.

"She's in shock. There is nothing more we can do until we get to Petersburg."

I looked at Levi. His face was grim.

I said, "Thank you. You saved her life. Have you dealt with bullet wounds before?"

"Several times, but this is the first woman. I'm going to check on Lorngren."

"When you are done there, Jock hit Al—you know him as Johnny Bishop—pretty hard. Better check him too. He's tied up in the engine room."

I planned to ask Levi what happened on *Teacher's Pet* later. He didn't look injured, except for a few minor cuts on his knuckles and wrists.

I lay down on the floor beside Cindy. I wanted to put my arms around her, but I was afraid of disturbing the wound. I took her left wrist and checked her pulse. It seemed weak, but at least it was there.

The ship's bell rang three times. All hands on deck. I had noticed the motion increasing. I got up and ran to the wheelhouse.

The wipers were running. The snow had stopped, replaced by heavy rain. Although the sky was getting lighter, visibility was poor. André was at the helm.

"Sean, I need you to man the radar and guide us into Petersburg. The visibility is so poor I'm not sure exactly where we are. I'm on a compass course for the channel, but I didn't compensate for the tide."

I looked at the radar screen. There was a lot of clutter from rain and waves, but the echo from Mitkof Island, where Petersburg is located, was stronger. I could see the gap we would have to enter, but we were off course, and about half a mile south of where we needed to be. I called out a new direction to André and went to the radio room.

I got the Coast Guard on the radio again. The Coast Guard cutter was still many miles away. But an Alaska State Trooper boat was heading out to meet us and lead us into the harbor where a slip was waiting at the fisherman's wharf.

Just as I went into the wheelhouse again, André spotted the approaching boat, a fast aluminum workboat with many antennas. They approached, circled to parallel our course, and slowed to our speed. I called them on VHF Channel 16.

"State Troopers, State Troopers, this is *Lady L*, *Lady L*, come in please."

"*Lady L*, this is *PB Sentry*, Alaska State Trooper patrol. Follow us and slow to seven knots, please. Place fenders and mooring lines on the port side."

Unlike the big SSB radio, the VHF was in the wheelhouse, and André could hear what was said. He rang the control, and the engine slowed.

Charlie and I went out on deck and organized the lines. Then I remembered we were still towing *Scurry*. I went aft, placed fenders, and pulled her up the starboard side of *Lady L*.

Ten minutes later, we were in reverse, slowing to come alongside the dock. André timed it correctly, and we threw our lines to the men waiting. Although it was very early in the morning, it seemed that a substantial portion of the population of Petersburg had turned out to meet us. On the street above, there was an ambulance with lights flashing. Two medics were on the dock with a stretcher. They came aboard as soon as I lowered the boarding steps.

"Where is she?" No introductions.

"Follow me!"

I lead the way aft to the saloon, where Levi was again tending Cindy. One medic used a stethoscope to listen to her chest. The other attached an IV to one arm. It wasn't blood, just saline solution.

"What's her blood type?" the medic asked.

I had no idea. It would have to be tested at the hospital. The next problem was how to get Cindy off the boat. Levi and I helped the medics get her on to the stretcher, which they carried to the back deck.

Lady L's railing was about seven feet above the dock. The boarding steps were steep and required a sharp turn to get onto them, not possible while keeping the stretcher level. Several people on the pier offered helpful advice, none of it useful. Finally, we placed her in a rowboat and used the davits to lower the whole thing. It was quite a production, and I was terrified that she would die before she reached the hospital.

At last, the medics got her up the ramp to the ambulance, and it drove off with sirens blaring. I wanted to go to the hospital immediately, but there was a small problem. As soon as Cindy was on her way, a uniformed trooper came up to me.

"Are you Sean Gray, leader of the salvage crew?"

I admitted that I was. He held up a badge and identified himself as officer Svensen. Then he read from a card.

"You have the right to remain silent. Anything you say can be used against you in court. You have the right to a lawyer before we question you. You have the right to have a lawyer with you during questioning. If you cannot afford a lawyer, one will be appointed for you. If you decide to answer questions without a lawyer present, you have the right to stop answering at any time."

"You are under arrest for assault. There may be other charges once we sort all this out. Do you have any weapons on you?"

"Yes. A knife in my left jacket pocket."

He took it and placed it in an evidence bag, then handcuffed me and took me to a patrol car. André was already inside, also in cuffs. I nodded but didn't speak. I was so miserably worried about Cindy, being arrested didn't seem important.

As far as I could tell, they didn't arrest Charlie, Levi, or Jock. This seemed odd since it was Jock who hit Lorngren and Al on the head.

When we got to the station, a rather plain building that could have been a school or an apartment block, Svensen took us to an interrogation room. He took off the cuffs and left us there, locking the door as he went.

I looked at André.

"How did we get to this? What happened in Thomas Bay before Charlie and I got back?"

André shook his head sadly.

"About an hour after you left with Charlie on *Scurry*, *Teacher's Pet* came in fast and dropped anchor in front of us. Simultaneously their tender came up astern of us. We all were up forward. I told Jock to hide in the engine room. Levi heard noise aft and ran back to intercept them. He had a pistol."

"I started blowing a distress signal on the horn, but it was futile. The next thing I heard was Lorngren telling me to put my hands up."

"Apparently they overpowered Levi and threw him in the tender and took him back to the tug. I don't know how he escaped."

Officer Svensen came back in with Levi.

"Sergeant Levine has explained what went on. I'm letting you go with him for now. We'll need a statement in the morning."

Levi said nothing, just gestured us to follow him. Once outside, we walked to the Medical Center, which was very close. He spoke to the nurse at the desk, then came back to us.

"She's in surgery, but they are almost done. We're to sit in the waiting room until they call us."

We sat for what seemed like hours, Charlie and Jock came in. Apparently, Lorngren and Al were in the hospital with minor injuries, under police guard.

I remembered Bambi.

"The story I told Lorngren about his girlfriend Bambi wasn't true. She was on board his yacht *Ponderosa*, anchored in Farragut Bay. We didn't disturb her. The marine patrol should probably go get her."

Levi went off to find a phone. The nurse called out, "Is there a Mr. Gray here?"

I stood up and went over to the desk.

"I'm Sean Gray."

"Doctor Emerson is on his way."

"Is Cindy alright?"

"I don't know. The doctor will brief you."

As she said that, a large man in blue scrubs came through a pair of swinging doors, undoing a surgical mask. He didn't look happy, and my heart fell.

"Are you Mr. Gray?"

I nodded dumbly.

"I'm sorry. We did everything we could…"

My knees buckled, and my eyes closed. The pounding of blood in my ears was so loud I couldn't hear anything else.

Gradually I became conscious that André and Charlie were supporting me, patting me on the back and laughing. I must have missed something. I managed to squeak out a question. "What did the surgeon say?"

"They did everything they could, but she'll still have scars front and back."

Levi came back, and there was much laughter and joy as Charlie explained my mistake. The nurse told us to return in about three hours when Cindy would wake up. We went back to *Lady L*, where André made us breakfast.

CHAPTER 31 – THE LAW

Over breakfast, I asked Levi a few questions.

"If you are an undercover officer investigating Lorngren, why join our crew?"

He looked at me without smiling and seemed to be thinking of an answer. Finally, he said, "Now that you know I'm a cop, I might as well tell you. I wasn't after Lorngren. I was after you, or more specifically, Lizzie. We suspect her of having Finnegan killed, of money laundering, and importing drugs. At first, I didn't believe this Alaska expedition was about the old safe at all. I thought it was a cover for something else."

This was a shock to me. I thought a bit before the next question.

"What will happen to Lorngren?"

"It's up to the Alaska State's attorney. He should be charged with unlawful restraint and attempted murder, but the arrest wasn't quite kosher since I have no authority here. I'm having a meeting with them in a few minutes."

André and the rest of the crew were inspecting the *Lady L* for damage from the collision. I went up the dock and walked to the hospital to visit Cindy. I hadn't slept at all, but adrenalin was keeping me going.

When I got to the nursing station, there was a young blonde nurse at the desk. Her name tag read Anita.

"I'm here to see Cindy Gray."

She checked her list. "There is nobody by that name here. What's your name?"

"I'm Sean Gray. I'm her husband. She was brought in during the night with a bullet wound."

She rummaged through the files on her clipboard.

"Do you mean Cynthia Lu?"

"Yes. We just got married, and her ID is old."

Anita got up and led me to the intensive care room where Cindy was lying flat, with tubes in both arms and wires on her head.

"She'll be groggy from the anesthetic, but she should wake up soon. You can sit with her until she does. The doctor will come and see you on his rounds."

Anita left me with Cindy, and I sat by her side. She was breathing steadily, and her face was peaceful. After about fifteen minutes, her head turned toward me, and her eyes opened. Her mouth moved a little as though she was trying to say something, but her eyes closed again. I squeezed her hand, and she squeezed back weakly.

After I sat there for a few minutes, a doctor came in. He was the exception in Petersburg, stocky with dark hair and eyes, and a handlebar mustache. I stood up, and he introduced himself.

"I'm Dr. Ruiz, the duty physician. Let me check on Miss Lu. Then we'll talk."

Ruiz efficiently listened to Cindy's pulse, took her blood pressure, and checked her breathing. After a couple of minutes, he turned to me.

"Her vital signs are okay. She's doing well. Did she wake up while you've been here?"

"Her eyes opened for a few seconds, but she didn't say anything. I squeezed her hand, and she squeezed back."

"That sounds good. She'll need to stay here for about three more days, then she can go home, but she'll need bed rest for a couple of weeks."

"We're from Vancouver. Will she be okay to fly?"

"I'd advise against it. She won't be in shape to sit up for long periods for a while."

Cindy's eyes opened. She spoke clearly but softly.

"I don't want to fly to Vancouver. I want to stay on the boat with Sean."

Dr. Ruiz looked surprised.

"A boat? Is it a fishing boat?"

It was the logical guess since about 98 percent of the boats in Petersburg were fishing vessels.

"No, the *Lady L* is a 110-foot motor yacht. It's pretty comfortable."

"Miss Lu will need someone to change her dressings and help with her other needs. Otherwise, the yacht should be okay."

"I'll make arrangements before she's released."

Cindy was asleep again, so I left. I stopped for a coffee in the first place I came to, a fisherman's café called the Net Loft.

Moments after I sat down, Darya walked in, looking just like she did the day I met her. She came straight to my table and sat down opposite.

"Hi, Sean. I saw you come out of the hospital, and I followed you here. I'm sorry about what happened to Cindy, but I hear she'll be alright."

I thought about that for a moment. I didn't see how Cindy could ever be the same carefree girl again, but I didn't want to get into a long philosophical discussion.

"She'll be okay. What are you doing here?"

"Lizzie sent me up to deal with the legal issues. Peter Lorngren is suing *Lady L* for ramming the tug."

"But isn't he in jail?"

"No. The judge let him out on fifty thousand dollars bail, and the rumor is that if he leaves Alaska, they won't chase after him. The tug was towed here and hauled out for repairs. Lorngren's yacht, the *Ponderosa*, is also at the marina."

"That doesn't sound good. I need to talk to Levi. Did you know that he's a cop? Sergeant Levine of the RCMP."

Darya looked surprised.

"I didn't know that. Why is he here?"

"He was investigating rumors that Lizzie had Fingers Finnegan killed, and that she smuggles drugs, and maybe other stuff."

Darya laughed.

"Lizzie asked me to start the rumor about Finnegan. She had nothing to do with it, but she thought the story would show she isn't to be messed with. It was intended to deter Lorngren and others like him."

"Wait—there are others?"

"Not that I know of, but Lizzie used that phrase."

"So, is the expedition over?"

"Did you achieve the objective?"

"No, but we located the safe. It's still there."

"Then, the operation is still active. Given the danger, I'm authorized to increase your budget to allow you to hire some protection."

"Thanks. Too bad we didn't have that before Cindy got shot. I still need to talk to Levi. He got me out of jail, so I suspect he is at least a little sympathetic. By the way, Cindy wants to stay on the *Lady L*, so we'll need to hire a nurse and someone to handle the cooking and housekeeping."

Darya shrugged and touched me on the shoulder as she stood to leave.

"Do what you have to. I'm going to a meeting with the public prosecutor. I'll try to get Lorngren's boat impounded."

I finished my coffee and headed back to *Lady L*. Time to make a plan.

CHAPTER 32 – EXPECTATION

Back at the dock, I found Charlie scrubbing the decks. André was hanging from the bow in a bosun's chair, touching up the paint scratched when we rammed *Teacher's Pet*. Jock was sitting on top of the wheelhouse, puffing on his pipe.

Walking down the dock, I called out, "Where's Levi?"

André looked up. "I fired him. He's in his cabin, packing up his stuff. We can't have an undercover cop on board."

I disagreed.

"He's not undercover anymore. And he saved Cindy's life. Let me talk to him."

André didn't look happy, but he mumbled assent.

Levi was in his cabin, but he wasn't packing, just sitting on the bed. He stood when I came in.

I folded him into a bear hug. It was like hugging an oak tree. He didn't hug back.

"Thank you."

He knew why I was thanking him. He nodded.

"Would you consider staying on? Lizzie still wants us to retrieve the safe."

"I'd like that. My RCMP mission is over because my cover is blown. But I do have a lot of leave due. I'll tell my boss I like Alaska and want to take a few weeks holiday up here. I'll be working for you, not the RCMP."

"Sounds good to me. I'll square it with André. I need to find some more help. We weren't prepared for an attack last time. My fault, I didn't take the possibility too seriously, and Cindy was the victim."

"How is she doing?"

"She's recovering. They say a couple more days in the hospital. She'll stay on board with us."

"Is that wise?"

"No, but it's what she wants."

I went back on deck to talk to André. He agreed to let Levi stay with us as protection. I told him I would need to hire a nurse and a cook.

André said, "Leave the cook to me. I'm particular about food."

That agreed, I headed back to the hospital. I was beginning to drag my feet, having not slept in over 30 hours. Cindy was sleeping, so I used the payphone to check my messages. Brenda again.

I called back, and this time, a woman answered.

"Hello?" Her voice had the croak of a heavy smoker.

"Brenda?"

"Hang on. I'll get her."

I could hear coughing and voices in the background. Brenda came on the line.

"Is that Sean?"

"Yes."

"About time. Where have you been?"

"Alaska."

"Oh. Well, I have some news you might not like."

My wife had just been shot, what could be worse than that?

"Yes?"

"I'm expecting."

"Expecting what?"

"A baby, you fool! And you're the father!"

My knees buckled. I needed to sit down, but there was no chair, so I sat on the ground. It took me a few moments to recover enough to speak.

"Uh…are you sure it's mine?"

"Well, duh. There was nobody else for a very long time, so you're it!"

I thought back to the night she came to my boat. I couldn't remember using protection. I couldn't remember much except…never mind.

"I need to tell you something. I'm married."

It was her turn to hesitate.

"You bastard. You should have told me that night!"

"I wasn't married then, not even dating."

"So, a whirlwind romance then?"

"I guess you could say that. I'm at the Petersburg hospital right now, where my wife Cindy is recovering from a gunshot wound."

Brenda softened, "Oh, Sean, I'm so sorry. Listen, I don't want you to marry me anyway, but I thought I should tell you. The baby is due about February, so this conversation can wait until you get back to Vancouver."

"Are you going to keep it? The baby, I mean."

"Damn right. Goodbye, Sean, call me when you get home."

She hung up. I stood up and replaced the receiver. I didn't think this would be a good time to tell Cindy about my impending parenthood, but I went up to her room and sat by the bed, holding her hand.

CHAPTER 33 – BETTER?

Around me was a stark white room with no furniture, just tiled floors, and a single door. A baby was crying on the other side of the door—squalling actually. I was wearing white pajamas with jailhouse stripes. The door opened, and Cindy was standing there in matching pajamas. The room beyond was just like the one I was in, with no other opening. There was a crib on the far side of the room. That was where the noise was coming from.

"Help me change this diaper."

Cindy held up a ragged piece of cloth and two safety pins. I went over to the crib and peered in. The screaming baby was naked and very fat. Despite visible male attributes, it had Brenda's face complete with a mop of blonde hair, green eyes, and angry look.

"Sean. SEAN. Wake up."

My eyes slowly opened. I had dozed off in the chair beside Cindy's hospital bed. She was sitting up and looked wide awake. The clock on the wall said 8:23. I didn't know whether that was AM or PM.

"How long have I been asleep?"

"I don't know, I was sleeping myself. I woke up and could see you were having a bad dream. If you're awake now, we need to talk."

I felt guilty. I really needed to tell her about Brenda.

"Okay. You go first."

"I have some questions for you. First, did you consider the chances of being attacked?"

"It was a calculated risk."

"So, did you?"

"Did I what?" I didn't like where this was going.

"Calculate the risk? Or did you just carry on regardless?"

I was being forced to confront my reckless way of life. I bowed my head like a five-year-old kid being reprimanded by the teacher.

"Umm…just carried on, I guess."

"Alright, we'll come back to this tomorrow. I don't have the strength to deal with it now."

I decided to clear my conscience. "Cindy, I have something to tell you. I had a one-night stand with Brenda just before I started dating you."

Her unsmiling expression didn't change.

"Who's Brenda?"

"I guess you never met her. She was the waitress at the Shipmate Café."

"The blonde? I've been in there a few times. Terrible coffee."

This was easier than I expected. Cindy didn't seem upset. I thought I better get the rest out as quickly as possible. I mumbled the next sentence quickly.

"She thinks I'm the father of the baby she's expecting."

Cindy sat up straight, grimacing in pain.

"Out. Get out."

I stood up to leave. I had nothing ready to defend myself, but my miserable expression must have said something. Cindy spoke softly as I neared the door.

"Sean. Come back tomorrow. Bring flowers and chocolates and be ready to kiss my feet. We'll talk then."

I nodded, still unable to speak.

Back at the *Lady L*, I found out that I had missed dinner, but I had lost my appetite anyway. The crew was playing cards again. I told them Cindy was doing better, and I went straight to bed.

I had trouble getting to sleep. My mind was racing, trying to make sense of my life. Only a few weeks before, I had been a carefree bachelor with nobody but myself to answer to. Now I had a wife in hospital, another woman pregnant with my child, and a woman boss. All of them wanted something from me.

I got up and took a bottle of rye from the bar. After a couple of drinks, I dozed off.

CHAPTER 34 – CINDY RULES

I was sleeping on my back on a rocky beach. I could feel something tugging on my arms and legs. I opened my eyes. Cindy was pulling on my left arm. Brenda was pulling on my right. Lizzie had hold of my left foot, but she wasn't pulling hard. Darya had my right foot. I tried to call for help, but no words came. All four women looked angry. They were yelling, but I couldn't make out the words at first. Then it became a chorus.

"It's all your fault, Sean. It's all your fault."

I woke up with the sheets twisted around my limbs. I untangled myself and got ready for what I was sure would be a stressful day. I got dressed and went to the galley. Ajax was on his perch, rocking back and forth, repeating the same thing over and over.

"Where's Cindy? Where's Cindy?"

I knew I wouldn't be able to stand much of that, so I told him in a loud voice, "Cindy's fine. Now be quiet."

To my surprise, he shut up, although he glared at me and clicked his beak a few times.

Nobody else was up. The days are so long up there in June I needed to look at the time. The ship's clock in the main saloon said 2:15, but it wasn't ticking. It had been Cindy's job to wind it.

I went back to my cabin and found my watch. It said 4:37. I went back to the galley and put on a pot of coffee then tried to make a coherent plan to recover the safe efficiently but found there were too many unknowns. When the coffee was ready, I lay down on the settee and drank it. It didn't keep me awake.

André shook my shoulder. I opened one eye.

"Time to snap out of it, Sean. There's work to be done."

Breakfast and more coffee awaited. Darya and Levi were at the table, and Charlie came in while I was getting up. Over steamed eggs and sausages, I found out Darya was joining the crew as the cook. We still needed a nurse for Cindy.

"Where is the most logical place to find a nurse to hire?' I asked, to nobody in particular.

"At the hospital." Levi and Darya answered in unison.

"Seems obvious when you say it like that. I'll ask around when I visit Cindy."

After breakfast, I walked up to the hospital. On the way, I looked for a candy shop but didn't find one. The pharmacy had chocolates. The best ones they had were imported from… wait for it… Norway. Melkesjokolade.

The lady at the pharmacy directed me to a florist shop where I purchased a dozen yellow roses for just slightly less than the price of a new car. I thought red ones might remind Cindy of blood.

When I got to the hospital, Anita, the young blonde, was at the desk. I asked her if she knew how I could find a nurse to hire for a week or two.

"Your timing is good. We just heard that because of budget cuts, two of our nurses are being laid off. I'll give you their contact information."

As she was writing down the info, a nurse came through the swinging doors. I had noticed her before. Probably the only one who wasn't of Norwegian descent. She was about forty, tall and slim, with brown hair and hazel eyes like mine.

Anita looked up.

"Speak of the Devil. This is Deena Ogilvy. She's one of the two nurses I told you about. Deena, meet Sean Gray."

I took her hand and said, "You don't look like the Devil to me."

Deena chuckled and answered with a slight Texas twang. "You must be Cindy's husband. She said I should watch out for you."

I blushed a little and dropped her hand. I said, "Good, you know Cindy. She'll be released soon, and we need to hire a private nurse to take care of her while we are in Alaska, and if possible, on the trip back to Vancouver. You'd have your own cabin on the yacht, and we'll cover your flight home afterward. Are you interested?"

Anita's ears perked up at the mention of the yacht.

"If you don't take the job, Deena, I'll be applying."

Deena grinned, "Let's talk to Cindy about it."

She led me down the hall to a different room. Cindy was no longer in Intensive Care, just a regular hospital room. When we went in, she was sitting up in bed. There were no more tubes in her arms. I leaned over, kissed her cheek, and presented the flowers and chocolates.

"Thank you, Sean. We still need to talk. I'll let you off the foot-kissing for now. Hi Deena."

"Deena is considering joining the crew of the *Lady L* to help take care of you. Would you like that?"

"Very much. Deena has been good to me. She even sneaked me some real food."

Deena's cheeks reddened, "Shush. Someone might hear. Although I guess it doesn't matter. I'm losing my job here anyway."

"Deena, I need to spend some time alone with Cindy. I'll talk to you afterward."

I sat down beside Cindy's bed, ready to catch hell. She reached out a hand to me, and I took it in mine.

"Sean, I'm sorry I lost my temper. It's a lot to take in. My life has had more major events in the last two weeks than I ever experienced before. I'm feeling stronger today. Tell me again about Brenda."

"The night after I met you at your café, Brenda let herself into my boat. It wasn't locked. She rang the ship's bell as I came aboard. She was wearing a robe, which she dropped as I went below. Nothing underneath. I told her it wasn't a good idea, but…"

"Okay, enough details. I take it you didn't use protection."

"Never thought about it, but I wouldn't have had any on the boat."

Cindy sighed, "Result, accidental fatherhood. Is she planning to keep the child?"

"Yes. She hasn't asked for help, but I feel I should do as much as possible. Can you forgive me?"

Cindy looked pensive. She opened the box of chocolates, took one, and offered the box to me. I shook my head. They were for her. She popped it in her mouth and ate it.

"These are excellent. Sean, before we talk forgiveness, I need to give you the rules for staying married and keeping me onboard *Lady L.*"

I nodded.

"Number one, I'll need my own cabin, you can go back to your old one."

I was expecting that. She still had some recovering to do.

"Number two, I want a proper plan for protecting the ship and crew, with round the clock lookouts, now that we know other people are after the safe."

I nodded again.

"Number three, I want to have a say and a veto on how we proceed. I love you, but you are reckless, and the rest of the crew are no better. From now on, things will be done methodically, with proper precautions."

What choice did I have? She was right. I agreed.

"Now fill me in on Lorngren and his gang."

"The tug *Teacher's Pet* is out of action for a while after we rammed her—the crew just kind of melted away. Lorngren was jailed and charged with attempted murder. His lawyer got him out on bail, and the rumor is the local court hopes he skips out and goes back to BC, so they don't have to bear the expense of a trial."

Cindy looked unhappy about that.

"Is there any way we can make sure he leaves Alaska?"

"I'll talk to Levi. He probably has some ideas. Did I tell you he's an undercover RCMP officer?"

"No, but Darya did. She visited me yesterday for a few minutes. She said he's going to work for you now."

"That's right. I'll arrange some additional guards. By now, half of Alaska probably knows why we're here."

Cindy said, "Start a rumor that you are hunting for traces of the Kushtaka and the ghosts of Thomas Bay. Anita told me the locals think the bay is haunted and avoid going there. Reinforce that."

"What's a Kushtaka?"

"According to Anita, the Tlingit believe it's a kind of half-man, half-otter, that can steal the soul. There are said to be many in Thomas Bay, although she has never met anyone who's seen them. Could be the creatures in the *Strangest Story Ever Told*."

"Good idea. I'll get the crew to help me create a rumor tonight."

"The hospital is releasing me tomorrow at 11 AM, so come and pick me up then."

I kissed her, said my goodbyes, and left. I met Deena outside and arranged for her to move her things aboard *Lady L* the next morning.

CHAPTER 35 – RUMORS

That evening, Darya made a wonderful meal of fried salmon and cou-cou (cornmeal and okra).

"Really should be flyin' fish, but one uses what one got."

Darya was relaxed around us now, and her British accent was slipping. I found it endearing. A lawyer who could cook. Her clothes had changed too. She wore jeans and a tee-shirt, just like the rest of the crew.

"Darya, Darya." Ajax croaked, perched on her shoulder as she fed him cou-cou. Fickle bird.

Levi helped with the dishes and cleanup, the first time I had seen him in the kitchen. He seemed eager to help Darya, so I sat at the table with the others. On my way back from the hospital, I bought a book called *Tlingit Myths and Texts* by John R. Swanton. I skimmed it, and though there were two stories about the Kushtaka or Land Otter as the author named them, it didn't have much we could use.

I showed the book to André, Charlie, and Jock, pointed out the two chapters, and then started the plan.

"This is Cindy's idea. She thinks we should start a rumor that we're in search of the Kushtaka. Tonight, we all go up to the biggest bar. We spread out among the locals and ask questions about the creatures and the haunted nature of Thomas Bay. If anyone tells you a story about an adventure or mishap, try and remember it and tell everybody later. Don't tell anyone that is why we're here. Let them reach their own conclusions."

André said, "We could add a few stories of our own. Nothing detailed, just noises in the night in Thomas Bay, stuff going missing from the boat, that sort of thing."

"So that's where my hairbrush went," Charlie said.

"My pipe wrench disappeared too...wait, the police took it as evidence," Jock muttered.

Soon Darya and Levi joined us, and many ideas and jokes followed. I could see that everybody was in the spirit. Before we headed up, there was the item of security to discuss.

"Cindy thinks we need around the clock security watches and protection in Thomas Bay. I'm thinking we hire a couple of fishing boats to anchor near the entrance to Thomas Bay, and radio us if anybody suspicious approaches. One good thing about the bay is there's only one way in, and that's narrow. Scout anyone likely at the bar. I'll ask around in the marina."

Levi added, "Tomorrow, I'll talk to the local police. They will know who we can trust for guard duty."

We headed up to the pub. Ajax hopped on André's shoulder and went along.

The weather had improved, and the sun was peeking through the clouds as we headed up. The docks were steaming as the sunlight evaporated the rain. Most of the boats were empty, but the odd one had someone puttering on board. We nodded and exchanged greetings with those we saw. I wanted us to come across as the good guys.

When we got to the Bergen pub, it was busy but not packed. Following our plan, we split up. Levi and

Darya stayed together, which made sense to me. She was the only black woman in the place, maybe the only one in Petersburg, and we had no idea what attitudes we would encounter.

With Ajax on his shoulder, André soon was seated at a table that included several blonde women. His French charm was in full flower.

Charlie found a table of slightly older, mostly male engineer types. I imagined they were discussing gear ratios and sinusoidal loading curves. We planned to make friends by treating the table we landed at to a round of drinks.

I hadn't yet found a place. Behind me, I heard Jock's Scottish voice. "Waiter, I dinna remember ever doin' this before, but this round is on me."

Jock had found a group of mostly older men with bushy beards and plaid flannel shirts. They seemed to be having a good time.

As I walked around, a voice called my name.

"Mr. Gray? Would you like to join us?"

It was Dr. Ruiz from the hospital. There were three other people with him at the table. One was Anita, the receptionist. The other two were a stocky native lady of indeterminate age and a blonde man about my age.

I went over and was introduced to Raven Petroikov and Bob Arneson. Raven wore a black tee-shirt and jeans. Bob had on a suit and tie, but the suit jacket was on the chairback, and his tie was loose.

I sat with them. After some preliminary chat, I asked if they knew about the stories surrounding Thomas Bay.

Anita said, "I've lived here all my life, and I have never heard any complete story, just talk of 'otter men' who can steal your soul."

Raven chuckled, "I'm Tlingit, and my grandmother told me about the Kushtaka or 'land otters.' She said they were family members who drowned or died without the body being found. They only appear to their relatives. It's a legend, part of our heritage, but not a real thing."

Here I tried to add something to the legend. "While we were anchored in Thomas Bay, late at night, we heard voices murmuring in the woods. We didn't see any creatures or people."

In truth, we had the generator running, so it wasn't likely we would have heard much.

Arneson laughed, "That's the glacier at the head of the bay talking. It's gradually receding, and as it does, it drops stones and gravel on the beach. From some distance away, it sounds like voices."

Ajax squawked and flew over to our table. As he landed on the chairback beside Raven, he let out a long wolf whistle. "Ajax, I'm Ajax."

He held out a claw, and Raven took it.

"I'm Raven. Nice to meet you, Ajax."

Ajax rocked back and forth and purred like a cat. He liked Raven.

The door of the pub opened, and three people came through. Ajax jumped into the air and flew like a hawk toward the door. I stood up to see what was happening. Ajax flew into the face of the first newcomer and apparently attacked him as there was a loud scream of pain. By the shape and size of the man, I identified Peter Lorngren. He dropped to his knees, trying to scrape the bird off his face. I could see blood spurting. Then Ajax took wing and resumed his place at our table. There was blood on his beak and feathers.

The whole place was in chaos. Some people left, others crowded around the injured man. The two bruisers who came in with Lorngren scanned the room for threats.

Dr. Ruiz excused himself and worked his way through the crowd toward the injured man. Raven used a napkin and water to clean Lorngren's blood off Ajax, who seemed calm. The police arrived first, followed by an ambulance. I spotted officer Svensen. He spoke to Dr. Ruiz briefly then made a beeline for me. I put my hands in the air as he approached.

"Huh. You again. Put your hands down. Is that your parrot?"

I lowered my hands and said, "His name is Ajax. He's the ship's mascot. Nobody owns him as far as I know."

At his name, Ajax looked up and squawked, "Sean did it. Sean did it."

Svensen laughed, "He isn't much of a parrot. More of a stool pigeon. I don't see how I can charge a bird with assault, but it's illegal to have pets in a place that serves food. I'll have to give you a ticket. The fine is fifty dollars."

Anita gave Svensen a friendly smile. "Arno, the bird flew in on his own. Sean never even touched him. I'm a witness. Here's my number if you want me to testify. And calling *lutefisk* food is quite a stretch."

She gave him a slip of paper. Svensen blushed and put it in his pocket. The paramedics walked Lorngren out to the ambulance. Ruiz came back to the table.

"He's going to need stitches. Do you know him, Sean?"

"You could say that. Lorngren's the guy that shot Cindy. He's out on bail."

"I guess that explains why Ajax attacked him."

Svensen decided not to write a ticket after Levi went over and had a little chat.

Levi told me that Lorngren would be going back to jail as bail conditions were broken when he went out drinking with a gun in his pocket.

After that, we said goodbye to our new friends and headed back to *Lady L*. Ajax sat on André's shoulder and tucked his head under his wing. Our rumor starting may not have been a success, but we were proud of Ajax.

Everyone was too tired to play cards, so we headed off to our cabins. Levi put his hand on Darya's shoulder as they went out.

CHAPTER 36 – HEAT

The sounds of sirens and loud voices woke me up from a deep sleep. I sat up and looked out my port. Outside there were dancing shadows interspersed with orange and yellow highlights. It was a vision from hell. There had to be a fire, but I couldn't see the source.

Quickly I pulled on my clothes and ran to the bow of the yacht. From there, I could see a burning boat being pushed out into the channel by fishermen with pike poles. It was *Scurry*. The wind caught her and blew her away from the docks. When she was a couple of hundred feet out, she exploded in a ball of flames—the fuel tank. Glowing embers shot skyward. Fortunately, they were carried away from us by the wind. In a few minutes, it was all over, and the remains sank with a hiss and a few bubbles.

Scurry was no more. Firemen stood helpless on the dock. The fishermen started back to their own boats. I asked a few of them if they had seen the fire start, but nobody had. The dock where *Scurry* had been tied up was slightly scorched, and her lines were cut. It was no accident. That would be too unlikely a coincidence. I felt a pang of sorrow at the destruction of a piece of history.

I didn't linger on those thoughts because I immediately thought about Cindy. If somebody was trying to attack us, she was the most vulnerable. By then, the whole crew was either on deck or on the dock. I told them I was going up to the hospital to check on Cindy. Levi offered to go with me, and I agreed. He ran back to his cabin for a moment, then we set off up the dock at a fast pace. The time was about four AM, and the sun was already peeking over the horizon.

It took only about five minutes to get to the hospital. The front door was locked, which I took as a good sign. There was a doorbell that I pushed. In a couple of minutes, a sleepy-looking night nurse came to the door. I told her why we were there, and she let us in. She didn't ask for ID, which wasn't such a good sign. We looked into Cindy's room. She was sleeping peacefully. I could see her chest rising and falling, so I knew she was alive. A huge weight lifted from my shoulders.

Levi said, "I think we should guard her until we get her back to the boat."

I agreed to take the first shift. Levi would take over at seven. He slipped me a small handgun. It was a bit unsettling that a cop would give a civilian like me a gun. It wasn't the time to question him, so I put in my jacket pocket. It was more symbolic than real protection as I had never fired one like it. I sat on a chair outside Cindy's room, unable to sleep. There were a few books in the nurse's break room, and I picked up Jack London's *People of the Abyss.*

London kept me busy until Levi arrived. I gave him back the gun and looked in on Cindy. Still sleeping. I told him I would come back shortly before she was scheduled to be discharged.

I walked back to the *Lady L*, intending to grab a couple of hours sleep. As I moved along the dock beside her, I idly counted the portlights in the hull. There were thirteen. This triggered something in my brain. I remembered exploring the whole ship on my first day aboard. I had made a sketch of the layout. I counted 12 portlights on each side in the lower deck. My memory was reliable for such trivia.

Things like that bother me until I find an explanation. Perhaps a necessary part of being a detective. I went aboard and found Jock. I told him about the ports and asked if he knew an explanation.

"No. The fuel tanks are at the aft end of the engine compartment and run right across the ship. There is no passage through there. You have to go up to the main deck. Maybe there are dummy ports?"

That seemed dubious to me. *Lady L* was large but not pretentious. The design was absolutely honest, with no extraneous decorations or glitz. Those big bronze portlights were expensive, and I couldn't imagine the designers and builders putting in two extra with no purpose.

I borrowed a tape from Jock and measured the length of the interior compartments on the lower deck. The ship was 110 feet long, but the interior compartments added up to 102, making some allowance for structure. Eight feet. The missing area had to be at the aft end where the fuel tanks were. I found Jock and asked him what the tank capacity was.

"About a thousand gallons in each. It isn't exact. There is no gauge, but each one has a sight glass where you can see the level."

He took me to the tank area. There was a metal bulkhead running right across the vessel, with various pipes and valves, which formed the front side of the fuel tanks. There were three large round openings about a foot off the floor, with a ring of bolts securing them.

"Jock, are there three tanks?"

"No, only two. You can see where the pickups come out."

"So why three cleanout hatches?"

"I don't know. I never noticed it."

I knocked on the fronts of the tanks with my fist. There was a dull sound until I got near the middle of the bulkhead. There was about a three-foot section that sounded hollow.

I did some mental math. The ship was 21 feet wide. Given the size of the fuel tanks, the length to contain 1000 gallons would only be about four feet.

"There's a secret compartment behind the fuel tanks. Get a ¾ inch socket wrench, and we'll unbolt this center hatch."

While Jock went to get the wrench, I scrutinized the bolts. All were clean, except one that showed a trace of oily residue.

When Jock arrived with the wrench, I showed him which bolt to try first. It turned easily, and the hatch swung open on concealed hinges. It revealed a passageway between the tanks. I felt around and found a light switch. At the other end, there were two regular size doors with rounded corners. Both were closed. I wondered aloud what could be behind those doors.

Jock said, "One way to find out."

The hatch was big enough for me to get through, but I had to bend almost double. My rotund friend would have trouble, so I went in alone.

Once through the hatch, I stood up. The passage was bare except for the light switch and an overhead bulb. The doors were varnished teak, just like all the others on *Lady L*. I grasped the handle of the port side one and turned. It opened outward into the passage.

I stepped through and looked around, finding another light switch. It was a narrow room with two bunks on the aft wall. The lower one had drawers underneath. Straight ahead were a marine toilet and a small sink. No door. A small shower was enclosed only with a curtain. The extra portlight was there, covered by a sliding panel. Everything was dusty but not dirty. There were no footprints or handprints in the dust except mine. I opened the drawers, but they were all empty.

It was a cabin that could be used to hide two people—or possibly more. I looked closely at the door. It could only be locked from the outside. I told Jock what I'd found.

I stepped out and tried the other door. Expecting a similar cabin on the starboard side, I was surprised to find a storeroom. There were shelves on both sides with a narrow walkway between. Dozens of cases of liquor would fit. Again, it was dusty, not used for a very long time. A piece of paper was on the bottom shelf by the door. It was a whiskey label—*Walker's Canadian Club*—dated 1933.

Lady L was equipped to smuggle booze and people. There was no way to tell how this ability had been used, but the label gave a good hint.

I climbed out into the engine room.

"Jock, I see a way we could use this space in case of another attack. It would make a good hiding place for the three women."

He looked at the dummy hatch. It could be locked from the inside, so the exterior bolt would not open it.

"Maybe. But it would be better if we prevent any attacks."

"Levi is working on that."

We called the rest of the crew to see the secret compartment, then closed it up. Jock cleaned the area, so there was no sign of the hatch being opened.

I looked at my watch. It was time to get Cindy.

CHAPTER 37 – THE RETURN

When I got to the hospital, Cindy and Deena were outside waiting. Cindy was in a wheelchair, but she stood up and stepped quickly over to me when I got close. She gave me a one-armed hug.

I said, "Shouldn't you stay in the wheelchair?"

"Great to see you too, Sean. I was shot in the shoulder, not the leg. I can walk just fine."

Deena stifled a laugh. She turned and rolled the wheelchair back into the hospital.

"Sorry. How are you feeling?"

"Pretty good. The shoulder is sore, and my arm will be in a sling for at least a week to keep from opening the wound. Deena won't have too much to do."

We started walking back to *Lady L*. I carried a bag of Cindy's stuff. It was light. I looked at her.

"You have new clothes."

Cindy did a little twirl. She was wearing crisp black slacks, a white tee-shirt, and a light-yellow windbreaker.

"The old ones were covered in blood, and the police kept them as evidence. Deena bought these for me. You owe her."

"Okay. Thanks, Deena. I'll pay you back."

"I don't mind. Cindy is terrific, and I love to help."

Another thought came into my mind.

"Cindy, I never asked you how you got out of the handcuffs."

Cindy held out her left hand and squeezed her fingers together. Held that way, her hand was no thicker than her wrist.

"When I was a little girl, the beat cop used to come to the café for lunch. He let me play with his handcuffs. I perfected that move long ago."

I laughed, "That's a useful skill for a criminal."

Cindy winked, "I have other skills…"

"We'll talk about those later."

I told Cindy about the secret compartment. By then, we were at the boat. Ajax flew out and landed on her shoulder, cooing and purring. She went to her room, and I gave Deena a quick tour of the *Lady L.* She had never been on a yacht before and was suitably impressed. We gave her the guest cabin next to the master stateroom. She went home to fetch her clothes and other necessities.

After Cindy settled in, I showed her the secret room and how to get into it. I suggested it as a retreat in case of an attack.

"No way. If the ship were to sink or burn, this would be a death trap."

As usual, she was right.

The rest of the crew had been out talking to the police. They came back in time for lunch, with Deena in tow. Darya had been shopping for food, and Levi was carrying the bags. I told them Cindy was in her cabin but would join us for lunch.

The crew and I moved to the wheelhouse. We had to plan our next move. I asked Levi to tell us what he had on security.

"Lorngren is in jail. His bail was revoked. Bambi flew home to Vancouver, and the rest of his crew have dispersed. The rumor is that he burned *Scurry*, but the state troopers have no evidence."

Charlie said, "Were you able to get any guards for us?"

"Yes, the local cops recommended a few locals that could use some money and can be trusted. I spoke to them and hired two boats. One is a wooden gillnetter, and the other is an aluminum crew boat capable of 40 knots. The speed could be useful."

André asked, "Are they armed?"

Levi chuckled. "This is Alaska. Everybody's armed."

Something was bothering me. I asked Levi about it.

"Levi, if you were planning to rob a salvage operation, would you attack them before the operation was complete, the way Lorne Greene attacked us?"

He thought for a second.

"Absolutely not. I would observe the action, but I wouldn't attack until the target crew found something. Most likely, I would attack when they were celebrating."

"That's what André said before we left Vancouver. Maybe Lorngren is an incompetent hothead. He still did a lot of damage, particularly to Cindy. Lizzie mentioned 'others' but didn't elaborate. What if the others are competent?"

"If they exist, and they are truly capable, we might not know a thing about them. They will either attack us right away after finding something or possibly wait until we're on the way home. There are a lot of very remote places between here and Vancouver, with no police or Coast Guard nearby."

That made sense to me. But we still had to beware of what might happen in Thomas Bay. We spent the rest of the day getting ready to move back there. Jock went over the mechanical bits. Charlie filled the water tanks and helped André clean the boat.

I went with Cindy to buy more provisions. She was in good spirits. The supermarket in town would let you take a shopping cart down to the docks. They had very little fresh produce but an excellent selection of frozen and canned foods. We were able to get onions and potatoes. When we were done, the clerk packed the food in cardboard boxes and loaded them in a cart.

As we rolled the cart down the street, several people I didn't know greeted Cindy by name, ignoring me. I didn't ask her about it.

Back at *Lady L*, Deena helped us get the provisions into the galley, then she and Cindy set about organizing. I met André on the bridge and worked on our strategy for Thomas Bay. We looked at the charts and picked a more open anchorage where we couldn't be blocked in. The plan was to head out early the next morning to catch the high tide. *Lady L* needed plenty of water under the keel.

Darya cooked dinner, and Levi helped her serve. They exchanged little touches and glances between the kedgeree and latkes, a combination new to me. Cindy ate one-handed, but it didn't slow her down much. Dessert was a Pavlova, made with canned peaches and fresh blackberries.

After Charlie and I did the dishes, we all turned in early. I went with Cindy to her cabin, where we kissed and talked about the future. I helped her undress for bed, but when I started to unbutton my shirt, she showed me the door.

As I left, I said, "I'll leave my door unlocked in case you change your mind."

She didn't reply.

I went to my cabin, where I read for a while, then drifted off to sleep. I awoke as my door creaked open. I assumed it was Cindy, but I pretended to be asleep. The room was dark, but light seeping in from the hallway revealed a slim female silhouette. She softly padded up beside the bed, looked at me, and turned away. Then she quietly opened the top drawer of the dresser and rummaged through the contents, namely my underwear.

I sat up in bed and switched on the light. She let out a startled, "Oh!" and turned toward me. It was Darya. She was wearing a long tight tee-shirt, which left little to the imagination.

"Hi, Darya. Ordinarily, I would welcome a visit from a lovely young woman, but I'm a married man now."

I'm sure she blushed, but it was difficult to tell.

"Sean, I'm so embarrassed. Cindy told me you had a box of condoms in your dresser. I knocked on the door, and when you didn't answer, I let myself in to look for them. Can I have one or two?"

"Sure. Check the bottom drawer."

"Thanks, Sean."

She turned around and bent down to open the bottom drawer. I never really appreciated Darya before.

She left, and I switched out the light. The second time the door opened, it was Cindy.

CHAPTER 38 – FOUND IT

A ray of sunlight through the portlight tickled my left eyelid. I rolled over and found Cindy curled alongside. She opened her eyes and smiled. I had a question.

"Did you tell Darya about the box of condoms in my dresser? She came in last night looking for them."

In answer, she rolled on top of me and kissed me on the lips.

"Good Morning Sean. What were you saying about Darya?"

"Never mind."

I let it go.

Later, after an excellent breakfast, we got *Lady L* underway for Thomas Bay. The security boats fell in line as we left Petersburg with sunshine and a light mist rising off rippled waters. The crossing was smooth, and the only other boats we saw were a couple of small trollers heading north.

Once in the bay, we moored in the spot we had picked out earlier. The two security boats dropped anchor near the entrance to the bay, and we arranged to keep watch on VHF channel 73.

Our fake rock was still in position, so we knew the safe was undisturbed. It was still early, so André suggested we make a start on the recovery operation. Charlie and Levi launched the Whaler, and they got their diving gear ready. The first step was to dive down and survey the situation.

I stayed aboard *Lady L* while Levi and Charlie went over in the dinghy. Levi strapped on his tank, dove in, and remained under for just a few minutes. Then they came back toward us.

Levi reported that visibility was reduced due to the falling tide carrying milky glacier melt. We would have to wait for the tide to turn, which would be about 3 PM. Darya fed us a simple lunch.

After a coffee, I suggested an expedition up the slope behind us to find the crescent lake and search for the box Jakob buried. André was interested, but Levi and Charlie wanted to concentrate on the safe.

A close examination of the large scale chart showed dozens of small lakes above Spurt Point, as well as one a bit larger, imaginatively called "Spurt Point Lake." I dug out Jakob's last letter and read it carefully. With the charts and the actual landscape before me, I tried to gain an understanding of where he had explored ashore.

He mentioned, "a curious cave, high up along the eastern side of a long narrow lake." I thought he must have meant Spurt Point Lake. There were other narrow lakes, but they were either tiny or much farther away. Measured on the chart, the distance from our anchorage to the lake was about a mile and a half. It was uphill, but not very steep. I figured a hike up there would take an hour or less.

Charlie and Levi took the Whaler and went back to the salvage operation. I talked André into joining me on the expedition. We borrowed a powerful lamp from Jock and dressed in long pants and long-sleeve shirts. We didn't have proper hiking boots, but we did have rubber sea-boots. We took a shotgun and a few shells as well as a coil of rope. Both of us had sailing knives.

Cindy saw us getting ready to leave.

"Sean, where are you going? Are you leaving us alone here?"

"We're going to find the cave. Jock is here. I'll show you how to fire the flare gun. If we see a flare, we'll come right back."

She wasn't pleased, but let us go after I showed her the flare gun. We lowered one of the rowboats, and I rowed us ashore where André tied us to a fallen tree. We landed just below the hiker's cabin we had spotted earlier. We had a look around the cabin, which was hardly more than a shed. It had a couple of built-in wooden bunks and a potbelly stove. Alongside was an outhouse. It didn't look like it had been recently used, as weeds were growing up through the porch. There were no footprints in the dust, except the ones we made.

There was a visible path leading in the approximate direction of the lake, and we started following it. It wasn't well maintained, with muddy stretches and fallen logs across the path, but it followed a gentle slope. Along the way, we saw no traces of birds or animals, but we did hear a woodpecker tapping in the distance. In about forty minutes, we reached the lakeshore.

The lake was indeed long and narrow, and we couldn't see the far end as it curved out of sight. The eastern side of the lake was very densely forested right down to the water, and I began to doubt that it was even possible to explore it. I wished I had brought a machete.

André crashed off into the bush to our right.

"There's a path here."

I followed him. There was a trail, although it was narrow, and we had to push branches aside to navigate it. The ground was wet in places, so our seaboots were useful. In some areas, the trail seemed to disappear where the surface was rocky, but each time after a brief search, we found it again. The path wasn't right next to the lake, but at times we could see sunlight glinting on the water.

After about half a mile, we sat on a fallen log for a rest. I took a look around. The forest was dense and the trees large, although they were not old-growth. A few huge stumps gave an idea of the forest giants that once populated the valley. It was darker on our right as a steep hill loomed up close by.

As we sat there resting, a strange sound rose up ahead. To me, it sounded like the last throes of a large dying animal. André turned in alarm.

"What the hell was that?"

A shiver ran down my back. I wasn't exactly scared, but I didn't feel confident either.

"I don't know. Maybe that's the sound Jakob heard from the cave."

André stood up and started walking in the direction of the sound. I stood up too, but stayed in place. André looked over his shoulder at me.

"Don't you want to find the cave? This is a clue to the location. We have to follow it."

Reluctantly I followed. About a minute later, the sound came again. This time it was louder, longer, and contained both a low rumble and a high screech. My heart was gripped in a vise, and I stopped breathing for what seemed like minutes but was probably seconds.

André stopped in his tracks too. The terrain ahead was rougher and the undergrowth thick.

I said, "We need a machete or an ax to cut through that!"

We used that as an excuse to turn back, vowing to return better prepared. Getting back to the beach took only half as long as getting up there. As I rowed toward Lady L, André pointed out that the Whaler was back.

"I wonder what they found?"

"I guess we will soon know."

I kept rowing until we were close by. There was nobody on deck when we came alongside, but Charlie came out to take our lines. I asked him what they had discovered.

"The safe is there. We cleaned off as many barnacles as possible, but there was nothing to attach the air bladders. We'll have to do some underwater welding to make some lifting points. I stole a few links of anchor chain for the purpose. We'll go back down at low tide, first thing in the morning."

Onboard, Darya had laid out a buffet supper with cold cuts, fresh-baked bread, vegetables, and cheese.

"We din't know what time you all back, so I made cold supper," She said in full Bajan dialect. The city lawyer was fading away as she got comfortable with us. I was about to help myself to the food when I realized Cindy was missing.

I went to her room to check on her. The door was open. Cindy was lying face down on the bed, wracked with sobs. I sat beside her and stroked her hair.

"What's wrong, Cindy?"

She slowly turned over on her back, wiping her eyes. When she spoke, her voice was bitter.

"Nothing much. I met a guy I liked. We got married. I was insulted in Prince Rupert, assaulted and tied up in Thomas Bay, then shot and nearly died. Now I'm stuck on a boat in some godforsaken bay. Sean, being married to you is dangerous. The fun is gone. I want to go home."

She was right. My adventure had been hell for her. I held her for a while, mulling over the events that led to this, then said, "I'll get a floatplane in here to take you home first thing tomorrow. Brice has the key to my boat, and you can live there until I get back."

"The same boat where you found a dead guy? No thanks. I'll go stay with my mother."

I couldn't argue. Cindy was safer right out of my life, at least until I got back to Vancouver.

She cleaned herself up, and we went to get dinner. After the decision to go home, she cheered up and seemed to be her old self again. I didn't feel so good. I was beginning to understand the trauma I had carelessly put her through.

The evening went smoothly, and we played cards after dinner. Cindy quietly told everybody, one by one, that she would be leaving the next day. Deena agreed to fly back to Vancouver with Cindy because she was still recovering from her wound.

I slept in Cindy's room that night, but there was no hanky-panky.

CHAPTER 39 – FOUND WHAT?

I woke up about 6 AM and looked out the side window. It was as though the world had disappeared, leaving behind nothing but an infinite gray wall. Behind me, Cindy was sleeping soundly. I used the head, got dressed, and made my way to the galley. Darya already had the coffee on. André was sitting at the table nursing his cup.

"Morning, Sean."

He swept an arm to indicate the fog all around us.

"I don't think Cindy will be flying out today."

I nodded my agreement and poured myself a coffee.

"I'm going up to the bridge to check the radar," I said. I went out, and André followed, coffee in hand.

Once the radar warmed up, we could see the outlines of the land around us. Everything looked fine at first glance. Then André pointed out that there was only one guard boat on station at the entrance to the bay.

I switched on the VHF and called the other boat.

"King of Salmon, King of Salmon, this is *Lady L*, *Lady L*"

There was silence for quite a while. I was about to try again when the radio crackled to life.

A deep-chested laconic drawl came on, "*Lady L*, this is King Salmon. No 'of.' What's up?"

"Your partner boat, Aleutian Bobber, isn't showing on the radar."

"That's 'cause he's rafted alongside me. His anchor started to drag last night, and he was too lazy to reset it. He's fine. We had a few drinks and played cards. I had my radar on all night with the alarm set for half a mile. Nothing."

"Okay. Keep the radar on. The fog is thick."

"Roger that. King Salmon out."

After that, we went back to the galley where Darya was making breakfast. The whole crew was there except Cindy. I went to her room to find her.

Cindy was in the shower when I got there, so I sat on the bed and waited for her. She came out wearing a thick yellow bathrobe and drying her hair with a blue towel.

"I guess I won't be flying out today," she said with a cheerful grin.

"Not unless the fog lifts quickly, and that doesn't seem likely."

"It's OK. I don't mind staying here a bit longer."

"Get dressed. Breakfast is on."

"You go ahead. I'll be there in a minute."

Breakfast was a kedgeree made with salmon instead of salt cod. Darya also had baked fresh cinnamon buns. The crew was chowing down when I arrived. I dished up a plate for Cindy and one for me.

"If we hurry, we can weld some lugs on that safe and get it ashore under cover of the fog," said Charlie.

"Good idea," André said. "Maybe we can get it open. If anybody is trying to watch us, the fog will work in our favor."

We ate up and were finished by the time Cindy arrived. She, Darya, and Deena sat together at one of the small round tables in the saloon while the rest of us got ready to work. Out on deck, Levi put on his wet suit, and Charlie prepared his welding torch. We also loaded the air compressor and two air bladders. Within a short time, Charlie, Levi, and I were in the Whaler heading for the safe. The fog was so thick we had to feel our way slowly, watching the sounder.

André and Jock stayed on the bow of *Lady L.* peering out through the fog. The plan was to run a line around a large tree and use *Lady L*'s powered deck winch to haul the safe up to the beach.

We found the fake rock and dropped the Whaler's anchor nearby. Levi put on his diving gear. We left the welding tanks on board. The hoses were long enough to reach the safe.

"We need a signal to shut off the gas to the welding torch," Levi said.

Charlie said, "Two tugs on your safety line, one second apart. Three or more tugs and we'll pull you up."

I kept quiet as I knew nothing about underwater welding. Levi gathered several chain links and welding rods and put them in a bag tied to his waist. He test lit the torch, but when he dipped it in the sea, it went out. After adjusting the mix and setting the flame hotter, it stayed lit when immersed.

Levi lowered himself gently into the water, which was reasonably clear on the rising tide. He was soon out of sight, but we could see bubbles rising. He was underwater for about ten minutes, then Charlie felt two tugs on the line and shut off the gas. Three more tugs, and we started pulling him in. As he surfaced, he tore off his face mask. He was laughing.

"An otter was watching me. Then he swam away and came back with his wife and three kids. They were nibbling on my swim fins while I worked. I wish I had an underwater camera!"

Charlie said, "But did you succeed in welding the lugs on?"

"I think they should hold. The only way to test them is to try to haul it up."

Charlie gave him an airbag, and three lengths of heavy rope. Then Levi went back down and tied the lines to the lugs. Back at the surface, he connected all three lines to a large bronze ring Charlie handed him.

We connected a hose from the airbag to the portable compressor, and Charlie started it. As the bag filled, we could see some movement of the safe, but it didn't float to the surface.

Charlie said, "It can't lift it completely but will make it easier to move."

Then we helped Levi back aboard, pulled up the dinghy anchor, and motored back to *Lady L.*

Levi went aboard to take off his gear. Charlie and I motored up to the bow where Jock handed us the end of a large hawser, a massive galvanized block, a tub of grease, and a machete.

"Pick a big sturdy tree, cut a groove in the bark a few feet up, and lash the block to it tightly. Then take the hawser through the block and tie it to the safe. We'll use the powered winch to pull it toward shore. Grease the block thoroughly before we try," Jock said.

We set out to do as instructed. I picked a spot for the safe to drag ashore where the beach had small round stones, which I hoped would act like ball bearings. The tree I chose was over six feet in diameter.

When we were all set, and the hawser was attached to the safe, Jock warned us to get well away.

"If something breaks loose, it will fire off like a cannon. You dinna want to be in range."

We motored the Whaler to the far side of *Lady L.* André went inside, and Jock stood behind the cabin, holding the remote cable for the winch. When he applied the power, the winch ground slowly, wrapping the hawser onto a large drum. It took a couple of minutes to draw the line tight. Then, the bow of *Lady L* began to move slowly to the side as the strain came on her anchor.

Once the line was tight, the winch slowed and began to growl with strain. Jock paused to see if it was overheating and squirted some oil into the bearings. From my vantage on the side deck of *Lady L*, I couldn't see any significant movement of the safe.

The ship jerked violently to starboard, and I grabbed the rail to remain upright. Jock stopped the winch.

He called out, "The anchor let go!"

After moving about ten feet back and to starboard, *Lady L*'s anchor grabbed again, and Jock resumed winching. With a loud groan, the line to the safe shifted a few inches, then began a steady crawl toward the beach. The airbag surfaced, and soon the corner of the safe appeared as the water grew shallower. In about twenty minutes, the safe was almost clear of the water, prevented from moving further by large logs and boulders.

Charlie, Levi, and I went ashore nearby and dragged the Whaler as close to the safe as we could get. It was lying face down, and we couldn't see the door.

I asked, "How will we turn it over to get to the door?"

Charlie answered, "We won't. The doors on these things are massive, but since they were made to be mounted in a wall, the back is much thinner. We'll cut through there."

He put on welding goggles, lit the torch, and started burning a hole in the back of the safe. There was an inward rush of air as the flame made its first penetration. The rusty steel was about half an inch thick, so it was slow work. There was an air of excitement as the hole, about a foot across, neared completion.

Charlie stopped cutting as he neared the starting point.

"When I finish the cut, the piece will drop through the hole. Should we try to prevent it?"

I said, "Sounds like a good idea."

Wordlessly Levi took a thin line from the dinghy and looped it around the cut plate. He held it from above as Charlie finished the cut.

The jagged chunk of steel came free, and a cheer arose from André and Jock, observing our work from the yacht.

I looked into the hole. It was dark and partly filled with water. I reached in to feel around inside.

CHAPTER 40 – SOLVED?

Just as I was reaching in to start removing the contents of the safe, Levi stopped me.

"Sean, let me do that. We should treat the contents as evidence, and I have forensic training. Any papers we find will be in a delicate condition and need to be kept wet until separated, so they don't dry into a clump."

On Levi's instructions, we took the Whaler to *Lady L.* We fetched a tarp to lay on the beach, a washtub, and several jerry jugs of water. When we got back, Levi had already removed three small, heavy leather bags from the safe. We laid those on the tarp.

I couldn't wait. I wanted to examine the contents. The bags were laced tight with leather thongs. There was no hope of untying them after many decades immersed in salt water, so I got out my sailing knife. Charlie stood by as I opened the first bag.

Even after cutting the thong, the leather was so stiff it took a lot of force to open the bag. I was expecting gold dust, but what I found was coins, formerly loose but now corroded into an almost solid mass. One of the visible coins had a square hole in it.

Charlie said, "Looks like Chinese money."

The second bag had coins too, but they were Spanish reales, of blackened silver. The third bag had British currency. Queen Victoria was recognizable on a couple.

Levi heard us talking.

"This must have been a trading ship. British and Spanish money was in common use along this coast in the 19ᵗʰ century. I would expect to find American money too."

Levi had removed four or five pouches, apparently containing documents, and a small wooden box. The box had been heavily varnished and was in surprisingly good condition. It had tarnished brass hinges and a brass catch. Levi loosened the catch and opened it a crack. Then he tilted the box to drain out the water.

Inside the box was a ship's chronometer, gimbal-mounted. The dial was visible under the glass. I had seen something similar in the Victoria Maritime Museum.

The fog was thinning, and we could see the bottoms of trees on the shore. It was time to get rid of the evidence.

I called a small meeting. Levi was to empty the contents directly into the Whaler, without further examination, and get it all onboard *Lady L*. I wanted the safe back underwater as soon as possible. I reasoned that the opened safe was as good as a signpost reading "TREASURE FOUND HERE."

The method we used for landing the safe would not work in reverse. We would have to tow it back out. The outboard motor on the Whaler wouldn't be powerful enough. The larger of our guard boats might do the trick, but I didn't want to get them involved. So the *Lady L* would have to become a towboat.

In a few minutes, the Whaler was loaded, and on its way back to *Lady L*. I stayed behind and removed the block and lines from the tree, refastening the rope from the yacht directly to the safe. The air bladder was still inflated, and I left it in place.

Soon I saw Charlie up on the bow explaining the plan to André. They moved the hawser to the stern. *Lady L* wasn't meant to be a tug, and there was no strong central point to attach the tow line. Jock fashioned a bridle out of the mooring lines and tied the hawser to the center. It ran to the stern cleats, which were large and well fastened.

Jock went to the engine room and started the diesel in reverse and let it warm up. This was to make sure it would start again when needed. Then he shut it down. Charlie went up to the bow to raise the anchor with the electric windlass. André was at the wheel, calmly directing the operation though the open door of the wheelhouse.

As soon as the anchor cleared the water, André rang for slow forward, and the big diesel rumbled to life. *Lady L* glided ahead, slowing as the strain came on the tow rope. I stepped back up the beach to watch. As the towline stretched, the safe tipped a few inches but didn't shift. André rang for more throttle, and slowly, with loud grinding sounds, the safe began to drag along the rocky bottom. Soon it was out of sight underwater.

André dragged it out to a deeper part of the bay, then cut the motor. Levi appeared on deck in his diving gear to retrieve the lines and the airbag. In the meantime, we re-anchored *Lady L* close to its original position.

The radio came to life.

"*Lady L*, *Lady L*, this is King Salmon. Everything OK? We saw you moving around on the radar."

André replied, "King Salmon, we are fine. The anchor let go, and we picked it up and reset it."

Which was true, more or less.

Darya and Deena served a hearty lunch. Cindy came in to join us. I noticed her arm was no longer in a sling.

"When did you stop using the sling?"

She grinned, "Two days ago. I'm surprised you noticed so soon."

Oh.

We talked about what we found so far. It wasn't of great value. The coins might be worth something, but they were not in mint condition.

After lunch, we all—Cindy included—started to go through the contents of the safe systematically.

Levi showed us how to separate a sheaf of papers underwater, then hang them to dry. We were looking for anything which could identify the ship, her purpose, and what cargo she carried.

I opened the second wooden box, which proved to be a brass sextant of British manufacture. After I cleaned it up a bit, I found the date "1842" engraved on it, along with the name "V. Sutherland." The maker was "Brown and Son of Southampton." It was far from working condition.

So the earliest possible date for the wreck would be the 1840s. As the others sorted through the papers, additional, later times emerged. Deena found the ship's registry. She was the *Elspeth,* a schooner of 120 tons, launched in Hong Kong in 1868. There was a crew list as well. The captain was Victor Sutherland, and there were 11 crew members in all. It seems she was a trading ship, not a passenger ship. The latest date we found on any document was October 1891. Cargo manifests showed spices and tobacco from Indonesia, ceramics from China, and bricks and machinery from San Francisco.

I said, "Looks like Lorne Greene was after the wrong ship. This one is from before the gold rush. No treasure."

André said, "The last ship's log and manifest would have been in the Captain's cabin. We won't find it."

One more leather pouch had a few American coins, again in poor condition. We gave up the search for treasure.

Outside, the fog had lifted, and the sun was peeking through the clouds. We needed a plan to move on. The disappointment onboard *Lady L* was palpable.

I said, "Let's call off the guards. That's the best way to send a message that we haven't found anything. If we announce it, nobody will believe us anyway."

André said, "What will we tell them?"

"Just that their services won't be needed anymore. I'll take the Whaler over and pay them what we owe."

"What's our next move?"

"Before we head south, I want to mount an expedition on land to find the cave, and the box Jakob spoke about. He was right about the safe, even if there is no treasure, so I trust his story."

This seemed to cheer up the crew. We still had hope for something to make the trip worthwhile.

Cindy and Deena were not in the saloon. I found them on the fantail, lounging in deck chairs, enjoying the weak Alaska sunshine filtering through the mist. I told them about the plan.

"We're going to hike inland to find the cave and the box Jakob hid. Maybe there is something of value there, maybe not. At least we'll clear up the mystery."

Cindy said, "Did you forget about my floatplane?"

"No, but it's still too foggy for them to land here. Maybe tomorrow."

She didn't reply, just laid back and pulled her hat down over her face.

Charlie and I got in the Whaler to visit the guard boats. I took enough cash with me to pay them off.

The two crews were glad to be going home. Although it paid well, guarding the entrance to Thomas Bay had proved boring and uneventful for them. Within minutes their engines were running, and we could hear anchor chains rumbling in as they got going.

Once we got back, I spent the afternoon in Jock's workshop with Charlie and Levi, organizing our supplies for the expedition ashore the next day. We packed spare clothes, and Darya would make us sandwiches and cookies. We also chose a few tools to take, including a machete, pliers, a hammer and chisel, and a small pry bar.

Charlie said, "What about weapons? There could be bears or cougars."

I said, "Probably, but three of us crashing through the bush will likely scare them off."

Levi said, "Grizzlies don't scare that easily. I'll bring a pistol, and that pretty shotgun."

I think he meant Purdey.

By late afternoon we were organized. Levi helped Darya make dinner, and I went to find Cindy. She and Deena were in the saloon playing cards. I sat down with them.

I said, "Cindy, I expect we'll be done here by tomorrow night, and we can head home. Are you sure you want to take a plane? It won't take more than a week to get back to Vancouver in *Lady L.*"

"I'll think about it and let you know in the morning."

She smiled at me, but it wasn't the warmest smile. I should have paid more attention, but my thoughts were focused on the adventure ahead.

That night at about two, I woke up to the sound of…nothing. It was eerily silent. It took a moment to realize that the constant hum of the generator had stopped. I was sure Jock would take care of it, but I got up and dressed anyway.

When I got down to the engine room, I found Jock and André there already. Levi was right behind me.

Jock was peering at the clear filter bowl of the generator.

André said, "What happened?"

Jock said, "I dinna ken. Usually, the only thing that stops a diesel is a fuel problem, and there's clean fuel in the filter. I'll try to start it."

After checking a few more things, he hit the starter switch—not even a click.

"Dead battery. But that wouldn't make the motor stop."

There was a crash from above. Before I could move, Levi leaped to the stairs and disappeared. I was close behind.

I went out the pilothouse door on the starboard side just after Levi went out on port. I looked up and down the side deck but saw nothing. Levi came back in with a shrug.

"There is nothing out there."

As he spoke, we heard the unmistakable sound of footsteps running along the roof above our heads. Levi ran up the stairs to the top deck with me just behind. This time we searched the entire cabin top, including the dinghies and storage lockers, but found nothing.

Levi said, "I'll get a flashlight so we can look for footprints. You stay here and keep a lookout."

I did as he said, but there were no more sounds. When he came back with the light, we found some footprints in the dew. Our own. Nothing else.

We went below and talked about it. Nobody had a good idea of what had been on deck. We thought it could have been a crew member, but whom? Soon we gave up and went back to bed. The generator would not be needed until breakfast time. The rest of the night was still as death.

CHAPTER 41 – DOUBLE HAPPINESS

The ship's bell rang at 5 AM. I turned over groggily in my berth. The generator was running, and I could hear pots banging in the galley. It had to be André. Darya was much quieter.

I got dressed and went to the galley. All the men were there, but the three women were still in bed. Jock saw me come in.

"Sean, you won't believe it. The genny started right up this morning, the battery was fine, no fuel problem. I dinna ken what stopped it, but it must have been a wee seagoing Dunnie."

Since I had no idea what a "Dunnie" was, and didn't much care, I nodded, grabbed a coffee, and sat in the corner with Charlie.

The plan was to have André ferry Levi, Charlie, and me to shore in the Whaler, where we would unload our gear and head inland. I had made a crude map based on our earlier attempt. This time we were ready for bushwhacking. When we came back, we would blow a handheld air-horn three times as a signal that André was to fetch us from shore.

André was a passable cook, and he served us a mess of eggs, bacon, fried potatoes, and onions. We were well fortified for adventure. Darya was up by then and made sandwiches for lunch with bread she had baked the day before. We packed our gear and went up on deck.

The first thing I noticed was a large fir tree which had fallen in the night. It stretched from the shore to close by the starboard side of *Lady L.* The topmost branch had broken off and was hooked on our railing. The tree had to be over 100 feet tall, as we were at least 80 feet from shore. The roots were jutting skyward. What caused it to fall was a mystery. The night had been calm.

Levi said, "That explains the bump in the night."

Charlie said, "How about the footsteps? I suppose a creature of some sort could have run along the tree and jumped aboard then returned the same way."

We discussed this for a bit. The general opinion was that it would have to have been someone or something very agile. Not a bear. Suggestions included otter, raccoon, and to my mind, most likely, a cougar.

André promised to move the boat away from the tree while we were gone. We gathered our gear and got in the Whaler. André dropped us on the rocky beach. We examined the tree, but there was nothing to indicate why it fell, except that the roots were relatively shallow. The soil was thin on that rocky shore.

We started off our trek along the same path we had followed before and soon reached the spot where Charlie and I had turned around the last time. This time there were no odd noises. Levi found a thinner area in the bush, and we began cutting branches to clear a path. After about thirty minutes, we were among such giant evergreens that little light reached the forest floor, and the underbrush was thin.

With Levi leading, we made rapid progress up a gradual incline. The forest was tranquil, with no bird or animal noises, only the soughing of a gentle breeze in the treetops. The silence seemed to affect our small team, and there was no conversation.

We crested a rise and came upon a small clearing, where mossy boulders were scattered, as though thrown there from afar. Several were just the right height to sit on, and the moss provided a perfect cushion.

Charlie said, "Fate seems to have ordained a lunch stop."

We were ready. The lunch pack contained six sandwiches on thickly sliced whole-wheat bread, a thermos of coffee, and three tin cups. Half the sandwiches had sliced ham with Cheddar, and the other half contained smoked salmon with havarti and dill pickles. I laid it all out on a convenient rock, and we each took a sandwich and filled a cup.

While we were eating, I noticed Levi scrutinizing our surroundings. He pointed to a large flat rock just north of us.

"I wonder what's behind that?"

He gestured with his sandwich. I stood up and walked around it. The rock was more or less oval, about twelve by eight feet. On the far side, it was undercut, creating a cave-like recess, but only a foot or so high. A man could just fit in there lying down.

I said, "This looks a lot like Jakob's description of where he left the box. Let's finish eating then investigate."

Charlie came around and nodded his head while chewing. We went back to our rocks to finish lunch.

There was a sack of fresh cookies, and we had one each for dessert.

After lunch, Levi opened his pack and extracted a small folding shovel.

"Israeli army issue bivouac shovel," he said.

The recess was dark, so I got out my flashlight. The ground in there was sandy with sparse vegetation. There was a very slight rise just left of center, with a few fist-sized rocks on top. I pointed it out to Levi, and he started digging there.

Twice he hit something hard, but both times it was a stone. On a third attempt, he hit something that sounded different from the clang of the first two objects. He started digging with his hands and soon unearthed a wooden box in a disintegrating leather pouch.

Charlie yelled, "We found it!"

Levi hauled himself to his feet. The box was covered in dirt. It was about the size of a shoebox but shallower.

Levi set the box gently on top of the rock and cleared away the remnants of the leather bag.

He reached into his pack and brought out a small bristle brush and a bottle of water. With careful strokes, he cleaned the box. It was sandalwood, carved on the top in an oriental pattern. A Chinese character was inscribed in a circle at the center. The corners were reinforced with tarnished brass. A brass catch was held closed by a bit of wood through a loop.

I pointed at the character on top. It was one of about three Chinese ideographs Cindy had taught me.

"Double Happiness."

As the words came out of my mouth, a long, very loud, groaning, moaning sound welled up from somewhere nearby. We all turned in that direction, eastward from our position.

Levi said, "What the hell is that? It sounds like a wounded dinosaur."

Charlie said, "That's the sound we heard last time, just before we turned back."

Levi put the box in his pack and stood up.

"Let's go find it."

He gathered up his gear and strode off rapidly in the direction of the moans. A couple of hundred yards east, we came to a very steep hill, almost a cliff. At the base, there were a few broken rocks that had fallen from above. No cave was in evidence. Levi started walking north along the hill, and we followed.

After about thirty paces, the sound came again, much louder and seemingly right behind us. The hair stood up on the back of my neck, and a shiver ran down my spine. Levi turned and took the shotgun out of its case. He broke it and inserted two shells.

"Just in case," he said. His voice was hardly above a whisper. We turned and walked along the wall in the direction of the sound. I was leading because I had been at the back, but I didn't want the guy with the shotgun behind me. I motioned Levi past, and he took the lead.

In a short distance, we came to an opening in the wall. It was behind some bushes, and if we hadn't been following the wall, we would have walked right past. The entrance was crouching height. Levi switched on his flashlight. As he knelt to look inside, the sound of a large animal sighing poured from the hole. It wasn't loud, but it was as if the poor creature had the entire weight of the Universe on tired shoulders.

Charlie and I instinctively stepped back. Levi held his ground and looked inward. In a few seconds, he stood up and handed me the light.

"Take a look, Sean."

I took the light and crawled a little way into the cave. There was an area about ten feet square in which someone could stand, and then the roof gradually dropped until it was no more than snake height. It looked completely empty. As I was beginning to back out, the moaning sound started again, with thunderous force. I could feel a large volume of air rushing into the cave. I stood up with such force that I banged my head hard on the overhang. A whole constellation of stars circled my head as I pitched forward on my face.

The monstrous sound lasted for several seconds, and then a gentle rush of warmer air came out of the cave mouth. I got up on my knees just as Levi was grabbing my feet to pull me out.

"I saw the creature!"

Charlie looked startled. There was a wry grin on Levi's face.

Charlie said, "What is it?"

"I can say without a doubt that it's an Aeolian Ventrilomax."

Charlie stared at me with skepticism. Behind him, Levi was stifling a laugh.

Charlie said, "Never heard of it."

As the words were coming out of his mouth, his eyes opened wide with comprehension. Charlie was an Engineer, so naturally, he lacked my Classical Greek education (which I got from a book by Joseph Campbell), but he did understand physics.

"So there is a vent in the cave, probably leading to the top of the cliff. When the wind blows strongly over the exit, the column of air vibrates just like blowing over a Coke bottle."

I said, "Got it in one. When the wind is gentler, you get the sighing sound we heard. The vent is probably oddly shaped with varying diameter, setting up sub-harmonics that account for the animal sound."

Moments later, another great sigh came from the mouth of the cave. Even though I knew what it was, it still sent a shiver down my spine.

Levi said, "That mystery is solved. It might also explain the lack of birds and small animals around here. Who would want to live next to that?"

Charlie looked at me.

"Sean, you're bleeding!"

I touched my forehead. It was wet, and my hand came away red with blood. I must have cut myself when I stood up in the cave. I suddenly felt faint and sat down on the ground.

Levi opened his pack and brought out a small first aid kit and the same bottle of water he used for cleaning the box. He washed off the blood and wrapped a bandage around my head above the eyes.

"That should stop the bleeding. You'll have a scar, but that thick hair of yours will hide it."

Charlie said, "We should start back. It's getting late."

Levi nodded agreement.

"We can open the box aboard *Lady L.* There may be delicate contents, and I have the proper equipment there."

They helped me to my feet, and Charlie produced a flask of terrible brandy which revived me, coughing and spitting.

Levi unloaded the shotgun and put it away in its carrier. We started down the hill, more or less retracing our steps. It seemed slow, but in a couple of hours, we were back at Thomas Bay.

As we emerged from the bush, the late afternoon sun reflected off the water into our eyes. The glare made it hard to see. I shielded my eyes with a hand, but there was no sign of the big yacht. *Lady L* was missing.

CHAPTER 42 –VANISHED LADY

We walked along the shore, looking for signs of what happened. The fallen tree identified the spot where *Lady L* had been moored. There were no signs of a struggle, and the rocky beach didn't reveal any clues.

I said, "The stern line is gone. If the ship was under attack, the crew would have untied or cut it and left it here. That tells me they left deliberately."

Charlie replied, "Maybe they were hijacked, and the ship was taken over. The hijackers didn't want to leave evidence."

"Could be. But who would the hijackers be?"

We searched further, but the sun was going behind the hills, and it was getting cold. We were not equipped to stay overnight in the wilderness. I took out the air horn and blew three long blasts. The sound echoed off the surrounding hills in a syncopated pattern.

We waited five minutes for a reply, then blew the horn again. I expected an answering blast from *Lady L*'s powerful fog-horn. Nothing.

Levi said, "We better make camp. Remember the hiker's cabin? We can bunk down there."

The cabin was only a couple of hundred yards away, and we were soon unloading our meager supplies. A few cookies represented our remaining food. We had two more bottles of water, and there were several streams nearby. Immediate survival would not be an issue.

The cabin held four bunks, hardly more than slatted wooden shelves. There were no mattresses, but the slats had a little give. Levi cut some dry kindling with the machete, and Charlie found some split wood piled behind the building.

I started a fire by piling some kindling in the stove. There was a box of matches in the cabin, but they were soggy and old and wouldn't light.

Levi produced a book of matches. It was black with red lettering that said "Zelda's Midnight Café, Marrakesh." I didn't ask.

Soon we had a cozy fire going, and the cabin warmed up. There were no windows, but we left the door ajar to let in some light. Levi went out foraging and came back with a bag full of blackberries, cloudberries, and what he called "beach greens."

"I didn't see any animals, so tonight we're vegetarian," Levi said.

There was a cast-iron frying pan under the stove, and we used that as a salad bowl, eating with our fingers. It was surprisingly delicious. We saved the cookies for later.

Charlie produced his flask again, and we each had a shot of brandy. It tasted better this time. Then we lay on the bunks swapping tales and speculating on the fate of *Lady L.*

I was worried about Cindy. Deena and Darya too, but mainly Cindy. André was a resourceful guy, but he wasn't an impressive physical specimen. Jock was older and out of shape. If attacked, I imagined they would surrender without a fight. There wasn't anything we could do until morning.

We each went into the woods and took care of business, then settled in for the night. It was getting cold, and Levi closed the door. He shone his flashlight until we were all in bed. We used our packs as pillows and settled into the uncomfortable bunks. With the light out, there was still a faint glow from the grill of the stove. I fell asleep almost immediately.

CHAPTER 43 – THINGS THAT GO BUMP

I was at the helm of Lady L. Ahead was a broad channel leading southward. My right hand was on the spoked wheel. My left arm was wrapped around Cindy's shoulder as she stood at my side. Suddenly she jerked away from me and pointed ahead.

She cried out, "Sean, Sean, wake up!"

Ahead there were breakers, and jagged rocks pierced the surface. I spun the wheel to starboard and rang for full reverse. The ship didn't turn, and the engine continued its forward thrust. Then we hit the rocks with a loud but muffled crash. Again I heard Cindy cry out in a deep, hoarse voice.

My eyes snapped open. It was Charlie shaking me.

Levi was by the door. A thump on the roof shook the entire cabin. We could hear large animals or people running around the tiny shack. There were voices too, but I couldn't tell if they were human or animal. Levi opened the door a crack, looked out, and closed it quickly.

"Get down!" he yelled. Charlie and I fell to the floor. Levi pulled a pistol from his pack and, without hesitation, began firing through the walls. He fired until the gun was empty, then reached for another clip. By the time it was loaded, silence reigned.

"Levi! What the hell was that about?"

I was pissed off. My ears were ringing from the loud gunshots. There were bullet holes in the thin plank walls, and a dim light penetrated from beyond.

"Sorry. I looked outside and saw these dark shapes jumping and running. I panicked and fired."

His voice sounded shaken and sheepish. He was embarrassed. I had never before seen him show the slightest sign of fear.

Charlie said, "What did you see?"

"I don't know. I didn't make out individuals, just a swirl of shapes and shadows."

The gunfire seemed to have frightened off whatever was out there. After a while, we all went back to bed. I slept soundly until a narrow beam of sunlight from one of the bullet holes played across my face. I looked at my watch. It was almost eight o'clock.

I got up and went outside. Levi and Charlie were beginning to stir. It was a glorious morning, chilly, with a clear blue sky and steam rising off the wet rocks on the beach. A low mist obscured the far shore, but the tall hills behind were crisply outlined by the sun. I was desperate for a coffee, but we had none.

The forest was quiet, and the fears of the night seemed distant. I heard the far off sound of an outboard motor. I went back inside to get the airhorn. Charlie and Levi were awake and gathering up their packs.

I said, "I heard a motor. I'm going to blow the air horn again."

I ran down to the beach. There was no need to blow the horn because André was heading toward me in the Whaler. I was glad to see him but also annoyed.

As I took the bow line he tossed, I yelled, "Where the hell did you go!"

His answer was mild. "Hi Sean, I have coffee and breakfast for you. I'll explain once we get you fed."

I dragged the dinghy to the beach and secured it to a tree. Then we unloaded a full picnic hamper.

Charlie and Levi came down, and we laid out breakfast on a flat rock. There was steaming coffee from a thermos, scrambled eggs and bacon wrapped in foil, and fresh-baked croissants, still warm from the oven. Tin cups, cutlery, and enamel plates were provided.

As we ate, André told us what happened.

"After you left, we untied the stern line and raised the anchor. We moved out into the bay to anchor away from the tree. When Jock went to lower the anchor, the power winch seized. The second anchor has a hand winch, but it hasn't been used in years. Jock couldn't move it."

"I was faced with going back to Petersburg where we could tie to a dock, or find some other way to moor. I didn't want to leave you assholes here alone, so we explored the bay until we found a bight where we could tie between the trees on adjacent points. It took ages to do, and by the time we were successfully tied up, it was nearly dusk. I came over here in the Whaler, but I couldn't see any trace of you. I figured you were still up the mountain. I left you a note on the fallen tree."

I told him we didn't find any note. He showed me where he left it tacked to the tree. The empty tack was there.

I said, "I blew the air horn several times last night. Didn't you hear it?"

André looked puzzled. "No. Maybe the engine sounds drowned it out. We blew the ship's horn this morning at seven. Did you hear that?"

Charlie said, "When Sean is sleeping, he wouldn't hear a cannon if it went off beside him. But I was awake then, and I didn't hear anything."

It was pointless continuing the discussion. Everybody was safe. I said, "Let's get back to the ship. When we are all together, we can tell you about our expedition."

We finished off our coffee and piled into the Whaler. The trip back to *Lady L* was longer than I expected, almost two miles. Considering the topography of the bay, it wasn't surprising we couldn't hear each other. We should have bought a set of CB walkie-talkies. Hindsight.

As we rounded a point, *Lady L* came into view. The ship was in a small cove, tied to trees with a spider web of lines. I marveled aloud at André's ability to fit her in such a tight space without running aground. He blushed.

"Um, we might have touched once or twice. I waited outside for low tide so we could see the rocks."

I blew a single blast on the air horn, and by the time we were alongside, Cindy, Darya, and Deena were on the back deck. Jock came out of the wheelhouse and down the side to take our lines.

Cindy was beaming as I came aboard and gave me a two-arm hug, with only a slight wince. There were a lot of questions and a few disorganized answers.

Finally, we all sat in the saloon, and I related the detailed story of our adventures in the cave, the Aeolian Ventrilomax, and the Chinese box we found. Levi held it up theatrically.

Then I told the story of our night in the cabin, with sound effects. When I came to the gunshots, I looked at Levi. He gave a single shake of his head, and I took his meaning. That part of the story remained untold.

Cindy was on the edge of her seat. "Don't keep us in suspense. What's in the Double Happiness box?"

CHAPTER 44 – INSIDE THE BOX

Levi got up and took a shopping bag from the pantry. He took out a white cloth and spread it on the saloon table. Then he laid out his tools like a doctor preparing for surgery. Tweezers, scissors, Q-tips, and tissues. There was even a scalpel.

We all sat around the table as Levi gingerly opened the box. The lid was tight, and he worked around the edges with the blade.

He said, "It's ready to open now."

I don't know what we were expecting. At best treasure, maybe jade or gold. At worst, papers and photographs. Not even close.

We all stood to get a better view when Levi lifted the lid. Deena sat down with a gasp. Darya put her left hand over her mouth and stepped back. Cindy leaned over to take a good look. Charlie was impassive. André and Jock looked amused. I leaned in like Cindy.

The box contained a human hand, cleanly severed at the wrist. It was desiccated, but paper-like skin clung to the bones. It was a right hand, and there was a gold signet ring with three Chinese characters in relief on a square plinth. There were some scraps of rotten cloth in the bottom of the box, suggesting it had once been wrapped.

Levi looked surprised.

"Not what I expected at all. We better preserve it carefully. It might mean something to an expert."

Cindy said, "I know what it means."

She didn't sound happy.

I said, "Well, don't leave us hanging. What does it mean?"

She hesitated a moment, then said something in Chinese. Then she continued in English.

"My father told me about this. In some religions, the right hand of a thief was cut off as a punishment. The criminal would be allowed to keep the hand. Some believed they needed to have the severed limb with them when they died. Then they could be made whole again in the afterlife."

A general murmur arose as we tried to make sense of this. Cindy held up her hand for silence.

"There's more!"

We hushed up.

"The person would have a wu—a shaman or sorcerer—place a curse on the hand so that anyone who disturbs it or separates it from its owner would be punished."

I laughed. I didn't believe in spirits or ghosts or supernatural punishment. Cindy looked daggers at me. Only Darya looked concerned.

"Dere is sumpin' like dat in Obeah too."

Her Bajan heritage was suddenly evident. Nobody asked her to explain.

Charlie said, "Jakob felt tremendous fear when he started to open the box. Maybe that was the curse working. He died on *Princess Sophia* soon afterward."

Levi said, "More likely, he caught a glimpse, or maybe a sniff of the contents, and that's what scared him."

I agreed with Levi, silently this time.

Cindy turned to Levi and spoke in a scornful voice.

"You think what happened last night outside the cabin was just coincidence? Just some of the local wildlife having a party?"

André said, "Don't forget Kushtaka and Bigfoot!"

Jock added, "And wee dunnies!"

The mood was broken, and Cindy was laughing with the rest of us. Only Darya still looked somber.

Levi wrinkled his nose and closed the box. Deena found him a plastic bag to wrap it in, and he put it in the back of the fridge.

Charlie offered to help Jock repair the anchor windlass, and they left. André and I sat in a corner to plan our next move. Cindy came over and joined us while Deena and Darya made lunch.

Cindy said, "I've changed my mind about flying home. This is too interesting. I don't want to miss out."

I had forgotten about calling an air taxi. Standing up and hugging her gently, I said, "I'm so glad you're staying!"

André said, "There is no more reason to stay in Thomas Bay. I guess we should start for home tomorrow."

I said, "Agreed, but let me radio Bryce tonight and bring him up to speed. We haven't talked for a few days."

We discussed possible routes to Vancouver. I suggested we bypass Petersburg in case any of Lorngren's henchmen were still around.

"If we went directly from here, we could stop at Wrangell for fuel then proceed directly to Prince Rupert to clear customs."

André shook his head.

"We don't need to stop for fuel. We have enough fuel and water to go all the way to Vancouver if need be."

"In that case, let's go straight to Prince Rupert. If we run at night, we'll be in Canada before anyone notices."

"Okay, I'll check the tides. I would rather leave here at high slack, so we have plenty of water."

André went to the wheelhouse. I went to my room to shower and change. While I was rinsing off, Cindy slipped into the shower with me. Life was good again.

In a short while we returned to the saloon.

Soon lunch was on the table. Jock and Charlie came in after washing the grease off their hands.

"We found the problem with the windlass. The gears were jammed with a nest of long black hair."

Everybody turned toward Cindy, who grinned and gave her long black ponytail a flip. She did shed a lot of hair.

Deena said, "That's right. I sweep up the hair off the floor every day and go up on deck to stuff it in the windlass. What is a 'windlass' anyhow?"

We all laughed. It was the first time I noticed Deena making a joke.

Jock said, "I don't think it's hair. Charlie is teasing. It looks like strands of black rope, maybe from a net. Once we cut it all free and put the covers back on it, the windlass will be good as new."

Charlie said, "After lunch, that is."

We all sat down, and Darya served us tuna salad sandwiches on fresh-baked bread along with a thick vegetable soup.

"Soup's from a can, but I added a few things."

It was excellent, as usual. André said, "For a lawyer, you're a fantastic cook."

After lunch, Levi helped Darya clean up. She was back to her usual smiley self, and the Bajan accent was subdued. The afternoon passed quickly. I scrubbed decks while Cindy napped. She still wasn't up to full strength.

Deena came outside and spoke to me while I worked.

"Sean, I don't think Cindy needs me anymore. Can you pay me off and drop me back in Petersburg when you leave?"

I told her we planned to go straight to Prince Rupert but would pay her airfare back to Petersburg. She accepted that gracefully.

Charlie and Jock got the windlass working, and André suggested we move the ship into deeper water. After that, we could readily leave at any state of the tide.

Using the Whaler as a tug, Charlie and I untied the lines and gently pushed the big yacht out of the cove where Jock started the engine. *Lady L* motored back to near where we had anchored before, but far enough from shore that a stern line wasn't needed. Once we were all back on board, Darya started making dinner.

I wrote an account of our land adventures to read to Brice. When I finished, I realized that I hadn't investigated the scene around the cabin. We were so eager to get back to *Lady L* that I forgot all about it. Some detective. I determined to revisit the scene after dinner.

Darya made a traditional British Sunday dinner with roast beef, Yorkshire pudding, and side dishes of scalloped potatoes and mushy peas. It was just like my Granny used to make. André found a couple of bottles of Château Margaux and uncorked them.

Jock said, "Darya, this is fantastic. Please pass the peas."

Charlie proposed a toast, "To a great adventure almost over, and a safe trip home."

We all clinked our glasses and drank up, except Cindy, who just took a sip. I limited myself to one glass so as not to interfere with my mission.

After supper, I announced my attention to go back and look for clues to what transpired at the cabin.

"Does anybody care to join me?"

Nobody jumped forward. After a few moments of silence, Cindy said, "I'll go with you, Sean."

We got in the Whaler with Charlie handling the lines. I insisted that Cindy wear a life jacket. On the short ride to shore, I showed her how to run the boat. She caught on quickly, and I let her beach it. I had to tip up the motor for her. Her injured shoulder was still a bit sore.

We tied the painter and walked up the beach. It was still bright, but the sun was about to dip behind the hills across Thomas Bay. In the quiet evening, the water was almost glassy, throwing dappled reflections on the cabin walls.

The forest behind the cabin was forbidding with the long branches of giant fir trees overhanging it.

Cindy said, "Maybe if a wind came up in the night, those branches might have hit the roof and made the noises you heard."

I was dubious.

"Perhaps, but there were voices too, and what sounded like running feet."

Cindy stopped short,

"Sean, are those bullet holes in the side of the cabin?"

I had no choice but to tell her how they got there. She smiled and cocked her head.

"So Levi panicked and shot off all his bullets at whatever was outside? I thought he was Mr. Fearless."

I said, "So did I. And he certainly stepped up at the cave. I'm considering it a one-off. He was embarrassed, I'm sure he won't do anything like that again."

We looked around the cabin carefully, but the only tracks we saw seemed to be from our crew's seaboots. There was no blood, so either Levi missed, or there was nothing there to hit. There was some otter poop nearby, easily identified by the crab shells it contained. Cindy spotted a tuft of brown fur on one of the low branches.

I said, "It could be from a bear or even a wolf. I don't know if there are any wolves around here."

"Don't they howl at the moon? I haven't heard anything like that."

As I was about to answer, the low moan of the Ventrilomax rose in the distance. Cindy moved closer to me.

"That's our friend in the cave. Nothing to fear."

"It's a scary sound, but not so much when you know what causes it,"

We walked around some more, then sat on a log to enjoy the sunset. A few small clouds drifted above the dark hills opposite with their undersides painted a golden orange. A light breeze rippled the water, and off in the distance, we could hear the hum of *Lady L*'s generator. Cindy rested her head on my shoulder.

She said, "Sean, what do you think is going on here? The safe is a dud, we have a box with the hand of a long-dead castaway, and Lorngren shot me over that? It doesn't add up. There has to be something else he was after."

I thought about that.

"If you're right, then we might expect him to try again. He's a wanted man in Alaska, but maybe not back in Canada. I'll ask Brice about it tonight."

As the light wained, we motored slowly back to *Lady L.* A card game was in progress, so we nodded at the crew to let them know we were back safely. I went to Cindy's cabin with her, but I didn't linger. I moved up to the radio room and prepared some notes for my call with Brice.

The radio worked well, and we had a fairly lengthy conversation. I brought Brice up to date and told him what to relay to Lizzie. I figured the severed hand would give her something to chew on. Not literally.

A long time before, probably as much as five days, I had asked Brice to check out Lorngren. My friend wasn't a detective by any means, but he knew a lot of people on the waterfront and was good at getting information. What he told me that night changed everything.

CHAPTER 45 – BONANZA

Over breakfast the next morning, I told the crew about my radio conversation with Brice.

"The story Lorngren told us about his family running ships on the coast in the last century is pure bullshit.' A load of old codswallop', as my father would put it. His family emigrated to Canada in 1921 and moved west to Vancouver in 1927. They didn't own any ships, they ran a small trucking firm, which became a large firm during the war."

"He inherited the company, and according to Brice, is running it into the ground with a playboy lifestyle."

"Anyway, my conclusion is that he was after something already onboard the *Lady L.* Something Captain van Zant hid and didn't tell Lizzie about."

Jock looked embarrassed. He said, "I might know something about that. When I joined the crew, a couple of old-timers told me to keep my eyes open. Old Knobby Pearson, the ship's chandler, said when he demanded payment for an overdue bill, van Zant replied something like 'Time to raid Fort Knox.' That started the rumor that he had a stash of gold somewhere."

"I don't know how the rumor changed to say the stash was onboard the ship. Everybody in the crew had looked, but nobody found anything."

There were a few seconds of stunned silence, then André spoke.

"I never heard about this before. Maybe there is nothing to find. The secret compartment might have held the stash at one time, and van Zant could have used it all before he died."

Charlie said, "That's a reasonable explanation, but you have no evidence."

Cindy said, "You guys don't know anything about hiding things. I spent my whole life hiding things from my mother, including Sean! I bet I can find the treasure if it's there."

Deena and Darya jumped up and hugged Cindy.

"Right on, sister!" said Darya.

Levi had been looking thoughtful. He said, "You do realize anything you find belongs to Lizzie? As a member of the RCMP, I am duty-bound to make sure of that."

Cindy turned on him. She said, "Levi, you sure know how to dampen the mood. I'm talking about the thrill of the hunt. I don't care about the treasure."

I began to worry. Maybe Cindy didn't care about treasure, but others might. I feared greed might rear its ugly head, particularly if the booty was precious. I decided to take charge.

"Okay, let's give Cindy a chance. I'll stay with her, but she'll do the searching. If any heavy lifting is needed, I will help."

Darya protested, "I'm Lizzie's official representative here. I should be included."

I said, "You have a good point."

Levi interrupted, "As Her Majesty's representative, I must insist on being present."

That was hard to argue with, and I remembered that Levi was armed and much more dangerous than me. So we ended up with a team of four, Cindy leading.

"Before we start looking," she said, "I have a few questions. Sean, if you wanted to hide something heavy onboard a boat, where would be the most logical place?"

"In the bilge, under the engine."

"Okay, I can cross that off my list. Rule one of hiding things is never put them in the logical place. Sean, remember that cocktail dress I wore on our first date?"

I nodded. How could I forget? She was dazzling.

"I hid that dress from my mother, who wanted to keep me from dating. I hung it in her closet, inside one of my father's suits. She would never touch his clothes after he went to the nursing home. If I put it in my own room anywhere, she would have found it in one of her regular sweeps."

Darya said, "We have the right leader here!"

Levi said nothing, but a slight smile touched his lips.

She had more questions about the construction and maintenance of the boat. André and Jock answered most of those, but nothing new came to light.

Cindy said, "Alright, Sean, let's go."

She led the way aft and started climbing the ladder to the upper deck. We searched the dinghies, and all the gear stowed up there. Cindy tapped and poked and prodded but found nothing. Next, we went into the wheelhouse.

"Sean, who besides pirates would van Zant be hiding the booty from?"

"The captain and crew, and his wife. If Lizzie knew about it, there wouldn't be anything here."

"Okay, so following my principles, I would search the captain's cabin first. Darya, would you go ask André for his permission?"

In a few minutes, André cleaned out a few personal items and gave us the go-ahead to search. It took Cindy six minutes to find something.

"Sean, the corner post at the foot of the bunk is hollow. Lift the mattress."

Levi helped, and we lifted the mattress so she could see underneath. The bunk bottom was made of white painted grooved planks, screwed down with two screws at the end of each plank.

Cindy said, "Sean, please unscrew that plank for me."

I went to the toolroom for a screwdriver. By the time I got back, the plank was off. Levi held up a Swiss Army knife. The top of the post was painted white and looked normal. Cindy stabbed it with the screwdriver, then peeled back the top, which proved to be thin cardboard. Then she reached in and came up with a gold coin. She handed it to me.

"It's a British pound, dated 1918, with the head of George the fifth on it."

I knew nothing about coins. That information came from reading what was written on it.

In all, Cindy found fifty of the coins in the hollow post. We all looked them over. The dates ranged from 1917 to 1928. I made an observation.

"The newest coin dates from 1928, the year the boat was built. Maybe they were placed there during construction?"

Levi said, "Of course, that's a possibility, but these are collector coins. I have never seen one in circulation, even in the UK. It may be simply that newer ones are less valuable, or maybe they stopped minting them in 1928."

"What should we do now?"

"Let's take them to the saloon and show the others, then put them in the safe."

I went to the galley and got a canvas shopping bag, and placed the coins carefully in that. Then we went back to the saloon. I gathered André and Jock on the way. Charlie and Deena were already there.

I had planned to spread them on the table dramatically, but I thought that might damage the coins, so I gathered everyone around.

"Look what Cindy found in André's cabin!" I said as I opened the bag, and everyone had a good look.

André cried out, "Oh, no! You found my retirement fund."

Deena said, "Is that Canadian money?"

Cindy said, "No, these are British coins."

Charlie said, "Those are gold Sovereigns. My grandmother had one with Queen Victoria on it. It was in a frame over the mantlepiece."

I said, "André, does the ship have a safe?"

"There's a strongbox. I keep the ship's papers in it, along with my passport, and my spare watch."

"Is there room in it for this bag of coins?"

"Yes, but if I put them in there, I ought to lock it. I lost the key a while back. It doesn't have a combination lock."

In the end, we decided to put the coins back where we found them. Cindy and I went to do that. Once we were alone, Cindy spoke in a low voice.

"Sean, the second rule of hiding something is always giving them something to find. I would leave a tube of lipstick under my mattress, or a copy of Vogue inside my pillowcase, so Mom had something easy to find."

I replied, "My mother was afraid to search my room. There were too many gadgets with wires and glowing tubes, and she was afraid of being electrocuted."

"You're missing the point, as usual. I think the coins were the easy-to-find stuff, and the real treasure is still hidden. After this, let's continue the search without Levi and Darya."

"Are you planning to keep it for ourselves?"

"Don't be silly. If we get captured by pirates and tortured to find out where it is, the fewer people who know, the better."

"Cindy, if someone tortures you, I'll give up the treasure in a second."

"So give up the gold coins, dummy. The others will do the same because they think that *is* the treasure."

This girl was devious. I didn't know whether to be proud or frightened.

When we got back to the saloon, it was lunchtime, and Darya was laying out a buffet. After lunch, André suggested we all retire for a nap, as we would be leaving at dusk and running all night. Everybody retired to their rooms. I went with Cindy to the master stateroom, but we didn't sleep right away.

CHAPTER 46 – MORE IS LESS

Cindy woke me up about 2:30 PM. She started talking while my brain was still trying to focus.

"Sean, how tall are you?"

"…um, about five foot thirteen."

"Smartass. Okay, have you ever bumped your head on the ceiling onboard *Lady L*?"

"No. It has seven feet of headroom pretty much everywhere."

"Stand up. How much height is there above your head in here?"

I spread my palm above my head. With my thumb touching my hair, my little finger just brushed the overhead.

"It seems about six inches."

"Okay, step out into the hall and try the same thing."

I did. Deena screamed when she saw me and ducked into her cabin, slamming the door. I guess I should have put on my pants first. Anyway, there was quite a bit more headroom in the hallway, about four inches. I was awake by then, and I grasped what Cindy was driving at.

I said, "There might be a false ceiling in the master stateroom. Let me check my room."

I got dressed and went to check the headroom in my cabin. It was the same as in the hallway. I rejoined Cindy.

"You're right. The ceiling is at least four inches lower in here. Let's look for a way in."

The overhead was tongue and groove painted white, just like the rest of the ceilings. It was slightly cambered, following the line of the upper deck, which was curved for drainage. I tapped each of the planks, in turn, looking for a loose one, but found none. Opening the ceiling would require removing trim pieces which concealed the plank ends and removing hidden screws that were under wooden plugs, painted over. There was no sign that they had ever been disturbed since the boat was built.

"Cindy, I don't think that area is accessible from here."

While I was checking out the ceiling, Cindy was in the head looking for access from there. She didn't find anything. There was a wardrobe on the aft wall with drawers underneath. Cindy's limited clothes supply was in there. I stuck my head inside.

"The wardrobe goes full height. I'm too big to get in there, but I bet there is an access panel to the hollow ceiling. Can you give it a try?"

Cindy was just the right height to stand on the drawers with her head almost at the top. She tapped at the upper part of the wall. It sounded hollow.

"Bingo. There is a panel here held by only two screws, and they aren't plugged."

I fetched a screwdriver and handed it to Cindy. She opened the panel, which was about two feet long. I gave her a flashlight so she could examine the area.

"Sean, this is odd. There are ten small cleats just inside the opening. One of them has a thin rope cleated off. The rest are unused."

"Where does the rope lead?"

"I can't get my head in there to look, but it goes outboard where the roof is sloped."

"So, pull the rope. It will probably ring a bell in the engine room, and Jock will come running."

She laughed, a gentle sound that never failed to lift my spirits. I could hear something dragging in the ceiling as she pulled.

"The line is attached to a burlap sack. It's pretty heavy. I'll hand it out to you."

She used both hands to give me the sack, with the line still attached. It was long enough so I could lay the bag on the bed. Cindy climbed out of the closet while I untied the bag. *It contained two gold bars, weighing about ten pounds each.*

Cindy stifled an excited scream. "What would these be worth, Sean?"

In those days, I could do math in my head.

"Last time I heard, gold was about forty US dollars an ounce. So estimating each bar at 160 ounces gives a total value of 12,800 dollars for the pair."

Cindy said, "That doesn't seem enough for this to be called 'Fort Knox.' "

"If all of the ten cleats were tied to a bag with two gold bars, that'd be well over a hundred grand. A pretty tidy sum. Maybe van Zant used all the rest?"

Cindy cocked her head and looked at me skeptically.

"Or…maybe, this is another decoy. Let's put it back and continue the search."

She put the gold and the panel bank in place while I thought about all the parts of the ship that I had observed, looking for anomalies. I thought of one.

Cindy came out of the wardrobe.

"Sean, what do you do when you find what you are looking for?"

We said it in unison:

"You stop looking!"

Cindy grinned, "Let's not give up yet."

I told her about the odd thing I thought of.

"That doesn't sound so odd to me, but it would have to be subtle, not obvious, so let's check it out."

The corridor was empty. We padded shoeless down to the engine room, where I found the correct wrench and opened the secret compartment. In the room with the liquor shelves, I pointed out how sturdy they were.

I said, "Cases of whiskey are heavy, and those shelves can take the weight."

Cindy said, "What's your point? They look about right."

"They are. Let's go to the bunk room."

In the other room, I pointed out that the upper bunk was supported by massive six-by-six corner posts on all four corners. Ordinarily, a top bunk would have posts one third that size, and they would only be on the outer side, leaving the back edge of the berth supported by the wall.

I removed the mattresses from both bunks and examined the structure. Both berth tops had transverse planking about 4" wide, screwed down on the ends.

I removed the top drawer under the bottom bunk and looked inside. Light was visible between the planks.

That wasn't the case with the top bunk. The underside was a solid panel, with no screws visible. I rapped on it and hurt my knuckles. It was thick metal.

"Cindy, *this* must be 'Fort Knox'. Most people wouldn't think of hiding something heavy like gold in the upper bunk."

"Are you sure? Better open it up."

When the first plank came off, it revealed neat rows of gold bars.

I dropped the screwdriver, grabbed Cindy around the waist, and lifted her up for a kiss. I would have spun her around, but there wasn't space.

Cindy pulled her lips away and giggled triumphantly. "We found 'Fort Knox!' "

As I put her down, I said, "*You* found it, I'm just the helper."

I went back to work and removed one more plank.

I said, "If this is full, I calculate it would be about four cubic feet of gold. At 1200 pounds per cubic foot, that's 4800 pounds. No wonder the construction is so sturdy."

"What is that worth?"

"Somewhere around three million dollars."

Cindy was silent for a moment, probably trying to imagine such a vast sum. I put the bunk back together. While I was doing that, I re-evaluated my position.

As a leader, I felt responsible for the safety of the crew. Having a vast sum of money on the ship was a huge risk. André and Darya were also Lizzie's representatives, but I was in charge of the expedition. I confided in Cindy.

"We can't keep this a secret. I have to tell André and discuss our next move."

Cindy had sobered up after the initial euphoria of the big find. She nodded and added, "It's over a thousand miles back to Vancouver, and most of the trip is through remote areas. Isn't there somewhere nearby where we could deposit the gold in a bank?"

"Good point. I'll bring that up with André."

We finished up and went back to the master stateroom without seeing anyone else. I went to find André.

CHAPTER 47 – JUNEAU

I found André in the wheelhouse, plotting a course to Prince Rupert. He didn't look up when I came in, so I cleared my throat.

He turned my way and said, "Oh, Hi Sean. Do you want to look over tonight's route?"

"Not exactly, Cindy and I have found something that might change our plans. We found 'Fort Knox.'"

"Isn't it somewhere in Kentucky?"

André could never resist a joke, but his huge grin and dancing feet showed he got the message.

I detailed our findings, omitting my valuation. André could guess that himself. When I finished, he looked a bit stunned. After a few minutes, he turned to the chart drawer and rummaged for a different chart.

He said, "We need to change our destination. We better go to Juneau. It's the closest place likely to have a safe that can store the gold. Maybe we can have an armored car meet us at the dock?"

I agreed, but there was more to discuss.

"André, who onboard do you trust completely?"

H grinned, "Pretty much everybody except you."

I said, "Be serious now. Who do you not trust?"

"Levi. He's a cop. Darya. She's a lawyer. I do completely trust Charlie. He doesn't even cheat on his taxes!"

I thought of my trust list.

I said, "I trust you and Charlie. Cindy, of course. I have never seen any reason to distrust either Levi or Darya."

As I said it, I remembered catching Darya searching my cabin. Maybe she wasn't looking for condoms. I didn't mention it to André.

I continued, "I don't know Deena well enough to judge, but she's the most recent addition of to the crew. Could be a plant. But she did ask if she could go home."

André said, "Since we'll be going past Petersburg, might as well drop her off. Let's do that before we tell anyone else about Fort Knox."

"Even after that, do we need to tell everybody? Right now, Cindy is the only other person that knows."

"We need to explain the change of destination somehow. Why go over a hundred miles in the wrong direction?"

"I guess we'll need to tell everybody. Before we do that, I'll find a way to lock the secret compartment."

"Good idea. Let's go to dinner." André always remembered his stomach.

At dinner, I told everybody that we had decided to drop Deena at Petersburg but didn't mention going on to Juneau after that. Deena was happy, and as soon as she finished eating, she went to her room to pack.

While Darya cleaned up the kitchen with Levi's help and Ajax supervising, Jock and Charlie went forward with André to start raising the anchor. I went aft and made sure the Whaler was ready for towing. We didn't plan to tie up in Petersburg. I would run Deena ashore while *Lady L* stood by. Then we would start heading west from Petersburg, crossing Frederick Sound to head north after dark.

It was still light when we got underway. The water was glassy, and the sky clear, with just a few high clouds. I went below to figure out how to lock the door to Fort Knox. The solution I came up with was simple. The bolts on the hatch were real, just short of engaging the threads in the metal bulkhead. They were held in with glue, which broke loose when I applied a wrench to them. I removed them and replaced them with longer bolts from the spare parts drawer in the engine room. After tightening them hard, I took the socket wrench and several other tools to my cabin. I hid them under my mattress.

It wouldn't stop a determined thief, but it would slow them down.

I returned to the wheelhouse as we were approaching Petersburg. I wished we could tie up and go ashore, rather than run all night, but we were on a mission. André rang for engine stop, and as we coasted to a gradual halt, I went to the aft deck. Cindy and Darya said tearful goodbyes and hugged Deena. Then I put her bags in the dinghy and helped her aboard.

It was a smooth ride to the fishing dock where we had last moored. Nobody was around as I let Deena off. I gave her an envelope with her pay and a two-hundred-dollar bonus.

"Thank you, Sean. It was a new experience for me, and I appreciate the opportunity you gave me."

She hugged me and kissed me on the check. As we separated, she slipped me a piece of paper with her address and phone number. I assumed it was for Cindy, and put it in my pocket.

On my way back to *Lady L*, I noticed that *Teacher's Pet* was no longer at the repair yard. I didn't see her moored anywhere either. That gave me an uneasy feeling, and I returned at top speed.

Charlie and Levi helped me onboard. We used the deck crane to lift the Whaler up to the top deck. It was safer not to tow it if the weather got rough. We still had about a hundred and twenty miles to go.

We headed west from Petersburg for a couple of miles, as though heading for Wrangell Narrows, then crossed the sound and headed north, hugging the eastern side of Admiralty Island. André was steering. I convened a meeting in the saloon for the rest of the crew.

To Cindy, I said, "Deena gave me this."

I handed over the paper. She cocked her head and looked at me oddly. She said, "Deena already gave me this information."

Cindy made a pot of coffee while I explained to the crew what we had found. I didn't mention the two gold bars in her room.

"We found more gold hidden in the secret compartment."

Darya's eyes flashed with excitement. Levi sat back and put his hands behind his head. His face showed no surprise. I looked at Charlie. He was leaning forward with great interest. Darya stood up.

"Sean, how much are we talking?"

"I didn't tally it up, but it's a lot. Gold bullion. Obviously, it belongs to Lizzie, and we have to safeguard it. André suggested we head for Juneau tonight instead of Prince Rupert. There will be a bank there set up to deal with gold."

Darya put on her serious lawyer's face.

"As Lizzie's representative, I have her power of attorney. I'll open a bank account in her name and deposit the proceeds."

I nodded.

"That's what I was expecting. We can phone from the dock and get the bank to send an armored car. I'll call Brice on the radio tonight and let him know we have left Thomas Bay, but I won't tell him our new destination."

There wasn't much more to say. Darya wanted to see the gold, but I told her I had closed up the hiding place and did not plan to open it until we were safely in port.

I asked Levi and Charlie to come with me to the wheelhouse to discuss our route and apportion shifts to steer.

In the wheelhouse, Charlie asked me with a grin, "So Sean, how much are you keeping for yourself?"

I chuckled. "Only half!"

André and Levi joined in the laughter. It was a joke, but it gave me an idea.

Charlie looked at the radar screen.

"Kapitan André, what is that blip on the screen?"

André said, "I can't look now. I just saw a big log. They are hard to spot at night. Sean, take a look."

I looked at the screen. The blip was coming up behind us. It was on the same course and about five miles away.

"Guys, another boat is coming up behind us fast. I'd say he's no more than half an hour from catching up. We better prepare ourselves just in case."

André called Jock up from the engine room. When he arrived, we had a conversation about our defense.

André said, "Jock, can you bring out the fifty-caliber and set it up on the bow mount? Charlie can help you. Levi, can you arm yourself and Sean in case of boarders?"

I took the big binoculars from the rack and went back to the fantail. At five miles, I should be able to see the running lights of the other boat. I scanned the area behind us for lights but saw only the Point Hugh light on the south end of Admiralty Island. I went back to the wheelhouse.

"André, whoever is following us is running without lights."

André reached up to shut off our lights. I stopped him.

"Don't do that. It will tip them off."

He nodded. Levi came into the wheelhouse with the double-barreled Purdey shotgun and a folding rifle with a scope. He handed me the shotgun. The rifle looked very military. He unfolded it and removed the scope.

"It's too dark to use the scope. I'll need to be quite close to be sure of hitting anything."

I said, "Let's hope it doesn't come to that."

Charlie came in and said, "We have the deck gun set up, but we don't know how to operate it,"

Levi said, "I do. I'll show you."

Jock came back and went down to the engine room.

They went out, leaving me alone with André.

I said, "Well, aren't you glad Levi is here to help us?"

André gave a Gallic shrug, "Maybe."

I rechecked the radar.

"They're less than a mile behind us."

André said, "The machine gun is up forward. If they come up behind us, they can stay out of the line of fire."

He was right. I said, "Turn around now before they catch up and head straight for them. When we get close, turn on the big searchlight. It'll blind them."

André said, "Won't it give them a target to shoot at?"

"Yes. We'll have to identify the boat quickly. What if it's the Coast Guard?"

"Doubtful. If it is, they'd call us on Channel 16. And they wouldn't run without lights. Odds are that boat is hostile."

I agreed. André spun the wheel. By the time we were turned around, we could see the white trail of the other boat's wake. André flipped on the searchlight and adjusted the aim. It was an aluminum crewboat, about 30 feet long. The bright light showed two men in the wheelhouse and two more on the back deck. The two outside both had long guns. The name on the bow was covered with masking tape.

André grabbed a microphone and activated the loudhailer. He suddenly sounded very forceful and official.

"This is Captain LaPalme. Stop your engine now, and come out on deck with your hands up."

A shot rang out. It missed the light but hit the fog bell with a loud clang. Our machine-gun rattled out a short but loud burst over their heads. The guy at the wheel started to turn.

André hailed them again, "Stop your engine NOW, or we'll blow you out of the water!"

This time they stopped. André rang for dead slow, and we circled the now stationary crew boat.

A big guy in the cockpit yelled out, "You're CANADIANS! You shouldn't be armed!"

André said, "Sorry. We missed that memo. Now step out on the deck where we can see you and throw your weapons overboard!"

Reluctantly, the men complied, grumbling among themselves.

They didn't look like hardened thugs, just fishermen, probably drunk. I felt a little sorry for them. We continued circling them slowly.

André gave another order, "Open the engine box and pull off the spark plug wires, then throw them in the water."

The guy who had been steering opened the box. He shouted back, "How will we get home?"

André said, "Use the kicker!"

There was a ten horsepower outboard on the swim grid. It would get them home, but slowly. The skipper complied. Ajax flew out of the wheelhouse and landed on the bow rail. He squawked obscenities at the hapless goons as one of them tried to start the kicker.

André straightened us out and headed back to our course. He switched off the searchlight, rang for cruising speed, and we were heading for Juneau again. Ajax flew back inside and sat on the dashboard, rocking back and forth.

Levi and Charlie came back in.

André said, "Charlie, would you get a tarp from Jock and cover the machine gun? Now that it's out, I think we should leave it in case there is any more trouble."

Cindy and Darya came into the now crowded wheel house together. Charlie saw the angry look on Cindy's face and went out the opposite door.

Cindy yelled, "What the hell was that?"

André was nonplussed. He shrugged and said, "We had to repel a small attack."

Cindy said, "I recognized one of those guys. He's Deena's boyfriend! You could have killed him."

André said, "She must have told him about the gold coins."

I still had the shotgun in my hand. I left the room to put it away. Levi had already folded his rifle and put it in the carrying case.

Levi said, "Cindy, nobody was hurt. André handled it perfectly. Thank you, Skipper."

I heard that as I came back in.

"Good boy, Skipper." I reached out to pat André on the head, but the look on his face suggested it wasn't a good joke.

I took Cindy by the hand and apologized for not warning her and Darya about what was happening. Jock came up from the engine room with a bottle of rum, and we each had a small swig by way of celebration. Cindy and Darya went back to bed.

Ajax squawked, "What the hell was that?" then put his head under his wing and went to sleep.

Levi, Charlie, and I took turns to steer through the night. At each shift change, André came out of his cabin to verify that we were on course and check the radar. We passed a tug and barge combination heading south, but they stayed well clear.

I was at the helm when the sky began to lighten. We were still about fifty miles from Juneau. Cindy came in with a cup of coffee and two slices of toast for me. She took the helm while I ate. The weather was gray, and whitecaps marched past us from astern. The Alaska state ferry, *MV Malaspina*, passed us slowly an hour later. André took over since he alone knew how to con the ship into the harbor.

I radioed the port of Juneau to secure a berth. They put us at the commercial dock as *Lady L* was too big for the yacht harbor closer to town.

At about ten in the morning, Juneau came into view. The small city was dwarfed by the massive mountains behind it. We radioed the port, and they assigned us a place at the cruise ship dock. The port captain told us we could only stay one night as a ship was due the next day.

Once we were moored up, Darya went ashore to call the bank and arrange an armored car and taxi to get there. While she did that, I opened the secret compartment and removed the bunk top to expose the gold.

The armored car arrived in about fifteen minutes. I asked Darya which bank she chose.

"Wells Fargo. It's the closest."

I said, "Okay. We'll use a bucket brigade to unload the gold. It will be me, Jock, Charlie, André, and Levi in that order. We'll take two bars at a time."

Darya said, "What about me? I'm probably stronger than Jock."

I looked at her. She did have a trim, athletic build, which couldn't be said of Jock. I said, "Okay, you go between André and Levi. I want Levi at the armored car end for security reasons."

The truck had a crew of three. There was a driver, a guard, and a loader. The loader did all the work while the other two stood guard. They both wore sidearms, and the guard had a small machine gun.

It wasn't heavy work, because we only moved two gold bars at a time, each weighing about ten pounds. There was a lot of it, and it took a while to load the truck. We stopped several times to catch our collective breath and drink water, which Cindy distributed.

Once loading was complete, I closed up the bunk and put the mattress back. Then I went out and replaced the bolts in the door.

I had told Darya that I intended to go to the bank, but when I went out on deck, both the armored car and the taxi were gone.

I turned to André and asked, "Did anyone go to the bank with Darya?"

He shrugged.

"Just Levi."

Alarm bells started ringing in my head. I flew down the gangway and looked around for another taxi. There wasn't a vehicle in sight. I could see the downtown area less than a mile away, so I took off at a run. I was never a runner, despite being in reasonable shape. Flat feet and deck shoes worked against me. Before I got halfway, a cramp in my side forced me to rest for a minute, bent over with hands on my knees. After that, I proceeded at a slower, long stride jog.

It took me around ten minutes to get to the Wells Fargo bank. I burst through the door and demanded to see the manager. A small man with round spectacles, wearing a three-piece grey pinstripe suit, came out of his office.

"How can I help you, Mr…?"

"Gray, Sean Gray. Did an armored car full of gold bars just arrive here?"

He almost choked with laughter.

"No way! I'm quite sure I'd remember that."

"Are there other banks in town?"

"Several, at least four in the downtown area."

I called my thanks over my shoulder as I took off to find the next bank. I was twenty minutes later when I got to the final and furthest bank, First National. The armored car was outside with back doors open. Nobody was on guard, so I knew it was empty.

It took a couple more minutes to locate the manager, a lanky man with thinning grey hair parted in the middle. He looked old enough to have been there when *Princess Sophia* went down. I almost asked about it before I remembered my mission.

"Are the people who brought the gold bars still here? A tall slim black lady and a cop?"

He looked down his long thin nose at me.

"I can't discuss their business with you, but I know who you mean. They left in a taxi about ten minutes ago. Are you by any chance Mr. Sean Gray?"

I nodded.

"Miss Hubert left an envelope for you."

He handed me a plain white envelope with my name on it.

I ripped it open. It was a wedding invitation, written in a beautiful looping hand on plain paper.

Sean and Cindy Gray
are cordially invited to the wedding of
Darya Hubert and Levi Strauss
Time and place to be ascertained

A rock dropped into my stomach as I understood what had happened.

Darya had chosen the bank farthest from the dock on purpose, and she must have given all the information over the phone, so the bank was ready with the paperwork when she got there.

With a sinking heart, I asked the bank manager, "Do you buy gold?"

"Yes, certainly, and we have done since the 1890s."

I didn't need to ask any more questions. I knew Darya and Levi had exchanged the gold for a bank draft. There was no proof of a crime. I turned and left. As I started the long walk back to the *Lady L*, I heard the roar of an aircraft engine. A small blue plane lifted off the water and flew over the dock where *Lady L* was moored. The wings waggled as it went over the yacht heading south.

I continued on my way back to *Lady L*. When I got there, I told the remaining crew what had happened. Everybody was surprised and angry, except André, who smiled and shrugged.

Cindy came to me and put her hands on my shoulders. She looked up at me with her eyes bright. She said, "Sean, you stink. You need a shower."

I went off to clean myself up. Alone.

After that, I had no choice but to phone Lizzie with the news. I broke it to her as gently as I could. She asked if we still had the gold coins. I said yes, and told her about the two gold bars in the master stateroom.

We agreed it was time to head for home.

CHAPTER 48 – VANCOUVER

Five days later, we were steaming under the Lion's Gate bridge in brilliant sunshine.

The trip back was fast and spartan. There were no gourmet meals or shared bottles. Cindy kept us fed and watered, and the rest of just hunkered down and did our jobs. The mood started out gloomy, and there were few jokes.

We stopped only once, in an unnamed bay south of Namu, to get a night of proper sleep and service the engine. Over breakfast, I had my only chance to talk to the entire crew.

"Guys, there are two things I need to tell you. I trust you all, and I think it will lighten the mood if I tell you now."

I showed the wedding invitation around without comment.

André said, "'Levi Strauss?' That sounds familiar."

Charlie said, "It's printed on your ass."

He pointed to the label on André's jeans.

André said, "The jean company? You don't suppose he's related?"

Cindy exploded, "You dolt! It's a phony name! And I bet he was never a cop either."

André held his tongue.

I put my arm around Cindy's shoulder and said, "It isn't good politics to call our esteemed Captain LaPalme a dolt."

"I'm sorry, André," she said contritely.

"Apology accepted. Sean, what's the second thing?"

I told them.

From then on, good cheer returned, and the remaining miles went by quickly. We played music using the cassette player and tapes Levi left behind, and Cindy tried on some of Darya's elegant clothes. They didn't fit well, but she had fun anyway, appearing in the wheelhouse in a silver cocktail dress once, and in a pinstripe suit another time.

When we got near the Royal Van, André blew a long blast on the ship's horn, then executed a perfect landing. We all had to stay on board while André went ashore to call Canada Customs for clearance and then Lizzie to tell her we were home.

When André returned, he said the customs guy would be along shortly, and then we would be free to leave. Lizzie would be coming down to welcome us. Cindy volunteered to make a final dinner for us all.

After customs came and went without incident, Lizzie and her driver came down the dock, and we helped them aboard. Lizzie was dressed elegantly in a flowered dress and a white straw hat.

After the welcoming greetings were done, I asked Lizzie if I could talk to her privately. We went up to the wheelhouse. I sat in the Captain's swiveling seat, and she sat at the settee.

"Lizzie, I have some news that I didn't tell you on the phone, because I wasn't sure who might be listening. We did find hidden gold, and Darya and Levi took off exactly as I told you."

Lizzie interrupted to say, "That Darya! I *trusted* her. She better not send me a bill!"

I chuckled and continued.

"I handled the unloading in Juneau, but I only unloaded the top layer of gold bars. There were two more layers, and they are still there!"

Lizzie leaped up and put her arms around me, kissing me on the cheek. The smile on her face was something special. It made her look years younger. It was the face of the vivacious girl who captured Captain van Zant's heart.

I suggested we arrange for an armored car, as we had done in Juneau, but this time Lizzie herself would accompany the gold to the bank. Since it was still early, she used the ship's phone, which was now plugged in, to call the bank and make the arrangements.

By late afternoon, it was all done. Lizzie had enough money to last out her days. She presented each of us with a gold bar, and two for Cindy.

"Consider the extra one a wedding present. And Sean, thank you for leading the expedition. Can you file a detailed report for me along with your invoice? I would love to find out everything that happened."

I offered her the sandalwood box with the hand inside, but she declined to open it.

"Dispose of it as you see fit."

I had an idea about that.

CODA

After Lizzie left, Cindy and I packed our belongings and walked around the end of Coal Harbour to get to *Tangled Moon*. I expected her to be covered in bird droppings and green algae, but she looked better than when we left. I knew it had to be Brice and Eva at work. There is no way to adequately thank friends like that, but I aimed to try.

Cindy called her mother, and I called Brenda. She was fine. I promised to have a lawyer contact her about child support.

After the calls, we started moving into our little home. Cindy seemed to have forgotten all about leaving me and going to live with her mother. We spent an idyllic weekend, mostly in bed or eating in restaurants. Cindy was tired of boat cooking.

On Sunday night, we took Brice and Eva out to dinner at Hy's and filled them in on our adventures. Cindy acted out her retort to the jerk in the Prince Rupert bar, which almost got us ejected.

On Monday, I looked up Lorngren Trucking and called for an appointment to meet the villain at his office. I gave Brice's name, in case he recognized mine.

When I arrived, I walked in with a package under my arm. The blonde receptionist looked at me suspiciously but waved me into Lorngren's office. He was sitting behind a big mahogany desk, leaning back with his hands behind his head, smoking a cigar.

He jumped up when he recognized me.

"What the fuck do you want?"

I raised my palms and said, "Don't worry, I come in peace. Lizzie isn't going to press any charges. I just want to tell you what happened in Alaska after you left. But first, I have a few questions for you."

He looked relieved and sat back down. I noticed a vee-shaped scab on his nose where Ajax had bitten him.

"Ask away."

"I know the story you fed us about your family claim to the safe in Thomas Bay was bullshit. We found the safe, but there was nothing of value in it. What were you really after?"

He said, "I guess I can tell you now. Business was bad, and I was desperate to raise some cash. I got a big contract last week that has solved the problem."

"I knew Captain van Zant fairly well. We used to have a drink together once in a while at the Sylvia. Once, when he was quite drunk, he told me he had a case of expensive wine hidden away, Château Margaux 1787. That stuff is worth maybe twenty thousand dollars a bottle. A full case of twenty-four bottles…"

I remembered the two bottles we drank at the roast beef dinner in Thomas Bay.

I laughed, "Twenty-two bottles!"

A horrified look came across his face.

"You didn't!"

"We did. Anyway, to show there are no hard feelings, I have a present for you."

I unwrapped the package and handed him the sandalwood box.

"This is the box Jacob found all those years ago. Lizzie doesn't want it. The contents will be of interest to you. I'll leave it here on your desk."

With that, I quickly took my leave.

EPILOGUE

Some mysteries remained unsolved. We never found out who killed Fingers Finnegan. And we didn't have a clue what it was that so frightened Levi in Thomas Bay.

Cindy and I spent the summer cruising the BC coast in *Tangled Moon*, and I showed her all my favorite spots. In the fall, she enrolled in the UBC business school, where she turned out to be a star pupil.

In February of 1969, Brenda gave birth to a strapping, healthy boy. We named him "Chandler" Gray, ("Chandler" being Brenda's surname). I agreed to contribute to his support and take him sailing with me every summer as soon as he was old enough

THE END

REFERENCES

Photos:
City of Vancouver Archives
commons.wikipedia.org

Books:
The History of Metropolitan Vancouver by Chuck Davis
The Strangest Story Ever Told by Harry D. Colp
Kushtaka: The Legend of the Bay of Death by Jay Border

ALSO BY GRAHAME SHANNON

<u>Tiger and the Robot</u> ISBN: 1541281594
Available in Paperback, eBook, and Audiobook formats.

Praise for Tiger and the Robot:

"Shannon has created a page-turner of a thriller and carved a small world's worth of fascinating and unique characters, pulled out of both high places and dark corners."
Chanticleer Book Reviews

"The personality of characters and descriptive text played a movie in my head as I read on. This is an easy read that I recommend, and I look forward to more books from Grahame Shannon!"
Patrick Chiu

"Great fun to read. A very entertaining and fast-paced detective story. Loved the BC and Vancouver Island references. If you like sailing and/or AI, you will particularly enjoy this book."
Amazon Customer

COMING SOON

Bay of Angels, third in the series. Expected publication spring of 2021.

PROLOGUE: BAY OF ANGELS

Tangled Moon heeled slightly to the gentle northwest breeze. A low patchy fog obscured the smaller islands, but taller peaks still poked above the mist. Chandler Gray sat on the bow, wearing a life vest and hanging on to the bow rail. He was five. His job was to watch for logs.

Chan leaped to his feet and waved his arms.

"A log! A big log!" he cried out.

At the helm, Cindy spotted the log. It was really a tree, with roots and branches. She didn't change course since it was off to starboard. As she was about to tell Chan it was okay, one of the branches waved. It was a pale human arm. Someone was clinging to the log. Cindy altered course toward it and called Sean up from below.

Sean was on deck in seconds. Leaving Cindy at the helm, he went forward, scooped up Chan, and carried him back to the cockpit.

As they approached the log, a small woman with long black hair streaming behind her was seen clinging on with her legs dangling in the water. She was naked in the frigid water of Caamaño Sound.

Cindy cut the motor on approach. Sean ran below and came back out with a big towel. As they came alongside, Sean reached out a hand to the woman. She said something in a language he didn't understand. He grasped her hand, then leaned over and picked her up under the arms, lifting her aboard like a child.

Chan's eyes were goggling as his father wrapped the naked woman in a towel and carried her aft. She collapsed in Sean's arms as he helped her below and gently lay her on the settee. Then he went back to the cockpit.

"Cindy, I'll take over out here. You go below and warm her up. Get some tea into her. See if you can find out what happened."

"Sean be quiet. I know what to do. Find us an anchorage."

That area of BC coast was a maze of islands, inlets, and channels. Many possible anchorages were available, and Sean chose the nearest, an unnamed nook on the south end of Princess Royal Island. He marked the chart with the approximate location where the woman was found.

After an hour or so, Chan took the wheel. His father dropped the anchor in the middle of the small bay. There were no other boats, and the only sign of life was an eagle soaring in circles above the tall fir trees lining the rocky shore. Moss clung to the limbs overhanging the sea.

Once secure, Sean and his son went below.

Cindy introduced the young woman, who was now wearing a pair of Cindy's jeans and a thick sweater. She smiled wanly.

"Sean, this is Minh Ha. She's Vietnamese and doesn't speak English. I think she fell off a ship. I tried to find out more, but the only phrase she kept repeating is bai dangles."

Sean said, "let's try writing it."

He got a notepad from the chart table and wrote BAI DANGLES in block letters and showed it to Minh. She took the pencil and scratched out BAY OF ANGELS in shaky block letters.

Manufactured by Amazon.ca
Bolton, ON